A PERFECT LOVE . . .

She began to twist her tumbled hair into its customary neat knot at the nape of her neck. 'You may not. *I care*. Taurus is the only thing I do care about.'

'Not me?' He barely recognised the sound of his own voice. 'Not me, one little bit?'

'Come on now, Naldo, that wasn't in the deal. *Pleasure*. That was the contract we made. Which you've had in good measure . . . running over the edges, so don't complain.'

'And what,' he asked ice cold and breathing hard, 'if your baby should be a girl?'

She shrugged. [illegible] always be another time . . . another [illegible]

JESSICA LAMB

Gemini in Taurus

SPHERE BOOKS LIMITED

Sphere Books Limited
27 Wrights Lane
London, W8 5TZ

First published in Great Britain
by Sphere Books Ltd 1987

To the men in my life; A Pisces, A Cancer and A Sagittarius.

TRADE
MARK

Set in Plantin

Printed and bound in Great Britain by
Cox & Wyman Ltd, Reading

Chapter One

In the summer of 1906, on the eve of his twenty-ninth birthday, Archibald Tallent decided to marry. A stocky man of middle height, short limbed and ginger haired, he resembled the indifferent family portraits hanging on the dining room walls of his grey stone house and took the responsibilities of a landowner seriously.

Taurus – no one knew the origin of the name and it never occurred to Archie to wonder why – was a prosperous but not extensive Somerset estate. It consisted of the house, home farm and half a dozen smaller tenanted properties. Archibald's grandfather had also acquired a tiny holding in the Vale of Athelney and a large Queen Anne cottage with a paddock on the outskirts of the nearby town of Somerton. Set in the mysterious heartland of the county where the green, willow strewn flatlands gave way with sudden gentleness to an escarpment of wooded hills, Taurus was a secret house. Tucked in the fold of a hillock, out of sight of the straggly, indeterminate village street, without an obvious or named entrance, many a stranger – and not only strangers – wasted whole half-hours driving down leafy side roads and along rutted lanes in futile search. Only when the branches were bare was it possible to glimpse the silvery walls and the duller gleam of grey roof tiles. It was also possible for someone standing at an upper window of the west wing to catch sight of the solitary peak of Glastonbury Tor, the ruined tower crowning its summit looking, in the swirling mists of winter sunrise, for all the world like a fairy castle.

Tallents had lived at Taurus since the middle of the fifteenth century when the first landowner built his stone long-house with its open passageway dividing the rooms in which his family lived from the byre and tethering posts that sheltered and secured his animals. The inheritance had passed, unbroken, through the male line now and again missing a generation or two. This consistency was surprising because Tallents lacked fertility. Even in prolific Tudor and Victorian times the number of their children tended to be small – rarely more than two or three with, inevitably, a single son.

Archibald had been an only child – his father dying when he was twenty-three. He had never considered matrimony whilst his widowed mother lived. Archie valued a quiet life and the autocratic old lady would have created domestic havoc with any but the most wishy-washy of daughters-in-law. Even after her death he didn't jump at the prospect of marriage. A bachelor's life was *comfortable*; only a sense of duty prompted him to take a wife.

Having made up his mind and not wishing to form an alliance with any of the local, county girls (another Tallent trait), Archibald wrote to a distant cousin living on the border of Worcester and Gloucestershire discreetly enumerating his predicament. Eleanor Truscott leapt at the chance of matchmaking. Archie was invited on a prolonged summer visit and, as discreetly, given the opportunity to look over all the eligible young women in Eleanor's not inconsiderable social circle. And, being nothing if not business like, she provided a list of those she considered most suitable. Magnolia King's name came halfway down, next to her best friend, Angela MacKinnon.

The girls were almost invariably seen together but not for reasons of affection. Magnolia was a cool, self-possessed seventeen-year-old whose strongest, undemonstrative, emotions were reserved solely for her twin brother, Reginald. It suited her to have an undemanding companion with whom to cycle, play tennis and talk fashion. For Angie, six months older, less assured, the motive was Naldo. Ever since, at the age of twelve, her parents had moved into the road adjacent to the King's home, she had been in love with Magda's twin. It made no matter that he treated her with a teasing indifference, Angela lived in fervent hope that one day he would take notice . . . realise how pretty she was. Prettier than Magnolia – but then, most people were.

Magda was a brunette just the other side of mouse. When good looks had been apportioned her brother got the lion's share. Angular features in a man could be an asset – they detracted from a girl's youthful charm and whereas Reginald's skin glowed warm and olive, Magnolia's by contrast was palely sallow. Dark brown, crisp hair sprang in a widow's peak from his high forehead, whereas the same hairline in Magnolia wavered indeterminately and her conventionally long tresses were finer, flyaway and lacking even the whisper of a curl. Only in the size and shape of her eyes did she score over her brother. Under thin, arched brows they were long lashed, very clear and grey, a colour that reflected any shade she wore leading to arguments as to their exact hue.

One attribute they shared – a long limbed, natural elegance of carriage. At school Reginald won a colour for fencing and, with greater application, could have earned the (unregretted) chance to represent his country. Magda needed no lessons in deportment or how to manage a train. People forgot the plainness of her face while watching her walk across a room and when the twins danced together most couples moved aside and left the floor to them. Naldo's laughing remark that they could always earn a living performing in the Halls displeased their somewhat stuffy father.

It was at the Mayoral Summer Charity Ball to which Eleanor had taken a small party that Magnolia was introduced to Archie Tallent. He was less attracted by her dancing than her suitability. He wanted a capable not a decorative wife and Magda's lack of girlish frivolity appealed to him. Her conventionally sober parents met with his approval and she possessed, for Archibald, one distinct advantage. She had no sisters. The last thing he desired being a horde of female in-laws invading the tranquillity of his home. Only her gigolo-type brother caused a twinge of disquiet – Archie instinctively distrusted any man who danced too well.

It was Ewart King who set his mind at rest – at a croquet

party held on Eleanor Truscott's lawn. Archie joined the older man who had moved a little apart in order to smoke a thin cigar. He declined the proffered case but took a cigarette from his own. They watched the match in progress – Naldo, flutteringly partnered by Angela, against Magnolia and the latest, local curate.

King said, 'My girl's going to be lonely when next summer comes along. Bound to miss her brother. Not sure *twins* are a good thing . . . tied too close. Don't know how ours came about. None in my family nor their mother's.'

Archie inspected the tip of his cigarette. 'Your son's leaving home?' The tone no more than mildly conversational.

'Going to Malaya . . . eventually take over my brother's rubber plantation. No son . . . not married, you see. Best thing for the lad – got no aptitude for the law. Army doesn't appeal . . . church out of the question. His mother's upset but she'll get over it and Magda's a sensible girl.'

Archibald said quickly, 'Much more than that, sir . . . charming.'

The older man cocked an eyebrow. Looked at the younger in a new, an *interested* light. 'How, Tallent, should I interpret that remark?'

'Seriously, sir. Most seriously.'

'And is Magnolia aware of your intentions . . . hopes?'

'Not unless she's guessed. I wouldn't presume to speak in any way without your permission.'

King exhaled a long, savoured plume of smoke. 'Most gratifying to know that some of you youngsters still observe the proprieties. It appears to me, Tallent, that if the choice were entirely mine you're just the sort of man I'd pick out as husband for my daughter. Pop the question whenever you wish . . . got my blessing.'

Taken aback by the speed of the other's approbation Archie stumbled, 'Surely, sir, you . . . you require to know in detail the extent of my income . . . ability to support your daughter?'

The cigar hand waved lazily. 'No need for that. Nellie Truscott's talked a bit about you . . . described your place in Devon.'

'Somerset, sir.'

'Well, the West country. Got a strange name . . .'

'Taurus . . . been in my family for more than four hundred years.'

'So I understand . . . backbone of England, you old families. Proud for my daughter. Mind you,' he leant close, 'if Magda don't wish to get engaged I'll do nothing to coerce her.'

'Naturally not, sir!' Archibald looked shocked at the suggestion but slipped in quickly, 'I would wish to be married within the year. Long engagements, I believe, can be unsettling.'

'Quite so . . . and she'd like her brother to be at the wedding. If Magda says "yes" we can start making plans right away. Do her mother good to be occupied.'

Magnolia's reply was made without hesitation and just the right amount of maidenly confusion. Laura King had prepared her daughter for Archibald's proposal with emphasis on her father's warm approval so it never occurred to the girl to refuse. She wasn't in love with Archie – her liking for him no more than lukewarm – but a good marriage was the only goal she knew in life and she experienced the heady satisfaction of becoming the first of her contemporaries to attain an engagement ring. A half hoop of five massive diamonds that suited her lean, rather large hand.

She did not, perhaps surprisingly, confide in or seek Naldo's approval. Both, on the edge of adult life, realised that their relationship was entering upon a new, a *separated*, phase and neither jibbed at its inevitability. Magnolia, as every successful daughter should, would marry; Reginald, unconsulted and secretly unwilling, would travel halfway across the world to learn the rubber planter's trade because Ewart King distrusted his son's insouciance and feared the consequences. To challenge parental manipulation was outside the twins' experience – in any case for Naldo *a quiet life* would always be the order of the day.

The wedding, as Archie wished, took place before twelve months was out – in early spring with the frost still glistening in the field furrows till well past noon. Laura King, to help ward off the impending pain of double separation, was determined that it should be the most spectacularly pretty wedding of the year.

The bride wore magnolia satin – a compliment to her name and bringing a needed warmth and glow to sallow cheeks and throat. The heavy train, appliquéd in cascades of silver threaded roses, fell from her shoulders and her veil (an astonishing break with convention) split out in a mist of petal pink tulle from a tiny wreath of myrtle flowers and orange blossom. Magda's mother was prepared to bend the accepted rules in the interest of flattery – the rather skimpy family lace would do nothing to soften sharp features and a lack of rounded girlishness.

Her bouquet was large – creamy, rose tongued orchids set in a shower of feathery, pale green fern and she wore her groom's wedding gift of drop pearl earrings and a matching single necklace rope.

Her five attendants – with the exception of Angela who was, anyway, a blonde – were chosen not for their depth of friendship but the colour of their hair. Collective fairness dramatically darkened, by contrast, the mousey brown of the bride's high piled and padded tresses. Dressed in ice white lace over underskirts of silver gauze, the flounced frills at neckline, hem and edge of three-quarter puffed sleeves trimmed in rose buds and tiny dark green leaves, they carried posies of white spring flowers tied with streamers of pink gauze ribbon and chaplets of artificial leaves and roses encircled golden heads.

Not all of the maids of honour favoured the bride's delicate choice – young blondes were inclined to hanker after shades of blue – but Angela, Magda's chief bridesmaid, spent the day in a kind of ecstasy. Ethereal gowns suited her frail, primrose fair prettiness better than most, and surely . . . surely, dressed so charmingly Naldo could not fail to notice her. It was galling to have to walk down the aisle after the ceremony on the arm of a stranger, a married friend of Archibald's but she accepted that it would be improper for the bride's brother to act as her groom's best man. However, it was not difficult, when the final wedding photograph was taken, unobtrusively to slide herself next to Naldo. Such unobtrusive slithering towards the achievement of her own ends was, as yet, an attribute unnoticed in Angela MacKinnon. Not unnoticed was the tendency for her china doll blue eyes to swim with unshed tears. Their sudden soft sparkle added appeal to an already piquant little face and aroused the protective instincts of both males and females – excepting those who knew her well.

Laura King, having dismissed the photographer, detached the girl from Naldo's side and, ignoring the anticipated rush of moisture, gently recalled her to the duties of chief bridesmaid. 'It's time Magnolia got changed into her going-away clothes. Take her upstairs – everything's laid ready in her room.'

Angela responded with a watery little gasp. 'Yes, yes, Mrs King. I'll go at once.'

It was in Magda's character to be already and without her mother's prompting, at the foot of the stairs. She handed over her bouquet in order to free her hands to lift heavy skirts. 'You must be sure, Angie, to come down before I do . . . to catch my flowers when I throw them over the banisters.'

Angela blinked, spiking her long, fair lashes with tear drops. 'It won't matter if I catch it or not. I shall not get married for years and years.'

'Nonsense.' Magda's words came drifting down above the rustle of stiff satin. 'Look at me. Eight months ago I didn't know such a person as Archie existed. Today I'm Mrs Archibald Tallent.'

Angela said nothing. It was pointless to tell unromantic Magda of her longing, her yearning, her hope that one day she would walk down the aisle in a cloud of white, lilies in her hands, to Naldo waiting at the chancel steps. Her dream lacked as much substance as her infatuation. Angela imagined the bliss of Naldo's arms about her; his voice murmuring undying love but his fantasy kisses never strayed from hand or brow. Sex was a word not included in her vocabulary and the facts of life never explained to unengaged girls.

Laura King's little talk concerning what she delicately termed the 'physical obligations of a wife' neither appalled nor dismayed her daughter. Magda's only reaction was one of curiosity. It seemed a strange way for God to organise the procreation of the human race but if Mama and her friends had survived the experience there was no good reason why she should not. Magnolia never wasted effort on the imagination of the unknown and Laura had been at pains to emphasise that Archie was a gentleman. *Gentlemen* required no more than compliance from their wives. The possibility of pleasure was never mentioned and Archibald Tallent would have been as shocked as Laura King at the suggestion. It was without a pang that Magda walked into her maiden bedroom for the last time.

It was Angie who looked tremulously around – at the pale, birds-eye maple furniture and the high, single bed, its white counterpane tidily strewn with going-away clothes. Amethyst wool travelling costume, pure silk underwear and stockings, and, resting on the pillow beside a pair of grey kid gloves, a small toque made entirely of violets.

'I can't . . . can't believe you won't sleep here anymore. That I shall never be able to pop round for a cosy, comfy chat!'

Bother! Magda thought, if her fingers are as shaky as her voice we'll be here for hours. She lifted her own steady hands and began pulling free the pins that fastened her veil. 'Oh, put down those flowers, Angela, on the wash stand and come and help. I've got a train to catch and a husband waiting.'

Angie fluttered across the room and laid the bouquet as reverently as a wreath onto the marble top. 'It's been a *beautiful* wedding. You're a *beautiful* bride. It seems such a shame to wear that lovely dress only once.'

'If you don't undo these buttons I shall probably wear it for the rest of my life.'

'Now you're being silly!' She took the veil and hovered indecisively until Magnolia exploded.

'Honestly, you're enough to try the patience of a saint! Bundle the thing up and put it at the foot of the bed. It will

be most unfortunate if Arc
saddled with an unpunctual
Angela's eyes began to s
and all my fault.'

'Not,' grimly cajoling, '
now.' Added a sting. 'I'm
Prudence Cooke to be chie

Her calculation was corr
to her side. Angie's helple
she wished.

'I know, Magda, you
sounded wounded but t
the row of tiny buttons f
quick. When she lifted t
lia's head she needed to
not a strand of hair.

Magda let her pettic
caught a glimpse of her
Will I, she wondered, look
how? It seemed unlikely.

Angela took deliberate care o
honour. Tears might brim a
another's brusque behest but she n
a secret, unguessed-at, self assertio
the little violet clustered hat at just the
the door opened without a preliminary k
came in.

'Nip off for a minute, Angie, there's a d
word with Mag.'

After she had gone he firmly closed the door
where he was, his gaze steady and unwavering. 'T
not been a moment, sis, to talk properly to you for we
You and Mama have been dashing here, there and every
where.'

Her responsive regard was as unmoving, unemotional. 'It was worth it. Everything's gone off splendidly . . .'

'And you look splendid.' He came close and kissed her, briefly, on the cheek. 'No time left now. Only for goodbye. You're off to the wilds of the West country and I to where I can't make any trouble.'

ıot the reason. You never do.'
ıan cure . . . our father's favouri-
gnation in his voice. 'I'll write to

ly. 'What's the betting, one letter to

bore. The flies are disgusting and the
g!'

to pick up a little reticule and checked
unnecessarily. Handkerchief and a tiny
salts. 'It will be strange not seeing you for
. . . school term used to seem an age. How

aybe six. Will depend, I presume, on Uncle
the natives. Whether I can get 'em to work

him a bright eyed glance. 'You've never had
e getting Angie running errands for you. Re-
we used to call her "your slave"?' She stood up
'Let's go down together. Angela, of course, will
g.'

course.' He laughed. 'Now you're a married woman
ps you could do some husband hunting for her.'

ot me, I wouldn't wish . . .' She let the sentence hang
began to move away from him but he caught hold of
shoulders and swung her round to look him in the
es. 'So long, sis. We both know *twins* never really say
oodbye.'

She tapped his chin with her purse. 'I wasn't going to . . . although it feels like it.'

He let his hands fall and she turned away, unhurriedly, to pick up her bouquet. 'I've got to throw this thing over the banisters. See if you can persuade Angela to go down and catch it.'

'Not likely, Mag! She'd believe I was duty bound to propose if she did.' He pulled open the door and called, 'Angie, inform the teeming multitude that Mrs Archibald Tallent is on her way down.'

Obediently, in a flurry of lace, the girl hurried to the landing rail and leant over. Breathlessly, just loud enough, her voice came, 'Everybody . . . Magnolia's ready . . . .'

Four figures, silvery pale, detached themselves from amongst the crowd of guests and came running into the well beneath the curving staircase. Their upturned faces looked pasty white and stupid – why Prudence even had her mouth half open. From her vantage point Angela felt superior, aloof and set apart. As brother and sister drew near she artfully slid into the place on Naldo's vacant side. Magda wasn't looking at him – both knew they would not look directly at one another any more that day.

Magnolia concentrated on the cumbersome bouquet, lifted it and sent the flowers sailing and plummeting into mid-air. There was a tangle of white skirts and a scrabble – two girls made the catch. She felt rather than heard his chuckle. 'Impartial as ever, Mag.'

'Too heavy to be anything else,' she replied moving towards the head of the stairs drawing Angela close so that her brother would walk alone behind them. Angela couldn't quite suppress a quiver of annoyance.

'See what I managed to get for you,' Magda held out one of the largest, most brilliantly tongued orchids. 'It seemed only fair as you hadn't the chance to try and catch the whole.'

'Oh, Magnolia . . . thank you.' No unshed tears came brimming. 'I shall keep it in my pressed flower book. On the page next to my coming-out lilies of the valley. And a freesia from my bridesmaid's posy.'

By the time they'd reached halfway down Magda realised that most of the younger guests had left the hall – gone, she guessed, outside on the driveway ready with packets of rice and paper petals. At the foot of the stairs, Archie waited and, a small distance off, her parents – everyone behind them in a blur. Beneath the osprey plumes dipping from the brim of her hat, Mama's face looked unnaturally pale. It was not until Archibald had gently pulled her arm through his own that Laura came forward to embrace and kiss her daughter goodbye. Her mother's lips felt as dry as withered leaves and she said nothing.

Papa was less inhibited and not at all depressed – she

smelt the whiskey on his breath. He clapped Archie on the back, booming, 'Not going to ask you to take care of my little girl. Wouldn't be standing here if I thought otherwise.' The scent of afternoon spirits and his exuberance were as uncharacteristic as her mother's silence. It seemed as though, somehow, her marriage had changed her parents into strangers.

Eleanor Truscott who, since taking her seat in the front pew on Archie's side of the church, had revelled in the role of unofficial groom's mother, pecked at Magda's cheek and murmured, 'Be happy, *happy*, dear. And, remember, I expect to be your *first* guest at Taurus.'

Then the front door swung open and they were walking past a river of smiling faces and good wishes, hurrying down the porch steps under a rain of confetti and a hail of rice pearls and up into the waiting carriage. The horses started almost at once, a final handful of coloured paper fluttered through the open window, Archie pulled it shut and suddenly the day had ended, was closed up, without time for so much as a backward glance. Not that she wanted to . . . Magnolia Tallent would never cling to the past – except when it came to stones and mortar.

The railway station at Somerton was spruce and serenely busy, its low buildings the exact colour of the clouds filling every inch of sky – an early twilight threatened.

Archie looked fussily up and down the platform. 'Greedy should be here.'

In the last ten days Magda had learnt that her husband, a generally calm and considerate man, took sharp exception to delay in his subordinates. The tardy services of a waiter at their lakeside hotel resulted in heightened colour and a bout of indigestion. Tactfully she arranged their move to another table.

She slid easily, without hesitation or selfconsciousness, into the role of wife. It was strange to share a bed with a warm limbed, gustily breathing man but proximity and a tendency to snore did not prevent her normal deep sleep. Neither did the 'physical obligations of marriage' – to use her mother's delicate words. Archie never turned on the light nor removed her nightgown. The whole indecorous proceedings lasted no more than five minutes – if those constituted the extent of male desire what was all the fuss about?

On the second afternoon of their honeymoon rain began to fall and went on falling, washing away any plan to walk beside Windermere's shores. Archie passed the daylight hours – with the assistance of another couple – teaching Magda how to play bridge. She was an apt pupil with an instinctive feel for cards. By the end of the week not one of the three was unwilling to take her for partner.

In the evenings, the men went off to the billiard room leaving their wives to chat, embroider and make, in the main, very amateur, music. Magda, being by far the youngest, was much petted although she steadfastly refused to play the pianoforte. The novelty of her position and staying in an hotel compensated for half a dozen dullish days.

The last three were spent in London – visiting the theatre, shops and a connection of Archie's mother who lived in a Grace & Favour apartment at Hampton Court. She was a General's widow and very deaf. She gave them seedcake, weak tea and an elaborately engraved silver salver as a wedding present. Wrapped in parchment coloured paper and tied with scarlet string Archie held it fiercely under his free arm as he helped her from the train compartment.

Hoping to soothe she said, 'Here's a porter, now.'

Archie grunted at the young man who was very tall and looked as if he were growing too fast for his uniform. 'All the luggage is in the guard's van. Three cases and a hat box.'

The lad touched his cap. 'Greedy's just arrived, sir. Lower road's flooded. Us 'ad a flash storm 'bout an 'our since.'

Archie's jaw relaxed a little.

The lad trundled off, his barrow to be immediately replaced by the station master – very straight without a speck of dust on tightly buttoned jacket and iron stiff trousers.

'Good afternoon, Mr Tallent, sir. And madam,'

continued in a spate of words to repeat the reason for Greedy's late arrival.

Archibald let him finish. 'This is Albert Haskins, Magnolia. He runs his station like a platoon . . . is one of my corporals in the County Volunteers.'

'Good afternoon, Mr Haskins.' She smiled but was still uncomfortably conscious of her husband's edginess.

The man gave a butlerish little bow. 'May I say, ma'am, how delighted we all are to have a lady again at Taurus.'

'Not so delighted as I shall be if we get there before nightfall.'

Archie stumped off in the direction of the exit gate, irritable fingers prodding the inside pocket of his jacket for the train tickets.

Haskins drew back to let Magda precede him and they walked together, the porter bringing up the rear. Some of her self possession began to evaporate. Despite the station master's courtesy she felt, now that Archie's back was turned to her, suddenly a stranger . . . unexpectedly swamped by the sensation of not belonging.

Archie was talking to a man in coachman's coat and hat – his words made no sense. 'You've brought the horses, then?'

The reply came halfway firm, halfway apologetic. 'Did'n seem fit, sir, for any other.'

'Quite right.' He looked testily up at the sky. 'See Morris gets the bags on quickly . . . don't feel like hanging about – had enough of that for one day.' Opening the carriage door himself and letting down the step he helped Magda inside. 'Had a surprise for you,' resigned exasperation tinged his voice, 'but it'll keep for another time.' He didn't join her at once but went round the back to supervise the loading of the cases.

She wondered if he trusted no one to carry out his orders unsupervised. Perhaps even the running of his home. Her sense of inadequacy grew and to push it away she sat forward and looked around the station yard. There were few people about, all dully dressed and mostly hurrying away but not without a covert glance or two in her direction. What whisper would go round the little town? 'Mr Tallent's wife's a plain slip of a thing'? She shivered and tried to stir up anger at so stupid a consideration. She was elegant, she was capable, she was . . . the realisation would not be crushed . . . eighteen years old and on her way to a house she'd never seen. To a life she had, until that moment, confidently contemplated. No more. It was a moment in which she would have welcomed anyone beside her – even Angie. Most of all Naldo.

Archie got in. His flush of annoyance had almost faded. 'Last lap, thank God. No more train journeys for me until we celebrate our silver wedding.'

She felt the miles to everything and everybody familiar stretching interminably into the distance.

'You tired?' An automatic question . . . no deep concern.

She nodded not trusting her voice.

'Pity about the weather.' Her husband leant back and closed his eyes. 'Not worth pointing out landmarks in this light. Soon be as familiar as roads round your old home.' Contentedly he added, 'It'll be cosy in the parlour. Started off as the cowbyre . . . more like a chapel now.'

She was lost . . . couldn't picture or understand his meaning.

A house called Taurus. Angie had said, 'What a horrid name! I'd be terrified.' It wasn't fright that kept her gaze fixed on the gloved hands lying limply in her lap but a total, empty loneliness.

The timbre of the horses' hooves changed, slowed down, came to a stop. Archie said, with matter of fact pleasure, 'Here we are.' Fumblingly she picked up her purse and prepared to follow him . . . a stranger . . . quite alone.

Unnoticed throughout their short journey the clouds had thinned, begun to drift apart. As she stepped down, her hand on Archibald's sturdy arm, a shaft of golden, evening sun broke through. It struck the west wing so that the front, which faced almost due south, was bathed half in shadow, half in diffused light. Silvery grey stone shimmered and to the left the deep set window panes glowed topaz yellow. There were twice as many and larger windows to the right, heavily mullioned, their glass untouched by the setting sun, remaining opaque and mysterious. The roof, apart from a tiny porch, was gently pitched, grey tiled and, except for the short length of the western wing, lacking dormer windows. There were four, not very tall, square stone chimneys, two sending plumes of wood smoke into the cool, damp air. Not a large house, not an impressive house . . . but an indefinably beautiful, *magic* house. It reached towards her . . . drew her loneliness away.

Archie shook her arm. 'Here's Mrs Bray.'

The figure in the dark blue dress standing by the entrance had gone unnoticed – Magnolia's eyes only for her new, beguiling home.

'Good evening, sir. Welcome, madam, to Taurus.' Even when they drew near the woman's face made no impression . . . Magda too dazed, too absorbed in a newfound joy to register the port wine stain that marred one cheek from eye to chin. She was, also, impatient to see inside.

The interior of the porch, being windowless, was very dim. In the hallway beyond, on the dark surface of a crudely carved, wooden dower chest, an oil lamp glowed. Its glass globe echoed the colour of primroses filling and spilling over the edges of a copper bowl, their perfume faint and very sweet. On the right, a wooden screen enclosed the drawing room which was entered by descending two stone steps and on the left a heavily panelled wall was broken by a door with massive latches leading to the dining room. A small passageway led straight ahead with immediately to the right a concealed flight of wooden steps. Magda was to find that Taurus was a house filled with fascination, twists, unexpected corners and almost hidden stairways.

Archibald said, 'Tea, Mrs Bray.'

'Yes, sir. Set ready in the parlour.'

He opened a barely visible door in the screen and led Magda down two shallow, stone steps into the drawing room. It was large and long, the outer wall broken by a pair of wide mullioned windows with firmly padded seats below. There was a huge, laid, unlit fireplace surrounded and surmounted by ornate pillars and mantleshelf. The floor was polished wood covered by two, pale blue, patterned carpets. Three settees were grouped around the hearth, one backed by a sofa table strewn with framed photographs and china bric-à-brac. In the dying daylight filtering through the windows the curtains and upholstery looked dingy, bluey-green. Oil lamps and creamy candles in silver candelabra stood here and there on tables and the mantleshelf.

At the far end of the room each wall contained a door. Archibald opened the one in the centre and stood back to let her through.

Here was lamplight and a log fire, sprinkled with fir cones and blazing in a brass fendered grate. The low ceiling was plasterwork – lozenges and roughly formed Tudor roses; the walls panelled in lime wood, linenfold; her feet touched rush matting scattered with little Turkey carpets. Both outer walls contained windows – larger, foliate mullions. But that facing her – the end wall of the house – was filled with panes of different coloured glass. Ruby, sapphire, amethyst and emerald not quite haphazard but set in no immediately recognisable pattern. They split a jewelled glow into the room. The air was incense musky with the scent of pot-pourri.

Archie said, 'Give me your coat and hat and come to the fire. Ethel will take them after she brings the tea.'

A loaded, three tiered cake stand had been placed close to the fireside chairs and a low table set ready for two. The china was the finest bone but of hideous design – swagged, banded and medallioned in green, gold and bricky red, the cups both wide bowled and tapering. Guaranteed to cool tea fast.

The maid, carrying a tray of Georgian silver, entered by a door Magda had not noticed. Archie accepted her surprise with a subdued chuckle.

'Taurus is full of unexpected entrances and little stairways. You're certain to get lost in the first few days.'

She said, 'Tell me about the house – *all* about it.'

He seemed more interested in the buttered scones. 'Not much to tell.'

'There must be . . . after four hundred years.'

He corrected her. 'And fifty. Probably the reason why – nothing much has changed for over three hundred. Except the kitchen block which in the middle of the last century was tagged onto the west wing which was built sixteen hundred and something. The ceiling and windows here are a bit earlier but originally this was where the Tallents kept their cattle. The place, you see, started as a farm long-house – the animals kept close by but not under the same roof. Then we got more prosperous,' he dug into the jam dish coming up with a top-heavy spoonful of bramble jelly which he spread thickly over a single scone, 'and more ambitious, moved the cattle out, added an extra storey to the old cowbyre and joined the whole lot up. We put in coloured glass and painted frescoes on the wall of the biggest bedroom. A bit later someone built on the porch with an oratory above – must have been one of the few "religious" Tallents. Just an alcove in the main upstairs corridor now.'

He reached for a plate of fruitcake, cut two slices. 'In the beginning this floor would have been beaten earth – now it's flagstones which is why we keep it covered up with matting. Oh, and the dining room furniture is Chippendale.'

Softly she remarked, 'Whilst this is best Maples.'

He looked around in critical surprise. 'Yes . . . I suppose it is . . .'

'And do we possess a *smaller* tea set?' She hauled up the massive, silver pot. 'This is far too large for two. And thoroughly uneconomical.'

'My mother always used it. But you must change things however you wish. You've got a free hand to refurnish exactly as you want – excepting my study. That's tucked away beyond the dining room and out of the general run of things.' He cut his cake into small pieces and went on, awkwardly, 'I think you'll find the staff cooperative . . . Mrs Bray wishes to retire as soon as you feel settled. You must believe me, Magnolia, I look forward to whatever alterations you may make.'

She answered quickly, 'I'm sure there are very few . . . how can there be in a house five hundred years old? And only to make you more comfortable and the house even lovelier.' She leant back contentedly. 'Caring for you and Taurus is my life now.'

Even more awkwardly, 'I hope it will be happy.'

She looked around the mysteriously glowing room and contemplated all the rooms she would wander through tomorrow. Pride of possession sparkled like champagne. 'Not a hope – a certainty.'

The confidence in her voice made him glance up. She was radiant – as he'd not seen her on their wedding day nor would again as everyday familiarity coloured his vision. Not apparent was her extreme youth nor the detached calm that added a hint of barbed chill to her personality. All was smooth, mature and utterly content.

Something of her pure happiness touched him – he leant forward, laid tentative fingers on her arm. 'Magda, I must apologise for my . . . irritation, bad manners a while ago.'

Puzzled and drawn from her dreaming she blinked at him.

'When we arrived at the station. I was disappointed . . . had planned to take you home in a different – a special – style.'

'How . . . different?'

Archibald looked ridiculously proud. 'In my automobile.'

Her gasp was gratifying. 'You own a . . . horseless carriage?'

Enthusiasm quickened his usually steady speech. 'A Standard . . . most comfortable and reliable and the sensation, I assure you, is exhilarating. To travel with no apparent means of propulsion! To jog along with *nothing* in front! It . . . it beggars description. And Greedy is becoming a most proficient driver although I think, secretly, he prefers his horses. Brought them this afternoon because of the hazard of the weather – didn't want to risk a breakdown or the chance of an uncomfortable ride. I must buy you a motoring veil, Magda, and a dust coat.'

She said, 'I've never ridden in a motor car. Papa did not approve. Do you drive also, Archie?'

"Great heavens, no.' He sounded shocked. 'Greedy is my coachman. I don't take the reins from his hands.'

Chapter Two

Magda, without recognising the sensation, had fallen in love. Not with her husband – her home. It was a passion that would increase with each successive year. Taurus was not merely beautiful – it represented continuity, unbroken belonging and the touch of immortality.

It took thirteen happily occupied months to bring the house to the point of her desired perfection. The changes she made were so subtle as never to intrude on Archie's consciousness until accomplished. The fresco room they shared she left untouched. The tapestry hangings to the Jacobean four-poster bed were still bright and strong and the window curtains to match had been ordered in the last century by a perceptive Victorian Tallent wife. Also the dining room, save for the cleaning of the family portraits, needed no improvements.

There were seven – none predating the late 1800s. All were unsigned, all male – excepting a young girl in a white, Regency ball gown – all with varying degrees of auburn hair. No Tallent had achieved fame or notoriety, entered politics or made a fortune and the need to record individual faces seemed unimportant. It was enough that their modest plaster tombs and stone plaques filled the little, grey stone church at the top of a wooded rise on the far side of the straggly village street and that the print of long dead hands lingered on the painted frieze in the medieval upper room and the linenfold panelling that covered every downstairs wall.

In an attic next to the maids's bedrooms, in the west wing, Magda discovered more evidence of generations past – an incomplete set of Queen Anne chairs and a Carolean cradle. She sent the chairs to be restored and reupholster-ed, picking up the colours of the parlour stained glass, and set them at uneven intervals against and around the pale brown walls. She discarded the incongruous three piece suite replacing it with comfortable armchairs of different sizes all covered in unbleached linen and scattered with cushions of all shapes and fabrics. The cradle she placed in the drawing room fireplace keeping it always full with cut or potted flowers.

Magda did not care for blue but the carpets were Aubusson and too valuable to be replaced. To soften the overformality of the drawing room she colour washed the ceiling in buttermilk and used a honey brocade delicately threaded with azure and gold for curtains and upholstery. She also exchanged the functional lamp globes for translucent and gilded glass. She placed blue, gold and amber lustres on the mantleshelf, reorganised the china ornaments covering most, flat, polished surfaces and cut down the number of photographs to Archie's parents, himself as a child in a sailor suit and their wedding group – Mama, Papa and Naldo. She found many fine copper bowls and jugs and dishes in one of the kitchen stores and a shelf full of cut glass vases and epergnes. It was her intention that, no matter what time of year, flowers would be found in every living room.

Once the house was arranged to her satisfaction she turned her attention to the gardens. Here the challenge was greater, the aspect very gently sloping but dull, ending in a border of trees – mostly beech – that hid a wall edging onto the village street. Not a single dramatic cedar or bank of flowers . . . just grass, evergreens and a bed of very ordinary roses. She engaged another gardener and set about replacing the evergreens with azaleas and rhododendrons, lilacs, laburnums and mock orange bushes. She planted a profusion of spring bulbs and roses, roses everywhere.

For early autumn she made beds of dahlias and michaelmas daises . . . a dazzle of colour and a host of butterflies. She paved part of the drive that swept past the drawing room windows turning it into a terrace on which to take afternoon tea and she trained yellow roses up and around the parlour window; wisteria she planted along the west wall. She encouraged the wild flowers – bluebells, jack-in-the-pulpit, even dogroses – that grew close to the trees and alongside the border wall and she turned the lower lawn into a tennis court. She was a patball player but a delight to watch.

She wrote, in detail, regularly to Naldo and received in return – as she had predicted – one letter to her three. He was an erratic, lazy correspondent and his powers of description minimal. She learnt nothing of his life beyond that he was well, the weather could be trying and Uncle Arthur very different from Papa – just how unspecified. Such imbalance mattered to neither – the ties that bound them might be finer than those of identical twins but strong enough to forge a tolerant understanding and unexpressed recognition of individual difference enmeshed in a shared but cool consanguity. A letter she sent, two and a half years after her marriage, contained the news that she was pregnant.

It was more with satisfaction than pleasure that Magnolia accepted her condition. She was not a maternal woman, she had no experience of babies but she knew it was her unavoidable duty to provide Archie with an heir and Taurus with a future. Some pleasure she experienced in being able to quell Mama's continual (almost monthly) questioning. 'Was there a baby on the way? Did Magda not think it time to seek expert advice?' The twins had been honeymoon babies – her daughter refrained from asking, Why no more?

Halfway through her pregnancy Ewart and Laura came to stay, Mama making it plain she would *not* be coming to Taurus for the birth. At her time of life home was the place to be in winter – one knew where the draughts came from. If the baby's christening were held over till the spring that would be a different matter. 'Before that, Magda, something quite astonishing is going to happen. Angela MacKinnon is engaged! The wedding day fixed.'

Magnolia, who was embroidering a tiny jacket, said, 'She hasn't told me.'

'Only just announced. This young man, David . . . Bland or Blane . . . a name like that . . . turned up at the

Staveleys. Minna Staveley's nephew by marriage, I believe. Swept Angie off her feet. She hangs onto him,' her lips pursed, 'like . . . like she used to hang on Naldo. Been on a visit to his mother. A widow . . . living in some dreadful place near Wolverhampton. But acceptable it seems. The MacKinnon's approve even though he works in Singapore. I think there's a fair bit of money . . . .'

Magnolia unpicked a stitch – in surprise she'd pulled a loop too tight. '*Angela* is going to live in Singapore?'

'Unbelievable, is it not? And such a rushed wedding! You'll be getting an invitation before long.'

'I won't be able to go – like this.' She smoothed the folds of her dark blue maternity dress. 'Do you like him, Mama?'

'David Bland? Nothing to like or dislike. He's a presentable – *handsome* – young man. Few years younger than Archibald I'd guess. Courteous, level-headed . . . daft over Angela.'

Her daughter looked up sharply. '*Level*-headed? AND daft over Angie? Naldo's what I call level-headed.'

Laura said reprovingly, 'She's a very pretty, gentle girl. Unlike Naldo this young man hasn't known her all his life. I'm sure I wish them very happy.'

Magda snipped her embroidery thread. 'I'm sure you do, Mama. No doubt with thanks.'

'I don't know what you mean,' her mother answered.

The baby was a boy – a sturdy eight pounder with a fuzz of auburn hair and a furious expression. As the weeks passed the indeterminate blue of his eyes changed to the amber that flecked his Uncle Reginald's. He thrived and gave no cause for parental anxiety – the perfect heir to Taurus. They called him Ronald after his Tallent grandfather and it was doubtful who was the more delighted – Archibald or Ronnie's mother.

There was a difference – Magda's happiness unalloyed; Archie's snagged by a thread of worry. For three years he had lived in the contented knowledge that he had picked as wife a woman whose sense of commitment to Taurus was as strong – maybe hotter – than his own . . . a matter for self-congratulation. But she was, after all, not much more than a girl – he shrank from putting that commitment and her maturity to the test; from the necessity to reveal the small but grinning skeleton in the Tallent's cupboard.

He waited until Magda had weaned the child – eight weeks she considered quite long enough to feed him. After that she handed Ronnie over to the full-time care of a nurse and cows' milk. Much as she loved her baby there were even more interesting things to do – hadn't played a *challenging* hand of bridge for five months and the herbaceous border needed replanning, last summer had been a disappointment. In the parlour, after dinner, she got out a pencil and paper to make a rough sketch of the flowerbed. She was too absorbed to notice that her abstemious husband refilled his whiskey glass.

'Magda . . . I need to talk about the boy.'

At once she put down her pencil.

'Not . . .' he swallowed, 'not Ronald specifically. The family . . .' Opening his cigarette case he offered it. Archibald did not object to women smoking – in private.

She shook her head – mind still absorbed in the merits of colombine and monkshood.

'Tallents show . . . sometimes an . . . eccentricity. We can be unpredictable.'

That caught her attention. Her husband was the most dependable of men.

'Now and again, there's no pattern . . . one of us – can be a man or woman – behaves . . . strangely. It's as if their energy gets bottled up and has to burst out. A sort . . . sort of frenzy. The need to rush about . . . break things. Gets worse if their will is crossed even unintentionally. Reason is nonexistent . . . for a while. Rarely lasts long, thank God.'

He drew deeply on his cigarette as if to find resolution for the next words . . . went on, 'There are exceptions. Aunt Phoebe died in a nursing home in Malvern and my great grandfather spent the last ten years of his life with two menservants in the cottage at Athelney.' Repeated almost pleadingly, '*Exceptions*, Magnolia.'

A little white about the corners of her mouth, she asked,

'How soon does this . . . condition . . . manifest itself?'

'Can't tell – that's the problem. Unpredictable as the state itself. Sometimes in little childhood, sometimes in adolescence, other times – like great Grandpa – not until the onset of old age.' He paused and bent down to pat her hand nearest to him. 'Mostly, thank God again, containable within the house.' He smiled as fleetingly as his touch. 'We're not known in the County as the "crazy" Tallents.'

When she didn't speak he went on firmly in an attempt to place his information into historical relevance. 'There's never been a murderer in the family and only one suicide and two accidental deaths. The first instance was recorded in the reign of Bloody Mary – a Thomas Tallent ran amok in church but that could have been a protest against the return of Popish practises – and why it persists is a mystery. Since the 1660s we've been careful never to intermarry.' Her continued silence unnerved him a little and he fidgeted remorsefully. 'Perhaps I should have told all this to you – or your father – before asking you to marry me.'

The briskness of her words reassured him. 'Nonsense! Everyone knows old families have problems with heredity. Why Papa said the new King's elder brother was next door to an idiot. I'm *proud* my son can trace his forebears back to the Wars of the Roses and as proud my name is Tallent. Of course I had to know but now let's talk about this bothersome herbaceous border. I don't seem to be able to get the blend of flowers right.'

In retrospect, the first four years of Ronnie's life seemed to Magnolia, like heaven. The only small sadness her parents' deaths within months of one another – even this tempered by the joy of Naldo's arrival on furlough. He spent part of the time settling their father's affairs and organising the disposal of the family home – 'Footloose, that's me, Mag' – and part at Taurus. He took detached interest in his nephew, went shooting with his brother-in-law, was much in demand at bridge parties, caused a flutter in a dozen maidenly hearts and left for the Far East expressing neither enthusiasm nor relief. He had, however, persuaded Archie to buy a larger car – the latest Sunbeam.

Four months after his departure, in the midsummer of 1914, Angela returned, from Singapore, with her husband, infant twin daughters and an *amah*. Her notion of romance had not survived the realities of the marriage bed and oriental, colonial life. She was determined never to go back. With concealed, crafty resolution that belied the dolly softness of her features she set about ensuring her intentions. At the homecoming party given by her mother she staged, in front of all the guests, a dramatic, physical collapse. The family doctor, summoned and clung to, prescribed immediate weaning of the babies and that, for a while at least, their mother be treated as a fragile convalescent. He also expressed doubts as to the competence of the childrens' Chinese nurse. By the end of three weeks Angela had succeeded in convincing him that to return to Singapore would put her health in permanent jeopardy.

David, accepting the manipulated inevitable, bought a house near Chester, packed the *amah* off on the next ship going East and settled down to spend his six months' furlough placating an apparently ailing wife, engaging domestics (including a composed, fourteen-year-old from a Dr Barnardo's Home called Caroline) and contemplating, with surprisingly little regret, his future bachelor existence on the other side of the world.

On 3rd August, the day before the outbreak of the Great War, Archie, a member of the Somerset Volunteers, joined his regiment. Two and a half months later, on the day David Bland sailed for Singapore, he crossed to France. Magda's personal heaven disintegrated into shreds. Four-year-old Ronnie roared with frustration and smashed all the nursery china because his father wouldn't answer when he called. The casualty lists in the papers contained too many names she knew and all her waking hours were spent waiting and subconsciously watching for the telegraph boy.

She was luckier than many. All her anxiety was centred on a single man. Reginald was safe – no chance of his returning from Malaya. With Kelly Watts, the farm manager, gone as well as Archie, caring for Taurus kept her busy from morning till night. She revelled in the responsibility and was glad that when on leave her husband wanted only to stay in his home or ride and stroll around the countryside. To the summit of Horn Tip Hill became one of his longer, favourite walks. The view was extensive – all Taurus estate and far beyond. He would sit on the short, flowerless turf not speaking, smoking cigarette after cigarette.

Action of the Western Front had left him quieter than ever. He bowled cricket balls to the boy, bought him a pony and spent hours on the garden terrace with a rarely touched whiskey and his cigarettes at his side. He rode around his land with the under manager, Bob, who had a club foot and was unfit for active service and whose admiration for the 'mistress' was direct and voluble. He read the Lesson in church, went into the village to talk to families whose sons had been killed and visited his tenants – all too often for the same reason. When he played bridge it was with abstracted concentration and by 1917 his fiery hair had turned quite grey and his cloudy eyes remote and faded. In July, 1918 he stepped on a mine and was blown to the four corners of that particular foreign field.

On her return from the memorial service, Magnolia found that Ronnie had rampaged all over the garden tearing off the biggest flower heads and strewing them along the paths – even roses. His hands were torn and streaked with blood. He was the last heir to Taurus and all Tallent.

She confided in no one – the truth was her's alone – but she consulted the Vicar about finding a preparatory school. Archie had attended an old establishment in Exeter but commonsense prompted that Ronald should not go so far away.

The Rev Martin Harris was a conscientious man. He gave the matter careful thought and prayer and made many, as careful, enquiries. Finally he recommended St George's at Bradford-on-Tone a village close to the county town of Taunton. It was small, the headmaster was married (which made for greater understanding into the emotional needs of little boys) and it possessed the added advantage of easy transfer to Kings College in the town when the time came to move on to public school. Six generations of Tallents had been educated at Blundells in Tiverton but the Vicar felt no twinge of surprise that so young a widow should express the wish that her only son stay nearer home.

Apart from the knowledge that Archie would never return to Taurus life continued little changed. Magda wore black – which did not suit her – for the customary twelve months of mourning and then gently reverted to the colours that did. To the safely returned Kelly Watts, she handed over extra estate responsibility and she gave the vacant tenancy of the Dundon farm to a cousin of Bob's who had been severely gassed and had three children to support. It was not an entirely charitable gesture – Bob, she knew, would ensure the land stayed in good heart.

She kept in constant but prudent touch with the headmaster of St George's, replaced Ronald's outgrown pony with a sturdy, peat brown Dartmoor purchased for him by Watts and took the boy on holiday to Goodwrington Sands and a visit to Angela.

It had been Magda's intention that the little girls and their mother should stay at Taurus. Even before Archie's death she had explained there was plenty of room for the children's nanny and Caroline, the housekeeper/companion Angela praised so fulsomely in her letters.

Angela procrastinated. She was still suffering, she wrote, the after effects of severe shock following her parents' deaths . . . it might be *two* years ago but felt like yesterday. Magda would understand having lost her own so similarly. And it had been necessary to dismiss the nursemaid on suspicion of thieving. Any such unpleasantness upset her and laid her low with migraine headaches. It was impossible to get through any day without spending most of it lying down in a darkened room. Poor Caroline had her hands full.

During her early widowhood Magda's vague wish to see her friend crystallised into mild compulsion. Her absorption with the running of Taurus and its future nudged her towards strengthening the only tie with her girlhood. Angela had two daughters . . . one day Ronnie would need a wife . . . Tallents always chose their brides from beyond the county boundaries.

On each of the two summers following the end of the War she sent off persuasive invitations – even going to the trouble of looking up and providing a list of train departure and arrival times. Angela's response was as twittery but less evasive. Dr Killearn was anxious as to the state of her nerves and forebade the stress of travelling . . . it was a great disappointment but it would be discourteous to ignore the advance of a medical practitioner who took such devoted care of her physical and mental welfare. Nor would it be fair if on reaching her friend's house she collapsed and spent the whole of the holiday in her room which was more than likely.

The next year's reply was even more definite and petulant. A journey of such length was out of the question – even the drive of seven miles into Chester was agony and sitting in a train, torture. Dr Killearn wanted her to see a specialist, but what was the use? The long boat journey back from Singapore had smashed her health to pieces. Since that time she had never enjoyed a single day without pain or nervous agitation. She added that David was due home on furlough at the end of the month and her mother-in-law had come on an uninvited visit and taxed her with being an unnatural wife and selfish woman!

It was obvious that if they were to meet, Magnolia would have to travel up to Cheshire.

They went during the Easter holidays, setting off for and staying two nights in London so that Ronnie could visit the Tower and Madame Tussauds, watch the changing of the guard and be photographed beside a mounted trooper on Horse Guards Parade. He was full of his experiences and boastfully vociferous. The little girls, Phillipa and Rosanna, stared at him with almond shaped, dark blue eyes and when the quieter ventured to ask if he'd seen Peter Pan's statue in Kensington Gardens he demolished her in two swift sentences.

'Peter Pan's for sissies. Fairies are a lot of bunk – like Father Christmas.'

The other girl's instant reaction surprised him. Without shifting her gaze Rosanna gently touched her sister's hand. 'Boys, Philly, only *think* they're clever.' Something in the cool expression on her face quelled the bluster of a reply.

Despite having to be polite to silly girls the visit was a considerable success. The Edwardian townhouse was spacious enough to absorb two families and as the cook and housemaid performed their duties without constant watching and the two ladies happy in each other's company, Caroline was free to devote herself to the children's entertainment. She was good at organising outings and careful no one got overtired. The acre of garden contained a neglected tennis court. She retrieved a shabby but serviceable net from a box in the summer house, got the gardener to mark out lines and bought four lightweight rackets. The game became something of a craze and the children in the neighbourhood drawn in. Having played a little with his mother, Ronald knew enough about the rules to assume a position of authority. The dry spring days held out – the plink/plonk sound of bouncing balls resounded from morning till twilight. Angela was persuaded to watch and Magnolia to referee. More than a week passed before Ronald began to get bored and crave other amusement. He lost two points in a row to unaggressive but deft Phillipa and flung his racket across the court snapping the wooden frame.

'It's over a fortnight since I rode my pony. That's real sport not this sissy, putrid pitta-patta ball!'

There was a riding and hacking stable half a mile away. Magda took him the following morning and watched him jog away with a cluster of other smiling children. When, two hours later, she went to fetch her son she found him confined to the owner's office. The ride had lasted twenty minutes. Almost at once he had defied the instructions of the groom in charge and set his pony into a gallop over stony ground. He ignored all pleas and reprimands and orders to return to the group. One or two were near novices and badly frightened when he circled round forcing the animal to rear. By the time he and his mount were under control the pony was covered in a lather of sweat and two little girls in tears.

'The only good thing about your son, madam, is that he has a firm seat.' The owner of the stables held his voice tightly steady. 'His hands are hard, his conduct dangerous and his attitude towards his mount unpardonably cruel. I will never permit you to hire a pony of mine for him to ride again. He's lucky I didn't thrash him the way he whipped the creature.'

Magda's lips were pale as her cheeks, the grey eyes colourless.

She said, flatly, 'It's as well you didn't. I shall deal with my son as I think fit. And your remark, I consider, obviates the necessity for an apology. Come along, Ronald,' she took the glowering boy's stiff arm. 'Your unfortunate escapade has caused quite enough bother for one morning.'

The man held open the office door. 'Take my advice, discourage your son from owning horses . . . his sort are likely to maim if not kill 'em.'

She flushed poppy pink. 'I paid for the use of your pony not your opinion. It seems a pity you did not place Ronald with a more experienced group. One where everyone was capable of being given their head. That would have saved us both a lot of aggravation and needless trouble.'

'Your boy, madam, is likely always to be trouble on a horse.' Sensing he'd gone too far he added quickly, 'It was not my intention to be offensive . . . talk it over with the lad's father.'

She gave him a straight, cool look. 'That will be very difficult. His father is dead,' and pushing Ronald in front of her, walked away.

Far from taking Ronnie to task Magda ignored the incident merely remarking that it was rather silly to let his impatience to gallop spoil the whole of a morning's outing but his conduct persuaded her it was time to go home. She told Angela of her decision whilst they sat drinking their after dinner coffee giving no details but implying that the visit to the stables had increased Ronald's fretting after his own pony. Angela, whose fingers had been dipping into a box of chocolates, dissolved into trickle of ladylike tears.

'I'd not realised until you came to stay how *lonely* I am. How *starved* of congenial companionship.' Sniff, sniff, dab, dab with a lace edge wisp of handkerchief. 'Caroline is a great support and comfort but one can't make friends with a servant. And my health's been so much better . . . not even a tiny attack of those terrifying palpitations or more than a weeny headache, since you've been with me. It's simply not comprehensible to those blessed with good health,' more dabbing, blue eyes brimming over, 'to understand *how* much I suffer. I try, I really *try,* to be patient and uncomplaining but ill health is so . . . so *wearing.'*

Gently bracing, Magda answered, 'Easy to get Caroline to pack and then we could all travel down to Taurus together. That way you'll still have my company and a change can only do you good . . . in a close friend's house.'

Angela shrank back against the sofa cushions, twisted her fingers in her handkerchief and closed her eyes. 'Impossible . . . the strain would be too great. And very old houses are *so* depressing . . . all those dark corners and horrid, dim corridors. Besides I can't leave home just now with David's mother so ill in hospital after that nasty stroke. No matter how cruel tongued and unjust she may have been in the past it's my duty not to desert the poor old lady.'

As the hospital in question was in Wolverhampton even self controlled Magda was unable completely to suppress a gasp of astonishment at so artlessly spurious an excuse.

Before she'd regained her breath Angela tumbled on, 'Promise . . . promise you'll come back . . . another time. Perhaps during a school term. The noise even a well behaved boy makes – and Ronnie is a well behaved boy – can be so very trying.'

Magda went back – once or twice a year, always alone. She recognised Angela's plaintive hypochondria for what it was – a means of getting her own way. She even felt a kind of sympathetic approval. Angela had never been the adventurous sort and if David Bland had failed to appreciate what type of wife he'd picked the fault was on his side. An adoring, wishy washy, clinging softhearted girl, but softhearted only up to a certain degree – past that, steel lay hidden under swansdown flutterings and the graceful posture of chronic invalidism. Even since Archie's death no one had challenged Magnolia's decisions or sought to influence her will and before that, Archie had had the sense to choose a wife complementary to his own ways and needs. Marriage was the only career for women of Magnolia's and Angela's generation – they never contemplated any other. Men must take the responsibility for incompatible alliances.

Steeped though she might be in her care for Taurus and sublimely contented in the trust she held on her son's behalf, nevertheless, it came as a relief, every now and then, to take the first-class journey northwards, to spend a few days in purely feminine company, to persuade Angela on shopping sprees to Chester, visits to the theatre and critically to watch the little girls growing up.

They were so alike physically it always took her forty-eight hours to distinguish Phillipa from Rosanna (and not then always correctly) but gradually she formed the opinion that the older, quieter would make the more suitable wife for Ronnie. Rosanna showed a hint of independance not greatly approved of. After they had gone to bed and Caroline tactfully retired to the kitchen, the two old friends would sit cosily together (Angela eating chocolates and sipping brandy – for stimulant's sake) making plans. Neither doubted that their offspring would fail to fall into line. Phillipa adored her mother and grew distressed when, inadvertently she crossed her will whilst Magda was convinced that, as long as Ronald had his horses to ride, she could impose her own upon him without more than a fleeting, shortlived challenge. Nor was she worried that he'd fall in love. Ronnie went willingly to dances and tennis parties but girls did not interest him. He rarely made a date and even more rarely with the same girl twice.

The problem would be getting the young people together. There was no question of Ronald travelling up to Cheshire. And Angie wouldn't budge. Magda didn't invite the twins to stay – there would be no point; Angela would object to being left alone and she preferred Phillipa to visit Taurus away from her stronger sister's influence. She guessed that when the girls left school, Rosanna would go away from home – to wait a while would be to everyone's advantage.

In 1932 the unexpected happened – Naldo sold up and came back for good. A slump in the rubber business threatened, Uncle Arthur had died and Reginald had had enough of the Far East. It was natural that on his arrival in England he should make his way to Taurus. And, as the months passed, just as natural that any serious consideration to buy a property of his own faded away. To live as a non-paying guest in his sister's home suited them both. It cut his responsibilities to a minimum and Magda, notwithstanding her devotion to her son, was grateful to have another man about the place. Especially one who offered undemanding company and no interference in the running of the estate. That, in theory, since his coming of age, lay in Ronald's hands but in practice the young man, interested in nothing save the horses he rode often and too hard, left matters to his mother and Kelly Watts.

Reginald had no intention of interfering in anything. He bought shop premises in Bath and Taunton and was content to fill his days dabbling in games of golf and bridge and the antique business.

Magda wondered if Naldo's presence would effect a not very welcome miracle and bring her friend to Taurus but Angie's only response came in an expression of good wishes . . . no mention for old time's sake. Magnolia, enjoying her brother's companionship, let a year lapse without a journey north. Rosanna's letter containing the news of her mother's death came as a shock if not bereavement. She sent a wreath of freesias but did not attend the funeral.

When she judged the poignancy of Phillipa's grief had subsided she wrote to the girl inviting her to Taurus . . .

and went on writing. The replies, in a wobbly, thin hand, were as evasive as Angela's until, finally, in Silver Jubilee year, an acceptance arrived.

Magda twirled the single sheet triumphantly. 'I *knew* no girl, no matter how shy, could turn down the prospect of a Jubilee Ball. Phillipa Bland is coming to stay!'

Naldo stirred his breakfast cup of coffee. 'Step into my parlour said the spider to the fly.'

His sister ignored his teasing, pretending not to hear. 'She asks, could I advise her as to the most convenient train to catch . . . hasn't the girl ever heard of railway timetables? Must check with Haskins. Says how happy it would make her mother to know of the visit. Always a dutiful daughter, Phillipa.' She looked more closely at the letter.'The writing's remarkably steady – why some of her lines are almost straight.'

Chapter Three

On the day Phillipa arrived Reginald drove into Bath. There was no arguable reason why he should call in at the shop on that particular afternoon – his manager, Luckes, was more than competent. He knew her train was due in Somerton at 2.57; that Ronnie had gone over to the far side of the county inspecting two hunters for sale and that in order to fetch the girl it would be necessary for Greedy to leave the vegetable garden, get into his chauffeur's uniform and the dark grey Rover out of the stable garage. A small devil of independence held him back from offering to meet his sister's guest – it irked him that Magda would not agree to taking driving lessons. He had, with little difficulty, persuaded her to exchange Archie's last purchase – the Sunbeam – for something more modern – 'You wouldn't, Mag, be seen *walking* around in out of date fashions' – but driving – no. Not even with himself as instructor. He couldn't credit the reason for her refusal to be respected for Archie's wishes. She had improved the plumbing at Taurus and installed a generator for the supply of electric light and greeted his surprised comment on these innovations with the remark that it was rubbishy sentiment to allow memories of the dead to impede personal comfort and convenience. He reached the conclusion that his sister relished one of the few remaining privileges of a '*grande dame*' – ordering the carriage.

Ronnie possessed a snappy M.G. sports car bought more to impress his contemporaries than for personal pleasure – he preferred riding horses to changing gears – and Naldo traded in his Alvis every fifteen months. His present model was black, the leather seats piped in brilliant green.

There were three couples in the shop. Luckes had

dressed one corner of the window with a collection of chinawear commemorating past Royal occasions together with two specially designed mugs for the Silver Jubilee of King George V and Queen Mary. These he had labelled – The Antiques of the Future. They were, he reported, selling like hot Sally Lunns. Naldo went into the back room to look over his manager's gleanings from a recent local sale. One small item caught his eye. He fetched brown paper and parcelled it up . . . would make an ideal gift for Magda. Not a placatory gift. To placate formed no part of Naldo's nature and certainly not his sister and twin – their relationship at once so close and impersonally affectionate, precluded such necessity. She would never reproach him for failing to offer to meet her guest; he would never apologise for not doing so. She knew him to be mutely annoyed by her refusal to learn to drive; he understood how conditioned she was by virtue of her position as mistress of Taurus.

He drove in by the back entrance and found Greedy in the stable yard rubbing down the Rover much as he would one of his carriage horses.

'Young lady come on next train,' he said laconically, 'They'm takin' tea on the terrace.' Looked critically at the dusty Alvis. 'Could give your'n a goin' over, Mr King. Not enuff day left to make it worth gettin' back to they vegetables.'

'Good of you, Greedy.' He picked up the parcel from the passenger seat and dropped half a crown in its place. It was not his habit to expect his sister's servants to do work for him for nothing and he knew that by nightfall his car would gleam like moonshine – worth every penny. It was an effortless way to ensure popularity.

He chose not to approach the terrace by the shorter route along the drive and past the parlour but by way of the tennis court and over the upper lawn – he wanted to take a long, unobserved look at the girl his sister had lined up for Ronnie.

His first impression was that she wasn't nearly as shy as Magnolia had led him to believe. True she sat stiffly in the middle and well away from the back of the white painted, iron Victorian garden chair – hardly the most comfortable of furniture unless wearing half a dozen petticoats although Magda had done her best with the addition of well stuffed, brightly coloured seat cushions. Reginald could see that her eyes were lowered but there was nothing gauche or awkward in her pose. From his sister's description he had expected the bent head and half hunched shoulders of the eternally self conscious.

She was a dark girl, wearing a pale summer dress and as he drew closer he saw that her hair was very glossy, parted in the centre and swept smoothly down and back into a coil at the nape of her neck – a style, the following year, to be much photographed but rarely copied as the general public became aware of a lady by the name of Wallis Simpson.

The two figures, set against a backdrop of silvery stone and dark, deepset, faintly gleaming window panes, separated by a table spread with the paraphernalia for afternoon tea, presented an almost magazine-type picture the composition and colour so exact. He could visualise the caption – Five o'clock in an English garden. Then the frame was set in motion – Magda waved and lifted up the silver teapot to fill his cup.

'Here's Naldo, Phillipa.' Her voice clear as polished glass. 'My brother, Reginald King. Naldo, meet Phillipa Bland.'

The girl tucked down her head and glanced awkwardly up at him under lowered lashes. Her saucer clattered as she set it down upon the table at her side. It was obvious she didn't know if she was expected to shake hands. He reserved his original opinion and to save her further embarrassment sat down in the chair opposite next to Magda.

'Hello, Phillipa. How was the journey?'

His sister answered. 'Poor child missed the connection at Swindon. Arrived nearly forty minutes late. I've sent her cases up to her room and brought her out here at once for tea. No one can pretend train rides are pleasant on warm, sticky afternoons'.

The girl said, 'I . . . I didn't m . . . mind. It was

interesting. I . . . I've never travelled so far south.' Her voice was very quiet and with a hesitancy almost but not quite a stammer.

He took the cup from Magda and stirred the sugar cube she had dropped in. 'But you have travelled . . . north?'

'N . . . no. M . . . mother didn't care to go away from home. Her . . . her health was never very good.'

He looked up to see that she was regarding him with eyes as dark as a midnight sky. Then heavily lashed lids dropped like a curtain and she fumbled again with her tea cup.

He lifted the brown paper parcel from the side of his chair and held it out to Magda. 'Little something for you, sis. Part of a heap Luckes bought at an auction at Long Ashton.'

Her eyebrows rose – it was not in Naldo's nature to be a bearer of unexpected gifts.

He grinned. 'When you see it you'll understand. Mag, I thought, will appreciate *this*.'

Slowly she pulled back the wrappings – the half hoop of diamonds flashing on her left hand. Beneath the brown paper was a fold of tissue paper. She twisted away the edges and drew into sight a single, terracotta tile. The raised impression of a full grown bull – massive shoulders, lowered head, tail swishing – filled a six-inch square.

She gave a little gasp of pleasure. 'It's . . . Naldo, he's a beauty. Perfect!'

'Not a chip or blemish.' Reginald's satisfaction in her evident delight warmed his usual tone. 'I'd like to know who made him. Victorian, of course, but what a craftsman! I wonder where the others are'.

Magnolia turned the tile over – the back smooth and unscarred as its upper surface. 'You think, originally, more than one . . . maybe the signs of the zodiac?'

'Most probably. A commission I'd guess. Too high quality to be a popular, commercial line. But Luckes says there was no evidence of any more. El Torro here was part of a lot of pottery urns and bits and pieces that come from God knows where.'

Magda said, 'Don't insult him with a Spanish name –

he's a very British bull. I shall have him set in the stone on the right side of the entrance porch. *Thank* you, Naldo.' She held the tile out to her guest. 'Don't you think he's gorgeous, Phillipa?'

The girl kept her hands in her lap. 'I . . . I'd rather not . . . I'm sure it's very precious and easily broken. I . . . I'd never forgive myself if . . . if I . . .' the words trailed into nothing.

Reginald heard his own voice, . . . comfortingly, 'Phillipa's quite right. Terracotta is fragile. Beats me how the thing's survived all these years.'

Her response surprised them. 'M . . . maybe he's been waiting to be found and brought to this h . . . house.'

Magda shot an astonished look in the girl's direction. 'Strange . . . the same thought had occurred to me.'

Naldo's laugh came gently mocking. 'Oh, dear, oh dear, how you girls love to make a mystery out of merest chance.'

Magnolia rewrapped her gift and placed it carefully on the tray beside the silver teapot. 'The survival of Taurus for five hundred years is not the merest chance.'

'Taurus isn't portable, Mag. But I grant you the survival. And here,' he nodded in the direction of the lower lawn, 'if I'm not mistaken, arrives the son and heir to prove it.'

Ronnie had come from the stables. He wore faintly grubby, fawn jodhpurs and a pale blue aertex shirt. He carried his jacket and an ivory handled riding crop.

His mother said, 'Be a dear, Naldo and ring for more tea. This is stone cold.'

Reginald got up and went into the house through an open doorway some distance to the right of the mullioned, drawing room windows. He was back and reseated by the time the ambling Ronald drew level with the little group.

'Ronnie, here's Phillipa.' Magnolia's words came chipped and very clear – the girl was reminded of the most assertive of the nuns at her school. 'I wonder if you remember one another.'

Ronald ducked his head in sketchy greeting and said, 'Hello, Phillipa.'

No one heard the whispered response.

He dropped his crop with a clatter onto the paving stones and flopped into the vacant chair. Screwing up his eyelids he contemplated the visitor just on the inside of discourtesy. 'Yes . . . I remember you. You're the one who never said anything but played the better tennis.'

She gave a little gasp and nodded.

'What happened to the other? Rosanna, wasn't it?'

This time the reply was audible . . . just. 'She's a n . . . novice . . . in a n . . . nunnery.'

'Good Lord!' Ronald squashed a laugh. 'I'd have thought it would be the other way round.'

The girl's head came up . . . she was looking at him with a strange expression that seemed to increase the brilliance of her eyes.

Reginald cut in. 'What a rude young puppy you are, my lad.'

'Nonsense, Nunki Naldo, we're old friends.' He stretched his legs and leant back against the painted iron-work.

'I agree with your uncle and only hope you haven't hurt our guest's feelings.' The lightness of Magda's tone not quite agreeing with the flicker of exasperation that crossed her features. 'I apologise, Phillipa, on this rough diamond's behalf.'

With eyelids lowered the girl murmured, 'There's no need Mrs T . . . Tallent. Ronnie's just being clever.'

The young man frowningly dragged up his head, stared at her . . . let it flop back again.

A maid came towards the table carrying fresh tea. He flapped one hand. 'Not for me, Mater. I'd sooner have a cool drink . . . glass of beer.'

She gave a repressive little laugh. 'At this hour of the afternoon? Don't be ridiculous. Bring a jug of barley water, please for Mr Ronald. And leave the fresh pot. Mr King will probably drain it dry.'

Easy and acquiescent, Naldo pushed his cup towards her. 'Gladly, sis, if you don't mind my smoking.'

'Ask Phillipa.'

'N . . . no.' She looked overwhelmed by the suggestion. 'Of course n . . . not.'

He took out his black onyx lighter and rolled gold cigarette case. 'Do you?', he asked expecting a shake of the head but Phillipa Bland said, 'Th . . . thank you, yes,' and helped herself with steady, peach tipped fingers.

She smoked like a schoolgirl – without inhaling, continually tapping the tip of her ash into the serpentstone saucer on the table. He was conscious of a lovely figure – full, small, high breasts, tiny waist and long legs modestly crossed above shapely ankles. Her dress, white cotton, sprigged in little sprays of green leaves, with a scooped but close neckline and narrow cap sleeves, was as demure as her tucked-in feet in their low heeled, round toed, ankle strapped sandals. When she spoke defencelessness slipped out but seated and silent her poise presented an enigma. It were as if she shared a secret with someone who wasn't there. He was puzzled by so fanciful a notion and intrigued against his better judgement. Aware of Magda's intentions he glanced in his nephew's direction. Ronnie was fiddling in the pocket of his jodhpurs with one hand, tilting a tumbler with the other. Reginald felt a uncharacteristic surge of distaste which lasted no more than a moment. Then his natural indolence came sliding back. Ronald's sexual proclivities, his sister's matrimonial plans and the girl's well being were no business of his. He would stay, as always, a comfortable onlooker taking no part in the game.

At 5.30, chimney shadows starting to poke dusky fingers across the smooth, green grass, Magda picked up her parcel and took the girl indoors.

She paused beside the doorless entrance to the spikey porch and held the Taurus tile at hand height against its grey right wall. A purist would have found the burnt honey square an incongruous, silly blot both wrong in date and false in colour but to the women the exuberant outline of the bull seemed, magically, to leap and merge and mingle with the silvery exterior as though it had been waiting for just such an addition to the harmony of stone and sunlight.

The younger, newly arrived and a little dazed, this time

kept the sensation to herself but Magnolia exclaimed outright. 'Sublime! Bless Naldo! It may be no more than a hundred years old but this lovely, *flaring* fellow is where he belongs – at Taurus! I shall get Greedy to fix him first thing in the morning.'

She led the way through the duskiness of the narrow porch into a hallway untouched by sunshine. The air was cool, adrift with the perfume of lilies of the valley. In a shallow, cut glass bowl a pool of white blossoms flowed over the surface of a sturdy, black wood dower chest. Magda placed the rewrapped Taurus tile beside them and took her guest along the passageway and up the stairs.

The room she had chosen was on the east side of the house – walls colour washed in primrose, counterpane and curtains honeysuckle patterned and the faintly tilting, polished wood floor scattered with rugs in bronze and cream and gold.

Of the girl's luggage there was no evidence save for her small locked dressing case set on the little, rosewood bedside cabinet. The room was full of angles and niches – one had been filled in with doors to make a hanging cupboard and in another stood a washstand with yellow china jug, basin, soap dish and tooth mug. Fluffy white towels hung on the brass rail alongside.

'The bathroom's at the end of the passage – the last door to the right at the start of the westwing corridor.' Magda checked all around with appraising eyes. 'We dine at seven-thirty. I'm sure you must be tired . . . would like a rest. One of the maids will bring up hot water at about six forty-five. I'll come along half an hour later and take you down. This house isn't big, but it is confusing. We always have cocktails in the parlour before dinner – Naldo likes to mix them. The men don't bother with dinner jackets but I always change into something long.' She paused at the doorway. 'I'm delighted you're here, Phillipa,' she said and was gone.

The girl stayed stranded in the middle of the room without moving. Then, like a whirlwind, she crossed the floor seizing and turning the key in the lock as silently as she was able. After a frozen, listening thirty seconds she stumbled back towards and onto the bed. Hunching forward she buried her face in gripping, anguished fingers. The minute hand of her small, gold wristwatch ticked round once, twice, three times before Rosanna Bland straightened up . . . stared blankly straight in front of her.

Angela's twins were indistinguishable. If both had been of a mischievous disposition the opportunity for playing tricks was endless.

In temperament they differed. Phillipa, the older by half an hour, was the gentler. Timid, biddable, fascinated from early childhood by all things religious and lacking curiosity she never once queried the exclusively feminine nature of their household nor felt any deprivation by reason of their father's continued absence abroad. Rosanna, possessing greater stamina, a marked degree of independence and a liking for change and challenge, thought God to be on a par with fairy tales and envied her friends whose fathers came home every evening. Also she dimly became aware that a special relationship existed between those friends' parents . . . a mysterious relationship somehow tied up with the fact that fathers were *men*.

When, eventually, David came home on leave her excited expectations were dashed and the mystery deepened. He was awkward with the little girls whom he had not seen since babyhood and Phillipa, unused to a man about the house and shrinkingly shy, added to that awkwardness. Passionately protective, as she was, of her frailer twin, Rosanna, for the first time in her life, felt a twinge of irritation at Philly's excessive sensitivity and David's natural confusion as to his daughters' individual identity inhibited his reaction to the one who wanted to be recognised and loved.

She was conscious, too, of a sense of friction – a twisted, evasive anger she couldn't understand – existing between her parents. An overheard conversation puzzled and troubled her. She kept the exchange to herself.

David was saying, 'Angela, for Christ's sake, anyone would think I was asking the earth – demanding an indecency. After all I am your *husband*.'

Mother's reply came plaintive and reproving. 'There's no cause to blaspheme.' She sighed. 'If only I were stronger. I fear, Davy, your wife's a poor, weak, useless thing. Dr Killearn says that to do as you wish would be injurious to my health.'

Father cut in. 'That's so much nonsense! I've spoken to Killearn. His opinion is that to sleep with me would do you a power of good as long as I didn't impose the strain of another child. I promise you that's not my intention.'

The following, frigid silence cut like an iceburg through the closed door separating Rosanna from her parents. Then she heard Mother's voice high pitched with a fury she recognised and dreaded. 'You have consulted *my* medical practitioner?'

'The *family's*.' Father's tone was just as angry but not raised. 'You and I have been apart for almost seven years – what could be more natural?'

It was her mother's turn to spring into quick speech. 'Don't pretend you've not had one little chi-chi during all that time.'

Sharp as a razor. '*I* pretend nothing. It was *you* who chose to stay in England. Did you expect me to live like a monk whilst on my own?' The anger faded. 'Now we're together I want only to make love to my pretty wife. But because she was reluctant I had the heart to discover if there was good reason why she should be so.' In the pause that followed the little girl sensed that he had come closer to the other. 'Tell me, truly, Angela, did I ever give you cause to tax me with lack of tenderness?'

Mother, clinging defensively to a single theme, cried, 'MEN! Trust you to hang together. I shall change my doctor . . . find a woman. One who cares . . . understands.'

A terrifying quietness preceded her father's words. 'Are you aware, Angela, that denial of marital rights can form grounds for divorce?'

A gasp came rattling – then nothing for a long time. Shakily and with a little laugh she heard her mother say, 'Don't tease, Davy. If Dr Killearn truly advises there's no harm of course I'll . . . agree to your . . . desires. Perhaps we could go away . . . a second honeymoon ...'

The response came unemotional and flat. 'You've just proved something to me. That you really are a bitch, my dear. I wouldn't have you in my bed if you were the last woman in the world,' and the door opened and he walked past the child looking straight into her face but unaware of her existence.

That night David packed his bags and went away. Rosanna cried herself to sleep rejecting Philly's puzzled attempts to comfort her.

Life returned to tame, maleless normality. Unknown to the twins a solicitor's letter arrived stating that the undersigned undertook to support his wife and children whilst, as the house was in his name, reserving the right to stay in the family home whenever it suited him on his furloughs to England without making any other demands on Angela Mary Bland, his wife. To Angela's chagrin it dawned that whilst separation was acceptable divorce would probably have ruined her husband's career – something David was unlikely to risk. Their final, humiliating exchange of words had been unnecessary. In a seething rage she took to her bed and sent for the new GP – Dr Isobel Brodie – who prescribed absolute quiet, light meals and a bottle of white wine per day. For close on a week Phillipa, Rosanna and Caroline crept around the house.

At the age of eleven, the girls were sent to a school run by the Wantage Sisterhood – St Oswold's Abbey.

It was a happy choice. For Phillipa, to be taught by nuns was to be close to heaven and even more heavenly the school chapel redolent with the scent of incense, awash with long, black skirts and dotted, in dim corners, with little, gilded statuettes. To the delight of both girls there were five hard tennis courts in the grounds – the games mistress had played for her county and Abbey pupils almost invariably winners of the inter-schools tennis challenge cup.

Situated at the end of the road next to their house it was

within easy walking distance . . . possible to eat luncheon with Caroline and Mother. Rosanna jibbed at this. She was beginning to find home stultifying and (an avid reader of the books of Angela Brazil) secretly longed to become a boarder. She grudged the forfeited half-hours of tennis practice and the other free time occupations that filled the luncheon break. Unwilling to accept the inevitable she set about hunting for a remedy.

'What we need,' she said, 'is to catch streaming colds. Lots of them. You know how scared Mother gets when anyone is really ill.'

'But we never do.' Phillipa was right – they were healthy little girls.

'We will if next time it pours with rain, we get a soaking and sit all afternoon in damp shoes.'

'That won't do, Anna . . . have to change into slippers.'

'They'll get damp as well if our feet are wet enough. We'll *jump* into every puddle, Philly.' Seeing the other's continued hesitation she added her persuasive, trump card. 'Sister Polydore holds prayer meetings in chapel on Mondays and Thursdays before afternoon class.'

Obligingly, because no heavy rain fell until the end of November, Caroline contracted shingles. Dr Brodie, aware of her employer's plaintively demanding disposition, sent the young woman into hospital for the total rest she needed. That left only cook and the daily housemaid to run the home. Angela dissolved into pretty, inadequately suppressed tears.

'How shall we manage? If only I were less weak . . . or the girls older.'

Dr Brodie had the answer. 'They attend the Abbey, do they not? Let them board until Caroline's back on her feet.'

The next two weeks were the happiest of Rosanna's schooldays . . . she 'lived' right at the heart of one of her favourite stories. A shrewd notion that Mother could easily be persuaded to make the arrangement permanent tempted her to try but not even the opportunity to attend three chapel services a day could compensate for Phillipa's homesickness every evening. She hated sleeping in a dormitory. Regretfully, and out of affection, Rosanna abandoned her scheme. But luncheon at school became a happy fixture.

In middle adolescence the twins blossomed into unconventional good looks. Not even heavy plaits and navy blue gymslips could obliterate the promise of something close to loveliness. 'Madonnas,' Sister Polydore called them, when out of hearing.

David came home in time for their fifteenth birthday and failed to recognise the plain little girls he'd left behind. Even by the end of his leave he still found difficulty in distinguishing one daughter from the other.

That was easiest in conversation. Philly's words got smudged now and then with the hint of a stammer whilst the other possessed ideas, the confidence to express them and a protective attitude towards her more vulnerable sister. He noted that neither ever opposed their mother but that it was Phillipa who always went to sit beside her. On leaving, he gave each a golden chain – with a cross for Philly and for Rosanna a locket in the shape of a rose. It never occurred to suggest to his younger daughter that she join him in Singapore when she left school and the girl lacked sufficient self assurance to ask the man who still remained a stranger. But she had no intention when the time came of staying at home. Philly wasn't likely to budge so Mother couldn't declare herself abandoned. (Phillipa prayed each night to be granted the gift of a vocation but kept her longing to become a nun hidden even from her adored sister).

Rosanna discussed possible careers with Sister Boniface who taught science and was fond of her. The choice was limited. University not considered – Rosanna doubted if her father would be willing to bear the expense; a secretarial course held little appeal and teaching even less. Which left nursing. The best teaching hospitals were in London, Bristol and Edinburgh. Edinburgh was furthest away. Although no vacancy fell due until well after her eighteenth birthday a desire to go as far as possible tempered her impatience to be off. Rosanna was prepared to wait until three months short of her nineteenth birthday to enroll as probationer at the Robert Carnegie Hospital.

Her last term at school was fraught with a domestic crisis. Staid, dependable Caroline had, out of the blue, announced that she was to marry a Barnardo boy to whom she had been writing ever since they left the Home and go with him to Australia. So shocked was Angela that she refused to speak for two days and never again addressed one word to the woman she now deemed and referred to as 'that traitor.' Adding bitterly, 'And she had the nerve to tell me *after* I'd paid her month's wage in advance.'

Rosanna, with a mildness she didn't feel, said, 'But, Mother, she'll work it through.'

'She will *not*. I've written a note informing her to pack and be gone first thing tomorrow morning.'

Both girls went very white. Rosanna muttered under her breath but so low only her sister could hear. 'At least she'll have a wedding present that way.'

Philly asked, 'Wh . . . where will she go?'

'That's no concern of mine. When I think what I've done for that young woman . . . she owes everything to me . . . to treat me like this . . . it's shameful!' Angela pulled out the ever available wisp of handkerchief and dabbed at her brimming eyes.

Rosanna rose abruptly, left her sister dropping kisses on their mother's hair, a consoling arm around her shoulders and went into the kitchen. The daily housemaid had gone, cook was washing up the supper dishes. She seized an entrée dish belligerently.

'If you're looking for Caro she's in her room. Packin' and cryin' most like.'

The girl said, 'I'm sorry . . . what I mean is I'm glad Caroline's getting married but where will she go tomorrow?'

'No need to trouble yourself about that, miss. Her fiancé's staying back in the Barnardo's so she'll go there. If they're short of room I told her my Auntie May'll put her up until the wedding. She's got *friends*, you know.' Clashing a couple of saucepans.

'When is the wedding?'

'Four weeks on Tuesday. I shall take the afternoon off and if Madam objects hand in my notice.'

'Oh dear.'

She looked hard at the girl. 'You *are* Miss Anna, Miss?'

'Yes . . . Phillipa's mopping up Mother.'

'She would be.' Vigorously wielding a scouring brush. 'The times I've seen Caroline do just that . . . on her evening off too, most likely.'

Rosanna said, as though thinking aloud. 'If you do leave it will make things very difficult.'

'If I stay, miss, it'll be for your sake and Miss Philly's.'

The correction came fast. 'Mostly for Phillipa's. I go to Edinburgh in a year or so . . . all arranged.' She swung back to the person uppermost in their minds. 'I'm going up to Caro's room . . . Mother will think I'm doing prep . . . ask if I can be bridesmaid.'

The occasion of Caroline's wedding was to be the only time in all her life that Rosanna Bland sought moral guidance. She went to Sister Polydore who, at first, thought her to be Phillipa. Quickly, she discovered her mistake. *This* girl was lucid, lacking the self-absorption that characterised her sister and troubled the nun a little – Philly showed herself more concerned with her own soul than other people's reactions. Also she remembered that Phillipa had been absent for the last week – the girls' mother was ill and needed her.

Rosanna's dilemma was straightforward and, in Sister Polydore's unexpressed opinion, shocking. Caroline, her pupil explained, had been the main, the *loving* prop in the home ever since the twins could remember. Mother ... Rosanna's hesitation though real enough lacked apology .... *believed* herself to be a semi-invalid. It had been Caroline who picked up the little girls and kissed them better when they fell; Caroline who held the basin when they were sick; Caroline who made sure their clothes were clean and aired, who took them to and fro from kindergarten, taught them the rudiments of tennis and all the while running the house, ordering the food, soothing Mother's nerves.

Mother said Caroline had been wickedly ungrateful and deceitful but surely she was entitled to a life of her own ... a husband if she fell in love? Would it be *so* wrong if she and Philly spent all their saved up pocket money on a wedding present? If she stayed away from school that one afternoon to go to Caroline's wedding? Philly couldn't be expected to defy their mother's wishes but if *she* were prepared to do so, wouldn't it only be just, be fair, be *kind* to Caroline who was so dearly loved by both of them?

Sister Polydore said a quick prayer not to prejudge another woman merely on a child's angry, hurt report. She acknowledged that the anger was suppressed but boiling underneath. She also caught a forward picture of Phillipa replacing the servant in her mother's life and made a resolve not to lose contact with the girl.

She asked, gently, 'You want, very much, to go to Caroline's wedding?'

'I want to be a bridesmaid but Caro says that would be inappropriate.'

The nun was surprised. 'She used that word?'

Rosanna bristled. 'She may come from a Barnardo's Home but Caroline isn't illiterate.'

Sister Polydore smiled. 'I'm sorry, my dear, it was not my intention to denigrate your Caroline. She sounds an admirable woman. And I think for honest affection's sake you should buy her the best present you can afford and go to the wedding. On Phillipa's behalf as well as your own. There can be, child, certain loyalties in life stronger even than those we owe our family. If necessary I will explain to Mother Superior that you have my permission to be absent on that particular afternoon.' With an almost imperceptible gesture she touched the girl's hand. 'You'll not want to wear school uniform ... come to my room to change. That I will explain to Mother Superior too, if the need arises.'

Caroline wore a suit of blue, artificial silk with a dipping brimmed hat wreathed in forget-me-nots. She carried a bouquet of pink roses and asparagus fern. Rosanna, chilly in lemon flowered ninon – the day was overcast but there had been room for no more than a dress in her school attaché case – sat in the left hand front pew together with the Barnardo Home house father and mother. After the short, hymnless service she went into the vestry and proudly signed the register. When photographs were being taken in the porch Caroline insisted on one of just bride, groom and Rosanna – the unofficial bridesmaid. As they drove away to the reception she couldn't attend, the realisation came flooding with a little spurt of tears that she would never see Caro again. The need to get away from home swelled like an aching abscess. She wanted to feel guilty because Phillipa's willingness to take Caro's place made her ultimate escape so easy but her twin's obvious contentment ensured nothing save a sensation of thankfulness.

'What about the nun thing, Philly?' She had, for her own peace of mind, to question her sister. 'I know you've never said much but I thought ... don't you want that anymore?'

'More than ever ... but not yet.'

'Mother's a creaking gate ... the sort who'll live to be a hundred. What chance of your vocation then?'

'You shouldn't talk like that ... I don't ask to look into the future. Each day, Anna, is God's. Consider the lilies of the field ....'

Her sister jumped in. '*We're* not lilies! Least I'm not. More the rampant bindweed! I must think ahead ... for the next four years anyway. The first will be a trial ... being with you the one good thing. After that, it's all exciting speculation.'

Phillipa lifted Rosanna's hand and held it to her cheek. 'You're not to worry about me, after you've gone. I know I shall become a nun when the time is right and, in four years, you'll be a nurse.'

'It's certainly my intention but ... but all sorts of things can happen whilst one's training. I'm not sure that it's not the unpredictability of life that I like best.'

Philly said, a little tremulously, 'You ... you will spend your holidays here? It ... it's going to seem so strange without you.'

'You bet! I'll probably find I can't get away fast enough after months of bedpans, nasal drips and dragons of ward sisters.'

'Perhaps you'll fall in love. With a handsome medical student.'

'Like they do in films? I doubt it. There'll be lots of competition. And medical students are *boringly* young.'

Chapter 4

She overestimated the strength of the competition but not one other thing at Robert Carnegie failed to reach her expectations. It was a relief and a delight to be somewhere new, exhilarating to be part, at last, of the quiet bustle of an institution and a pleasure to wear the lilac and white uniform of the first year student – a colour combination not popular with everyone. She was lucky, too, in that her dark, smooth hairstyle ideally suited the probationer's stiff, small cap – girls with curls quickly became untidy as the starched, white linen slid askew.

She rapidly recognised how callow the majority of medical students and, almost as swiftly discovered that the probationers in her year divided neatly into two categories – those who wanted to fall in love with and marry a doctor and those who believed the care of the sick to be as much a vocation as taking religious orders. Rosanna fitted into neither. This did not make for popularity. The husband hunters were piqued by the effortless ease with which she attracted masculine eyes, whilst the dedicated, resented her calm efficiency on the ward and high marks in the classroom. This did not bother her at all. She made a couple of cool friendships, staved off the most persistent admirers and wrote each week to Philly dutifully enclosing a note for Mother. At the end of her first twelve months she came top in her year. Happily she went home on long vacation to find Phillipa as happy and her mother looking genuinely frail and shadowy around the eyes. But four days of Angela's querulous, self-indulgent conversation were sufficient to quash any concern she originally might have felt. She played, on fine days, as a guest at Phillipa's tennis club, was entertained to tea by a new, attentive aquaintance of Angela's, a middle-aged widow called

Sophie Kennedy and accepted, with courteous indifference, a dance date and an excursion to the Chester theatre. On parting, she allowed the young man to kiss her chastely on the cheek.

She returned gratefully to Robert Carnegie, easy in her mind as to her sister's well being and eager for the next year's challenge. Home was stifling – the breeze that swept through Edinburgh's wynds blew more than cobwebs and discontent away. It was spiked with the scent of heather and salt and a promise of the unknown.

The first duty of her second year was on Mackintosh – a chest/heart ward. She reported, immaculate in her new, crisp, butterscotch uniform, at eight-thirty in the morning. Sister Findlay, fortyish, skinny, grey streaked curls edging a starch-stiff veil, said, 'So you're Bland.' No hint of fussiness stained angular features but her dark eyes were taut at the corners. 'I've two experienced staff sick. Just hope you're as good and reliable as your report implies.'

Rosanna said nothing. 'Yes' seemed inappropriate.

Sister led the way to a side ward. 'This is Mr Sewerin's patient. Mr Sewerin is here as one of our consultants because he has perfected a new method of thoracic surgery.' Her tone ambiguously flat. 'Mr Sewerin operated on this man last night. He needs constant watching. You are to relieve Nurse Aberfeldy.'

The woman by the bedside got to her feet. 'No change, Sister.' She looked close to retirement age and very tired.

'No need to touch him, Bland. Keep an eye on the drip and the urine bag and constantly watch his colour and respiration, just ring the bell if you judge anything's amiss. I repeat JUDGE – not imagine.'

The patient was propped up, greyfaced but breathing normally.

Rosanna said, 'Yes, Sister.' Whatever apprehension she had experienced when following the other through the door began to fade. Responsibility would never overawe Rosanna, and although she hadn't expected to start her second year of training all alone, if that was the way the coin fell, so be it.

Sister Findlay was regarding her with something less than a narrow bootface. 'If you've any reasonable doubts, Bland, press the bell. It is your first day ....'

'Thank you, Sister.' She sat down in the just vacated chair and studied her patient. He must be young because his hair was gold as corn dust but he looked very, very old. What did one think of while watching a maybe dying man? Nonsense! It was to make as sure as was possible that he wouldn't die that she sat by his side. Positive thoughts ... positive ... fill her mind with all the *plus*, the vital, living things whilst all the time on guard. Look at the colour of his skin – the ease with which his chest went up and down and think of running, running to meet the sun ... of warmth and snowdrops pushing up through a blanket of snow.

She was as unconscious of the minutes passing as was her patient – it could have been fifteen or fifty when the door opened and she saw Sister standing on the threshold a little behind and to one side of a tall man with silvery blond hair and a side buttoning white coat.

'Well, Bland?'

'No change, Sister, except I think he seems a little more relaxed.'

The man was looking straight at her – his eyes the colour of faded violets. He said, 'You're new.'

Sister Findlay put in defensively. 'Bland joined the ward this morning. I've one Staff Nurse sick and a third-year student on compassionate leave, otherwise I wouldn't have assigned her this responsibility. She came top probationer in her year.' She made the last words sound like an alibi.

Rosanna moved back so that the surgeon could come close to his patient without the hazard of the drip stand. He made no effort to touch the man but stood looking down at him for a long, silent moment.

'Good ... your nurse is right. Stiffness in the neck easing.' The foreign accent in his voice was only just discernible ... more a lilt than mispronunciation. 'We've pulled him through the worst hurdle ... the first twelve hours. If he can hold his own as well during the remaining twenty-four *we* can start to breathe more easily again. I'll be in to see how he does between five and six o'clock'. Without looking back he left the room.

As she followed Sister Findlay gave the girl an unsmiling nod which the more optimistic could have interpreted as approval.

Rosanna did not at once return to her seat. She moved down to the foot of the bed and lifted off the clip board of temperature chart and case notes. The patient's name was Jamieson Black, thirty-three years old, a steelworker. The operation had lasted three hours and a quarter.

She was in the act of reattaching the clip when a voice behind her made her jump.

'Sister says you're to go to coffee. And then report to her. S'my stint here, now.' The voice's owner had red hair, freckles, a wide, smiling mouth and blue striped third-year uniform.

The blue stripe checked Rosanna's angry retort. What if in surprise she'd clashed the board against the bed rail jarring the patient? But it was best not to antagonise a senior on the ward. She kept silent.

The smile broadened showing a gap between front teeth. 'I'm Lawson. You're Bland – right? Don't upset yourself if nothing pleases Sister this morning. Sh'always crabby whenever handsome Carl has a special patient. Most people'ud die for Sewerin – not Sister Findlay.'

Rosanna said, with truth, 'I don't upset easily.'

'Don't be too sure with the fiendish Find.'

Work on Mackintosh Ward was demanding and Sister Findlay as demanding as the work. A chilly woman who froze completely during Carl Sewerin's rounds she never gave praise and rarely criticism – reprimands came from necessity. Only with Douglas Laing, the senior surgeon, did she evince a touch of warmth. Rosanna enjoyed the challenge imposed by her high standards but days off came as a relief.

There was, on the corner at the top end of Princes Street within five or six minutes walking distance of the Nurses' Home, an exclusive tea room – Flora's. Once or twice a fortnight Rosanna treated herself to Ceylon tea and pastries oozing cream. Usually she went alone. Few of her colleagues were prepared to pay the prices written on the gilt-edged menu cards. Only two or three could, in fact, afford to do so.

On the afternoon of her first free day from Mackintosh the room was already full. Instinctively, she slid her eyes towards her usual table in an alcove. It was occupied by a single man – looking straight in her direction. Carl Sewerin rose, bowed a little and indicated the empty seat beside him. A little dazed and aware of the click of her high-heels she crossed the room.

She wore a dress and jacket of soft, hyacinth blue wool with a little halo hat. She carried a navy blue clutch bag that matched bow trimmed, four-inch high court shoes. Required to spend all her working hours sensibly shod Rosanna, no matter how far she had to walk, always chose frivolous, feminine footwear.

Even without make-up her creamy skin and wide eyes had caught his attention – now her rather too full mouth was tinted a rosy pink, curved cheekbones blushing a little beneath a hint of rouge and her long lashes darkened and glossy as her neat, smooth hair. Watching her – full, small, high breasts thrust even higher by the tilt of the high-heels she wore – he felt a surge of delight ... excitement.

When she reached his side he repeated the little, continental bow. 'Please, Miss Bland, join me. This place is unusually full. I am expecting no one.'

'Thank you.' He held her chair till she sat down. 'You're very kind.'

'Not kind at all. I dislike eating by myself even at four-thirty in the afternoon.'

What then, she wondered, was he doing in Flora's tea room?

He answered her unspoken question. 'I have a sweet tooth – crave rich cakes.'

As if on cue, the waitress placed a stand of fancies on the table and stood waiting expectantly. 'Madame? ... Sir?' She was a heavy girl, the lace frill of her uniform cap rested unbecomingly on a broad brow.

Rosanna said, 'A pot of Ceylon tea, please.'

Sewerin. 'My usual coffee.'

She turned the cake stand more to her satisfaction and went away.

Keeping her eyes on the retreating back Rosanna said, 'You're clever to know my name.'

'Not clever, I assure you. I try always to remember names – often without success. Your name was easy. It does not suit you. Unruffled, competent as a good nurse should be, but '*Bland*', I doubt.'

The girl's eyes widened on a new consideration. 'Names are . . . just names.'

'And rarely like their owners. How many Blacks have you known who are swarthy?'

That brought a picture of the man in the sideward. He was able, now, to talk a little and in a day or two would be moved out into the main public ward.

Once more Sewerin picked up her imagination. 'You see – our brave patient in Mackintosh hasn't a wisp of black hair on his head.'

'But a chance to live!'

He smiled gently at the youthful passion in her voice. 'He was a good subject for the operation. Technique and aftercare can only play so much a part in success. That man, as they say up here, is a 'bonnie fighter'.' His smile deepened. 'You're not a Scot?'

'No . . . I live near Chester.'

'Why then come to train in Edinburgh?'

'To get away from home.'

He looked amused. 'There are good – the best – teaching hospitals in London.'

'Not far enough.'

'I was right about your name,' he said. 'Perhaps your *first* name is more appropriate.'

The waitress came with their orders and when she had gone Sewerin asked, 'What is it?'

'My first name? Rosanna.'

'Pretty but not pretty enough. I shall call you Rüslein.'

The implication of intimacy in his words dizzied her. Hastily she replaced the teapot glancing at the man to see if he had noticed her trembling fingers but he was preoccupied with filling his own cup. Carefully he dribbled in a teaspoon of cream and a few grains of dark, brown sugar and looked around the bright room filled with discreet chattering.

'This is the one English – no, pardon me, we're north of the border – *British* habit to which I cannot grow accustomed. *Teatime*.'

She laughed and the sound brought his eyes round to her.

'You're here!'

'To drink *coffee*. These are the only people in Edinburgh who know how to make a decent cup – these and my wife.'

She felt as if a tiny, cold hand had tweaked her heart. Blindly, she took a very white meringue from off the plate he proffered.

Cutting into a millefeuille, he asked, 'Are you never homesick, Rüslein?

She shook her head. 'There's too much going on. Sometimes . . . not often . . . I miss my sister. We're twins. Her name's Phillipa.'

He regarded her with sharpened interest. 'Phillipa . . . the stay-at-home one?'

'She looks after Mother. Mother is – or thinks she is – a semi-invalid. Philly's . . . religious. She goes to church at least twice a day – at least she does when Mother's feeling 'strong' enough to let her go. One day she'll take vows . . . become a nun.'

'And your father?'

'We never – hardly ever – see him. He works in Singapore. Mother couldn't stand the climate.'

The picture was more vivid than the girl intended. He glimpsed a querulous, sexless, selfish wife and a husband who, sensibly, cut his losses, made his own bachelor life abroad with little interest in his daughters.

Ingenuously, because she felt she ought to make a positive contribution to the conversation, she said, 'Your home must be even further away.'

'My home, Rüslein, is here.'

Startled she stared at him. 'You won't go back?'

'To Germany, no. My wife is half Jewish.' And saw from her blank eyes that she didn't understand – the almost inevitable, British reaction.

'You don't mind?'

'For myself, not at all. For Irma it is different. She misses her family and friends, the home we've had since we first married and the streets and shops she's been used to all her life. It should be better when I get her younger brothers over here, though having them in the house won't improve her spoken English.'

She said, impulsively, 'Your English is marvellous! One can hardly tell you . . . ' blushed as she bit off the patronising end to her sentence.

'Don't look so confused. It would be disgraceful if it were not so. My grandmother was English.' He selected a petit four in the shape of a rose and dropped it on her plate. 'She met my grandfather when he came to London with our Prince Frederick for his marriage to Queen Victoria's Princess Royal. We used to spend holidays with uncles and aunts by the sea in Sussex and in Cambridgeshire. After,' he hesitated a little over choosing his next words, 'I had been a doctor for five years I took a post-graduate course at St Bartholomew's in London and then spent six months in the United States. When my old chief at Bart's – who is now at Carnegie – invited me to demonstrate the new technique it was easy to arrange a permanent appointment. In a few years' time, I shall apply for naturalisation papers. In a generation or two, no one will realise Sewerin is a German name.'

She asked, 'Have you any children?'

'No.' The monosyllable only. She regretted asking.

Sewerin drained his coffee pot and placed it, empty, back upon the table. 'What plans, Rüslein, does a probationer nurse have for the rest of her day off?'

The dizziness was not as great – she had half anticipated the question. 'Perhaps the pictures . . . .'

'Time enough for that when the evenings draw in. Do you know Glenspeysie House?'

Everybody did. By name if not experience. The most

expensive country hotel within fifteen miles of the city, overlooking the Firth of Forth.

'I'll take you there. A walk in the fresh air will do us good after all this delectable, unhealthy sweetness.' He signalled for the bill. 'Don't worry, little one, about getting back. I'll deliver you safely before nightfall and the Nurses' Home is locked.'

Now the dizziness came sweeping but she managed to ask, 'What about your wife?'

'Away to Glasgow. Irma's an opera singer . . . gives recitals.'

The picture of a heavy *hausfrau* with faded blonde, tight twisted plaits faded.

He paid the bill and put his fingers round her elbow. She felt a little tingle akin to a mild electric shock and remembered deriding such a description in romantic novels.

When they reached the entrance to the street, he held open the door but did not touch her again.

His car was parked down a side road – a gleaming, silvery grey Bentley Coupé. Used only to the Austins and Lanchesters driven by the parents of her friends the size and magnificence caught her breath.

He asked, 'Do you like her?'

'I don't know . . . so grand . . . .'

'I would prefer,' he said, assuming she would understand, 'a forty-horsepower tourer in British racing green but, for a German, the colour would not be diplomatic nor the style decorous enough for a Consultant Surgeon.'

'Are Consultant Surgeon's never indecorous?'

'Certainly not on duty . . . this one out of working hours . . . .' he let the sentence slide.

Once the city limits were behind them, he drove fast. She was caught up in a new experience of speed and exhilarated not only by the rush of air outside the car but the controlled sense of power that could cleave a passage through real but invisible space. She clasped her hands together. '*Now* I know how Toadie felt!'

The man laughed and cried, 'Poop – Poop!'

The gates of the hotel came all too soon – tall and imposing. Almost immediately Sewerin turned off the main drive and down a narrower, tree-lined way.

After about one hundred yards they drew level with the first of five little, timber cabins, each one secluded amongst a copse of shrubs and pines. Sewerin's was the fifth. He pulled onto the greensward by the front door and cut the engine.

'Welcome, Rüslein, to my retreat.' Wondered whether to kiss her then and there . . . decided not.

The inside consisted of one room – pine walled, pine floored, pine ceilinged. There were scatter rugs on the boards and bright curtains pulled well back from the two pairs of windows. A desk, the top tidily stacked with files, papers and a blotter, stood beneath one and at the back, to the left, a waist high screen serving also as a bookcase, hid the tiny kitchen. The other, inner wall contained a door leading to bathroom and storage space. There were two bamboo and canework easy chairs – one a rocker; a table with three backless stools pushed underneath; a big divan strewn with a polyglot heap of cushions and a drinks cabinet. She was reminded of a stage set just after curtain rise – the heartbeat moment before the play begins.

He moved past her. 'If we are to take that walk we must go now . . . before the sun sinks. Those pretty shoes of yours are useless. Take them off. I'll find something more suitable.'

Obediently she sat down on the stable chair, placed her handbag on the seat of the adjacent rocker, pulled off her hat, dropped it on top and began wriggling free her toes. When Sewerin returned from the inner room he carried tennis shoes, a pair of grey silk socks and a pale fawn Burberry draped over one arm.

'Here you are Cinderella Rüslein. They may be a little large but the socks will help to fill them out.'

Rosanna, loathe to touch anything belonging to his wife, hesitated. Alert to her reason he reassured her with a half lie. 'My predecessors here had a daughter who was mad about tennis. They left things behind but no forwarding address.' Irma had never been to the cabin and didn't play tennis – a previous, careless girlfriend did and, because of the carelessness and lack of discretion, was a girlfriend no longer. He had no notion who rented the place before him.

They went out by the back door beside a little boiler-house. Sewerin explained that in winter the cabins were centrally heated – a man from the hotel coming down morning and evening to stoke the furnace.

'There is not one chilly corner. I have sat at my desk in shirt sleeves and the ground outside with snow.'

Rosanna suspected that the description held a tint of something more fundamental and not only for himself. She blushed. He smiled down, delighted by her quick, charmingly confused perception.

They walked to the river over grass that led through a thicker copse to a newly varnished gate of cedarwood. High above the water, the right-hand side of the path ended in a sheer, sharp drop edged with a mat of wind-blown wynbushes. On the other, a stone topped bank rose almost level with undulating, pale green grassland. The hotel, Sewerin said, stood even higher – tree-screened from view.

The path was stony but wide enough for two to walk without touching. Lazily it twisted to the left and when the apex of the curve was reached the solid, dominating span of the Forth Bridge swung into sight . . . massive humped ironwork burnished bronze by the rays of the setting sun. On the smooth water below a single yacht meandered eastwards, its triangle of sail no more than a dab of Chinese white upon a painting.

In her too-large shoes the ground was hard going. She stumbled . . . righted herself before Sewerin could touch her.

'It's . . . stupendous! That glorious light . . . .'

'Man builds bridges . . . the light comes from nature or heaven . . . take your pick.'

'Man could reproduce it in oils . . . if gifted enough.'

'Are you an artist, Rüslein?'

'Not me . . . that's Phillipa.'

He asked seriously, 'Do you love your sister more than anyone else?'

'So far, yes.'

'Which means?'

His tone was bantering but she took the question gravely. 'Because she *is* my sister. We're half of one whole . . . she's always *been* there. But now we're parted I'm no less than a whole person . . . one who can choose whom she should love.'

He matched her gravity. 'Are you sure "choice" forms a part of loving?'

'Perhaps not. But chance must.' She twinkled up at him. 'Whenever I play Monopoly and I pick the card TAKE A CHANCE OR GO TO MARYLEBONE, I never choose the station.'

He laughed with pleasure and caught at her hand. 'How old are you, Rüslein?'

'Nearly twenty.'

'A blessed age . . . the beginning.'

Shyly she asked, 'Where were you at twenty?'

He replied obliquely. 'First year in medical school. Wondering if I was in the right place.'

'You had doubts? Why?'

'Such hard work and,' wryly, 'too little time for girls. The second year was better.'

She gave a satisfied little sigh. 'I think so, too.'

He teased her. 'Because of Mackintosh Ward?'

She answered, 'In three months I shall be moved . . . perhaps to Casualty.'

'You'll enjoy that?'

'How should I know . . . until it happens?'

'Have you thought – way ahead – when you are qualified what will interest you most?'

She frowned. 'Theatre perhaps . . . it's too soon.'

'Marriage?'

She blinked. 'I expect so . . . and a baby. What point is marriage without a child?'

Her youthful knowledge hurt . . . he slackened his grip upon her fingers. Unwilling to let him go instinctively she tightened them and, following a deflected, personal train of thought asked to his surprise, 'Why does Sister Findlay so dislike you?'

'You haven't guessed? Carl Sewerin is a German.'

Genuinely puzzled she looked up into his face. 'I don't understand.'

'What age is Sister Findlay? Thirty-nine . . . forty? An old maid. Just one of a generation who, in your country and mine, have lost their menfolk and any chance of real happiness. Probably she started nursing as a VAD. You cannot conceive, Rüslein,' the faded violet in his eyes darkened, 'what immeasurable, inexcusable suffering girls like Agnes Findlay saw every day. And after it was over – what had they left? No man, no home, no babies. Only the extension of a career begun amongst bloody, shattered limbs and crying, broken minds. Findlay's done well . . . she's respected; Mackintosh Ward is a model at Robert Carnegie; she is expert and unstinting in the care of her patients but she's dead inside. And I'm a German. No matter how many lives we save together every time she looks at me, she sees the man who pulled the trigger . . . or set the mine . . . broke her heart . . . turned all her days to dust.'

Rosanna cried aloud. 'That's dreadful! Wrong! To live in a past that won't – can't – happen again!'

He stopped and pulled her close to him. 'Rüslein, *ich sehe schlimme dinge kommen; tod und verderben . . .* '

Not understanding but happy to be near him she stayed within the circle of his arms, his heartbeats hard against her own.

After a long moment he pushed her gently away and held her at arm's length searching her face with importunate eyes.

'I want to make love to you.' Drawing the back of his hand across her brow he slid it, barely touching, down the edge of her cheek and chin, along her neck and, softly, over the roundness of shoulder and breast until dipping and pressing harder above her waistline he plunged a groove into the hyacinth wool between her thighs. 'I want you, Rüslein. I want you tonight . . . my exquisite, enchanting, beguiling innocent.'

She was too dazed . . . too deliciously disorientated to utter a rejection or response.

He placed an insistently restraining fingertip upon her lips. 'You must not say, "We met only this afternoon" . . . that is not true. You and I have known each other all our lives. We were with Hannibal at Carthegena and in Rome when Peter the Fisherman was martyred. I held you in my arms at the Court of Charlemagne; gave you a child the day before Joan of Arc stormed Orleans. Wc were lovers as the Spanish Armada sailed in a crescent up the channel; you belonged to me when Malbrock went to war. Tonight may only seem the first time but it will be a culmination . . . the most beautiful of all.'

The sun dipped behind a cloud and she shivered suddenly. He pulled the raincoat off his arm and, cherishingly, wrapped her in its folds.

He touched her hair gently . . . almost as a mother would reassure her child.

'Forgive me, Rüslein. I go too fast. We will walk back to the cabin. You shall put on your pretty high-heeled shoes and we will drive to the hotel. We will eat well and drink a little, cold, golden wine. Then I shall take you back to your Nurses' Home but in the car I shall kiss you three times . . . like this.' He pressed his mouth lingeringly on each eyelid; demandingly upon her lips. 'Tomorrow, when I do my rounds in Mackintosh Ward I shall look at you as I look at all the others . . . with courtesy – no more. But *you* will know that I want you . . . I love you.'

Chapter 5

Philly wrote faithfully once a week – usually on her return from Sunday Evensong. She was able to attend the last service of the day because Sophie Kennedy, the one neighbour Angela could tolerate, kept her mother company. When she got back she would find the two ladies engaged in a furious game of Double Demon which stopped only when Phillipa wheeled in the supper trolley set with sandwiches, small fruit tarts and cheese biscuits. The game over, Angela displayed the one domestic gesture of her week. She pushed the dirty dishes into the kitchen and made a pot of coffee. Then, it was back to the game and Phillipa, free to retire out of notice but not beyond call, sat in the corner of the sitting room with her writing pad. On Tuesday midday, or Wednesday morning at the latest, her letter would be delivered to Robert Carnegie Nurses' Home. That particular Wednesday, in the pigeon hole marked B, there were two envelopes for Bland. One addressed in Philly's rambling writing; the other narrow, made of expensive, pure white paper and typed.

Rosanna went into the dining room, fetched a bowl of porridge, found an empty table and read her sister's letter.

It contained the usual gossip – who was going out with whom at the tennis club; Ma Kennedy's latest millinery creation (it was a joke that all her numerous hats were homemade); plans for this year's Harvest Supper. Also one piece of news. Magnolia Tallent had been on a visit.

She'd hired a chauffeur-driven car and persuaded Mother to spend a day in Knutsford, talked constantly of Ronnie and Taurus and how well he managed the estate and after she'd left, Mother had gone all confidential over the evening brandy and chocolates. It was the two friends' dearest wish and fondest hope that Ronald would marry one of Angela's daughters.

'Which means *you*, Philly,' Rosanna muttered. 'Over my dead body.' She reached for a piece of toast, slit open the second envelope before spreading the butter.

It contained a single sheet handwritten in a distinctive style based on unfamiliar Gothic script.

> *Rüslein, I have to be in London for two days. On Friday afternoon at three o'clock I shall be waiting around the corner from Flora's. Don't bother with flat-heeled shoes but please, please, wear a pretty gown that buttons high up to the neck. You are adorable.* *C*

She thrust the paper down into her apron pocket. No high buttoning dress hung in her wardrobe and although Friday might be her day off the morning was scheduled for a lecture on the dietetic treatment of diabetes. She frowned. Shopping was out of the question. The nearest thing would be her cream, crêpe-de-chine blouse with the Peter Pan collar . . . .

Lawson, who possessed the capacity for appearing whenever her company was least wanted, plonked herself down opposite.

'Penny for 'em, Bland?'

'Not worth much more . . . just clothes.'

'Got a heavy date?'

'Not a date exactly . . . .'

She walked up to the Bentley at exactly three minutes past three. To arrive early would be a disclosure of naivety; late discourteous.

Sewerin smiled his pleasure and opened the passenger door. As she settled, he looked her over from head to toe.

She was hatless, the usually severe hair fluffed low on the nape of her neck and caught in place by a garnet, velvet ribbon. Her two-piece suit was made of honey coloured tweed flecked in cream and turquoise, the petal-led collar of a creamy blouse softened the topmost edge of the wide revers. Her silk stockings were pale and her shoes dark brown, high-heeled and tied with dainty laces just above the instep.

'Enchanting, Rüslein,' he said.

Her doubts about her dress began to fade but not quickly enough to check a soft apology. 'This is the best I could manage . . . I know you wanted . . . .'

He started the car. 'What I want is you, *enchanting* Rüslein.'

She relaxed back against the soft, smoky leather and shyly studied his profile. His forehead was high, eyebrows and lashes darker than the original barley gold of his thick, yet fine hair, now threaded with pure silver. His nose was very straight and somewhat sharp, chin well defined but not overemphasised and the lower lip of his mouth full in comparison with the upper. His very fair skin was neither florid nor porcelain pale and he kept his faded violet eyes fixed on the road ahead. Not surprising that he was known as 'Handsome Carl'. As though reading her thoughts he turned and smiled at her. She blushed and subsided even further into her seat. But when they left the city by an unfamiliar route she sat up enquiringly.

'I have a patient to visit . . . a very important patient who lives in a castle. She will be delighted to meet you.'

'But . . . but how will you explain?'

'Never *explain* anything, Rüslein. Only infer. You are a nurse at my hospital. I bring you. That's enough.' The smile he gave her was tenderly reassuring. 'The need for professional attendance is past. I visit her because she's old and lonely. Both sons killed in the War; her only grandchild at school at Harrow and a daughter-in-law who dislikes life outside a radius of twenty miles of London. She lives in the castle and oversees the boy's inheritance. When he comes of age she will probably die.'

Rosanna said, 'That's terrible.'

'No, little one, that's life . . . *her* life. She accepts it – without whining. The last thing she wants is pity. Remember that when you meet. Her greatest pleasure now is to encounter, talk to the young, the uninvolved. I have given her no hint of how things are between us but she will guess and be glad for our sakes.'

Sewerin was driving even faster than on the road to

Glenspeysie – she felt even more exhilarated and breathlessly excited by his speed and purpose. Suddenly, as they swung in through a half open, iron gated entrance worthy of any Hollywood film set, he asked urgently, 'Tell me, Rüslein. I know the answer, but *tell* me . . . you're a virgin. I shall be the first?'

Astonished at her self-possession she heard the answer, 'If you know, Carl, why put the question?' and his accompanying, near to triumphant laugh.

The drive was straight and very long – the castellated building at its conclusion vaguely familiar. She was reminded of a newspaper photograph . . . the Duchess of York and her two, Princess daughters dwarfed by a large doorway in an even larger, rounded tower.

Cannily he caught the thread of her remembrance. 'Glamis Castle . . . this is a Victorian copy, no more than half the size. The title is but two generations old, founded on coal mines and the building of dreadnoughts. But my lady, the Dowager Countess is the real thing . . . family reaches back to the reign of Charles II.' He smiled lopsidedly. 'For all that, Rüslein, descended from a bastard!'

The butler, it seemed, was in evidence even before he'd applied the brakes. A lean man with faded, dark brown hair and a limp not even a lifetime of strict deportment could disguise.

'Her Ladyship, sir, is in the turquoise drawing room. Expecting you.'

'Thank you, Bisset, I know my way.'

As they walked along a green carpeted, vaulted corridor Sewerin said, 'You wouldn't guess that fellow was once the fastest quarter miler in the East of Scotland. Took a packet just below the knee at Ypres. Whoever put it together deserves an accolade but Bisset's running days are over.'

The turquoise drawing room was well named. The architraves and panels of walls papered in watered silk so pale as to be fading into eau-de-nil picked out in gold; the curtains, upholstery and cushions a deeper, jewel shade and the Aubusson carpet a mix of all three colours. The woman, seated just out of the sun in a straight backed chair set at an angle to the long French window, was very thin with coal bright eyes, Queen Mary frizzled grey hair and skirts down to her ankles.

Sewerin kissed her skinny right hand. The left was loaded with diamonds and a mixture of multicoloured stones.

'Countess . . . how are you today?'

'The same as last time. Old . . . surviving.' She shot a sharp glance past his shoulder. 'Who's this?'

'Rosanna Bland . . . one of the nurses on my ward. I brought her for propriety's sake.'

'Fiddlesticks! *Whose*, I ask? Fat lot you care for propriety and my maid's within call if such a thing were necessary. You want my approval.' She leant towards the girl. 'What's your name again?'

It was difficult not to feel intimidated but at the same time a prickle of independence spiked her. 'Rosanna Bland.'

'Doesn't suit you. The Bowes-Lyons had a girl called Rose . . . pretty, round faced, always smiling . . . named the little Princess Margaret after her.'

Independence surged uppermost. 'No one has ever called me Rose. But my own name seems, somehow, out of favour. First Carl and now you, my lady, find it inappropriate. I think I shall have it changed – by deed poll.'

The flashing hand came out and touched her own. 'No need for that. Your name will be different . . . before you're twenty-one.'

'So soon!' Her surprise was genuine and ragged with disbelief.

The Countess laughed – a little, bubbling chuckle. 'I'm no Highland seer, my child, but young women who look like you don't stay single.'

Without prior thought she answered quickly, 'Nor need they marry unless and until they choose to do so!' She sensed Sewerin's approval and blushed because she guessed its reason.

There was a little pause, infiltrated by the Countess' voice, 'Go out into the garden, Carl. The michaelmas daisies are especially beautiful this year. I want to talk to this girl .. she interests me. When I've done I'll send her out to join you. I'm sorry there's no invitation to stay for tea. I expect the Procurator Fiscal and,' with a resigned shrug, '*his wife*. One of the water bailiff's boys is in trouble . . . want to get the thing settled out of court.'

He gave a rueful grin. 'I'm not sure that I trust you, Countess, to guard my best interests.'

'I trusted you to guard my life . . . away now.'

With the little bow that would always set him apart from every Englishman he went towards the French window, opened it and, turning left, was hidden at once by the heavy drape of brocade curtaining.

The old lady patted the sofa at her side – nothing persuasive in the touch; a calm assumption of compliance. Rosanna sat down reluctantly, fascinated against her will. She had thought, in her time at Robert Carnegie, to have come to recognise authority. Here was a different kind. Sewerin walked away without protest; the Procurator Fiscal was coming to tea in order, if not to bend the law, certainly to smooth its edges. It was surprising that she didn't feel intimidated either by the old woman's title or the piercing blackness of her eyes. Perhaps because there was nothing grim about the corners of the thin, carefully pink tinted mouth.

No time was wasted in the preamble. The Countess said, 'Carl's in love with you.'

'I hope so.'

'Hope has no part in it. It's as plain as the nose on my face that he's crazy for you. And you are dazzled by him.'

'No . . . if one's dazzled . . . can't see straight.'

'Meaning?'

'I know he has a wife.'

'That doesn't hurt?'

'Of course it does . . . but not enough to spoil what I could have.'

'Which is?'

'Whatever Carl chooses to give me.'

The black eyes narrowed. 'You'll sleep with him without hope of marriage.'

She answered on a little spurt of anger. 'It seems to me

all too often sleeping together has nothing to do with marriage. If my mother had been willing to share my father's bed he might not have decided to live half the world away.'

'Ah . . . ' said the Countess, 'now I begin to understand.' She looked reminiscently past Rosanna's shoulder. 'You could do worse, my dear, than taking Carl for your first lover. He's infatuated and accomplished and you obviously have no belief in the sanctity of marriage vows.'

The girl cut in. 'I believe in nothing save the sanctity of life.'

'I'm talking of life, my child. Believe me, there's always a risk in losing one's virginity. For some women, their first lover is also the last – no matter how many men sleep in their bed. And if he's clumsy she may never – ever – love a man. Carl's not that . . . no English Public School ethos to inhibit him. An *accomplished* lover,' she spoke the word again with a hint of warning she knew the girl would neither comprehend nor heed. A weariness crept over her thin features. She let her tissue thin, blue veined lids droop, blotting out the brightness of her gaze. 'Run along to him, now. Be happy and try not, too completely, to lose your heart. Next time he brings you, we shall have tea together and I shall see how things are by the look in your eyes . . . and his.'

The spread of the grounds was enormous, seeming to stretch into tree edged infinity. Her relief at seeing Carl close by a river of mauve, violet, purple and magenta blooms afloat with butterflies was so great she went running towards him. He caught her hands and pulled her close.

'She didn't scare you?'

'No . . . she blessed me, in a roundabout way, I think.' Secure within the circle of his arms a quiver of mischief prompted her to add, 'Told me I could do worse than take you for my lover.'

'I swear, my girl, you'll never take a better.'

She thought he would kiss her but he merely stroked her cheek with one hand and cupped her breast in the palm of the other.

'It seems, Rüslein, that I must bring my plans forward an hour or two. It shall be *afterwards* that we will eat our wedding supper.'

At Glenspeysie, Sewerin ignored the road to the cabins and drove directly to the hotel.

'Stay put, Rüslein. Be back in a couple of minutes.'

He was – followed by two porters, one carrying a large, stiff cardboard box and the other a bottle of champagne in an ice bucket. Both were placed reverently on the back seat and floor of the car.

When he drew up on the grass before the cabin, Carl handed her the front door key.

The first thing Rosanna noticed was the cinnamon sweet scent of carnations. An arrangement of pink blossoms stood at one end of the mantleshelf and on the coffee table a posy bowl of smaller, paler flowers.

Sewerin came up behind and past her – lowered the box upon the small dining table top. 'Open up . . . see what we have for supper. If the Countess hadn't been engaged in rescuing her peasants all would have been set out ready for our arrival.' Seeing the girl was, charmingly and appealingly, at a loss, added helpfully, 'The sides fold down.'

Rosanna lifted the lid, turned back each stiff side. The meal was held secure in little, separate compartments. On a silver dish, a salmon trout all whirled and twirled and starred with different coloured piping; on another quails in aspic, tiny pink and orange flowerlets gleaming through the jelly. There were half a dozen individual salads arranged like a bouquet, a cut glass bowl of fresh strawberries (in September!) with matching cream jug and sugar dredge and an oval, fretted platter of miniature meringues, éclairs, maids of honour and petit four fruits.

She exclaimed out loud. 'It's too pretty to eat!'

'That would insult the chef. Never bite the hand that feeds you, Rüslein.' In passing he dropped a kiss on the nape of her neck between the soft, fluffy edges of her hair and the cream collar petals. 'Put the dishes on the table while I open the champagne.'

She glanced at her watch – just past five. 'Isn't it a little early to drink champagne?'

'Nonsense. At wedding receptions at three . . . four o'clock. Remember . . . this is our wedding.'

Foolishly, 'But I don't have a ring . . . '

'Oh, but you have.' He took a slender, ambiguous twist of silver from his pocket. 'When the table is set and the bottle opened I shall put it on your finger.'

Her hands, so steady when changing dressings or packing the steriliser drum, felt clumsy and difficult to hold steady when touching the intricate dishes. As the champagne cork went 'pop' she almost dropped the strawberries. Sewerin filled two gold edged, thin stemmed goblets, placed them on the coffee table close to the divan, turned on his desk light and a standard lamp . . . pulled the curtains. Automatically she stowed the empty food box out of sight and, turning, saw him standing in the centre of the room.

He neither moved nor spoke but she read on his lips the three words, *Come to me*. The scent of carnations grew heavier . . . all pervading. Drenched in perfumed dizziness and unaware of any conscious effort she found the space between them, suddenly, existed no longer.

He lifted his right hand, twisted apart the single frog fastening of her costume jacket and pushed it down off her shoulders. Then, as deliberately, his faded violet eyes never leaving her own, he undid the half dozen buttons of her blouse. Only when she was completely naked did he kiss her . . . gently on her mouth, ravenously on each breast tip.

'Rüslein . . . Rüslein . . . you are a goddess made of lilies.'

He drew her down upon the bed, reached for a champagne glass and held it to her lips. 'First you . . . then me . . .'

She drank, her huge eyes softly bright above the golden rim . . . tasted only the sparkle of the wine.

When it was finished he said, 'Now you must give me mine,' but as she stretched towards the table he clasped both her breasts between his hands, pitched her over onto her back and covered her mouth with his own. He touched no other part of her until she was gasping with aroused, voracious need and, yearningly compliant, lifted herself to meet him. Then, in a single thrust, he entered her and for Rosanna all feeling and the world became a maze of shooting stars. She didn't see or know that he was smiling because he had judged her response so exactly.

They ate supper at seven – Rosanna engulfed in a pair of Carl's dragon patterned, Chinese silk pyjamas, the gold thread nowhere near as shining as her eyes. She sat at the table and demolished most of the salmon, half the salad and two-thirds of the strawberries. Her ingenuous remark, 'Making love makes me hungry,' tugged at his heart. At that moment he forgot he was the conqueror and would have indulged her every whim.

She declined to finish the champagne saying, truthfully, that she preferred water and when, after the meal, he made coffee and filled liqueur glasses with Kümmel she sipped at her's and shuddered.

'Ugh . . . shades of Baroness Lehzen.'

He reproved her. 'Rüslein, Queen Victoria's governess *chewed* caraway seeds . . . this is a distillation taking years of perfection.'

'She probably suffered from chronic indigestion and couldn't afford anything else . . . the Kent's were hard up, were they not? I don't . . . suffer from indigestion – do you?'

'I do not suffer from anything except, I think now, a chronic deprivation of you when we are apart.'

She looked up quickly. 'How soon can we . . . ?'

He smiled. 'Very soon . . . when I have finished my drink. But, first . . . have you forgotten . . . I promised you a ring?'

'No!' Her cry was urgent. 'That was a childish thing for me to say! *Before* would have been different but now . . .

now I want nothing to show that I am yours except . . . except what cannot be changed.'

He was arrested by the hectic ardour in her voice; understood at once that to slip the encircling twist of silver threads onto her hand would be insulting. He had judged the glorious depth of her latent sexual passion but failed to apprehend the passion of her independence. Whereas he thought it was he who had seduced her, he now realised that seduction to be mutual, albeit instinctively on her part. He wondered, with a twinge of apprehension that turned quickly into exultant anticipation if he would ever be able to discard her.

As though reading his thoughts she dropped the bright silk to the floor and, slowly, stood up, pale and importunate, willing him to take her without a word of love, preamble or finesse.

At nine o'clock she awoke from a short, sweet sleep to see Sewerin, fully dressed, seated at the desk, writing a letter.

Drowsy with remembered pleasure she asked, 'Is my honeymoon over?'

He smiled without looking at her. 'For us, never, Rüslein. But it is time to go.'

Her clothes lay in a neat pile at the foot of the bed. With a pang of deprivation she pushed aside the covers, yearning to stay all night in his arms.

He addressed, blotted and sealed the envelope and, picking up her bag, slipped it inside.

'Rüslein, there are two things we must talk about. Firstly, how to keep you safe.'

She looked up from fastening her stockings, mystified.

'From conceiving a child . . . I have written to a colleague who has no connections with Robert Carnegie but consulting rooms in his private house. Go there between two and four o'clock any afternoon except Fridays, give the note to his receptionist and he will arrange matters – show you how to avoid becoming pregnant. In the meantime, if your period is late . . . '

She was in the process of fastening the collar of her

blouse when her fingers rose in surprise. 'You mean it's possible to get a baby the *first* time?'

'My enchanting innocent . . . yes. And remember it was not just once but twice . . . '

She blushed as pink as her carnations . . . sunk her teeth into her lower lip.

He came close, clasping both her hands. '*That* time, for me, Rüslein, was the best.' Dropped them and took over the task of fixing buttons. 'If it happens, how will you feel?'

'Stunned . . . such a thought never entered my mind.'

'You must think of it now. If you miss a period, my colleague will be prepared to take away the trouble. It's a simple enough process, without risk, if taken early enough. Forty-eight hours in a nursing home, that's all. Would it trouble you?'

She was wriggling into her skirt, aware of an exciting tenderness deep between her thighs. 'No. Should it? If you tell me there's no danger?'

He gave a sigh of relief she didn't hear.

'The second thing, Rüslein, is that I shall buy a little car . . . pay for lessons to teach you to drive'. 'No!' He baulked her cry of protest, 'The car will be mine not yours. I've been considering for some time to get a runabout. I shall garage it a short walk from the hospital. You know I have to be in London almost every other week . . . if you can meet me here, Rüslein, there will be many more hours that we can be together . . . so much more loving we can share. I shall grudge every minute we're apart.'

'I think,' she said, 'everyone will be able to read what has happened tonight in my face.'

'I know better, little one. You possess not only total absorption in the moment but a calm ability to keep a secret.'

It snowed on the twins' twentieth birthday. They caught the early train to Chester under an opaque sky and with Angela's peevish protests whimpering in their ears. Philly would have abandoned the excursion; Rosanna overrode her.

'Mother is perfectly all right with Ma Kennedy for company *and* Cook and Gladys in the house. We've got a fat cheque from Father to spend and seats booked at the theatre. We're entitled to one day out together on our birthday! Wouldn't be the end of anybody's world if we got snowed in and had to spend the night in town!'

Phillipa cringed. 'Might not be the end of the world but I'd never hear the end of it from mother. And truly, Anna, I think she's unwell. She picks at even the things she likes and she pants a lot after walking upstairs.'

'Rubbish, Phil! Just trying something new. I spend all my days with people who are *really* ill, so you must believe me.' Seeing the other's worried face she said soothingly, 'If you're anxious we'll call home after the matinée, just to check.'

'No, no, we mustn't do that. If the phone rang unexpectedly and one of us were on the line she'd jump to the conclusion there had been an accident . . . the other maimed or dead. You can't imagine the aftermath of a jolt like that to her nerves!'

'Oh yes I can!' Rosanna kept the grim adjoiner, *I don't believe Mother possesses any*, to herself.

They passed the morning shopping in Browns. Rosanna spent all her birthday money and some more on a short, squirrel fur jacket and jaunty matching hat. She disapproved of Phillipa's contentment with a lavender lambswool jumper and cardigan.

'Honestly, Phil, it's not much of a present. Father intended you to do better than that.'

The reply came quietly stubborn. 'A gift is given without strings . . . I'm saving the rest.'

'For something special?'

'My dowry.'

'Your WHAT?' The words were startled out of her.

'When I enter the convent I shall need to bring a sum of money. No specified amount . . . whatever each postulant can afford. It's called a dowry.'

A prickle of distaste made Rosanna shiver. 'You mean . . . like a bride in olden times?'

'Exactly!' She turned ardent eyes towards her sister. 'I shall be a bride. The day I take the veil will be my wedding day . . . '

A picture of *her* wedding night swam before Rosanna's. She looked hard at Philly. Had she guessed? Carl was the one unshared confidence in their lives. She felt no sense of guilt only a little apprehension lest her sister had surmised the truth and found her deceit hurtful.

But Phillipa's returned gaze was limpidly unaware. 'You'll marry too, one day. A *proper* wedding with a human groom. That should make Mother happy,' she gave a naughty, twisted smile, '*if* she can support the strain of the ceremony.'

Now the grim reply was open. 'Oh, she'll do that all right. Won't miss the chance to be the frail, the pretty, wisp of the bride's mother . . . prettier even than the bride.'

A hint of apology in Philly's voice. 'She *is* prettier than either of us.'

Rosanna opened her lips to quote Carl's words, 'Mere prettiness is boredom,' but substituted, very fast, 'But who will be the bridegroom . . . that Tallent boy?'

The blue eyes clouded over. 'Not for you, Anna. But Mother and Mrs Tallent do so wish it . . . keep hinting . . . . '

'Let 'em keep on . . . the days of matchmaking parents are over.'

The reproof came mildly. 'They're not exactly matchmaking. It's understandable that two such old friends should hope when their children meet they will . . . . ' she left the sentence hanging.

Rosanna was brisk. 'As Mother can never manage without you long enough to let you travel down to Somerset and Ronald never makes shift to come up here, a meeting isn't likely. Just as well – one look and he might fall madly in love with you!'

Phillipa failed to respond to her teasing tone and answered gravely, 'Young men don't fall in love with me. For you it's different. Perhaps not madly but very much.' She gave a strange little sigh. '*One day* you'll know how much.'

They spent the afternoon engulfed in the easily remembered tunes and schmaltz of a touring company's production of Noel Coward's 'Bitter Sweet' and finished the day off with an old fashioned high tea at the Queen's Hotel. Halfway through the meal the threatening snow began to fall – soft, blobs of white drifted past the dining room windows. By the time they reached home it was an inch thick on the ground but the sky above clear again.

They walked up the street arm in arm, Rosanna singing, with inappropriate zest, 'Play to me beneath the summer moon, Zigeuner Zigeuner . . . ' She didn't hear Philly's little gasp of fright.

'Mother!'

Even though it was barely eight o'clock a light shone in Angela's bedroom window.

Phillipa wrenched her arm free and ran up the garden path, fumbling for her key to the front door and, when it was open, straight upstairs without removing her hat or coat. Rosanna said, 'Damn,' and didn't hurry. She closed the door with an unnecessarily loud click and carried the furrier's box into the drawing room where she tried on the jacket – looking with satisfied pleasure at her reflection in the overmantle mirror – before going into the kitchen.

Cook was a comparative stranger – had been in Angela's employ for less than two months. She was a heavily featured woman with a light hand at pastry who never mistook the twins.

'Madam's been mopy all day, Miss Ros.' It was one of her quirks to abbreviate every name. 'Left most of her lunch tho' I'd made the favourite Miss Phil ordered. Complained, afterwards, she'd got heartburn. Said she couldn't concentrate on cards so Mrs Ken read the paper to her. Thought for sure she'd take some tea . . . made a specially *weak* pot. Then at half past five – palpitations. Quite frightened Mrs Ken but Glad said she'd seen Madam worse and,' the woman sniffed, 'usually when

Miss Phil'd gone out somewhere – like today. Anyhow, we finally found the smelling salts she wanted.'

'Where was the bottle?'

Another sniff. 'Pushed right down under the cushions on the side of the sofa madam *never* sits on. Then we got her up to bed. Wouldn't let Mrs Ken send for the doctor . . . kept saying she was just a silly, old woman who'd be quite all right once her girls got safely home. Then she'd stop worrying. Mind you, Miss Ros, she *did* look bad.'

'People can,' Rosanna said, 'if they make themselves gasp long and hard enough. It's called hyperventilation.'

She was smoking a cigarette and idly watching the flames in the drawing room grate when the telephone in the hall rang. The unexpected sound of Sewerin's voice set the room whirling. She clutched the receiver.

'Happy Birthday, Rüslein! Take the train to London tomorrow. We'll drive back to Glenspeysie together. Stay one night near Leicester, the other at York.'

Her sudden longing for him took her breath away and smothered speech.

'Rüslein, Rüslein, why don't you answer? Is anything wrong?'

Her words came with an effort. 'I don't know, Carl . . . Mother isn't well.'

A touch of asperity in the answer. 'From what you tell me whenever is she otherwise? Don't you want to come to me? I'm hungry for you . . . it's been seven days since . . . too long, Rüslein, far too long.'

She could hear Phillipa and Mrs Kennedy coming down the stairs, their voices murmuring. She said, very fast, 'I want, of course, I want. Yes, Carl, I'll come.'

'Good, lovely girl. I shall be at Euston station at two-fifteen . . . waiting under the clock. Waiting until three hours and a half . . . for you. What could be more perfect than two whole nights together? Did I not tell you our honeymoon would never end?' and he hung up without saying, or giving her time to say, goodbye.

Rosanna turned abruptly, the ear piece of the telephone

still in her hand. It was important that Philly knew, at once, that she was leaving.

'I have to go back tomorrow.'

Her sister's clear, blue gaze showed neither surprise nor dismay. It was Mrs Kennedy who exclaimed, 'I trust you'll do no such thing with your mother so unwell!'

Still holding Philly's eyes she answered, 'I have certain . . . obligations. Mother's not alone . . . Phillipa's here.'

'Well, I declare! And you a nurse, Rosanna!'

Phillipa said, firmly quiet. 'It's because she's a nurse that she must go. Mother doesn't need both of us and it would be unwise for Anna to stay longer in case the weather should close in.'

Mrs Kennedy snorted. '*Trains* always run. You're too soft, Phillipa.'

The correction came gently. 'I'm not *soft* at all. I – and Rosanna – know exactly what is best for Mother. It would fuss her to have *two* people caring for her, especially,' her mouth twitched in a little smile shared with her sister, 'when, even now, she's never quite sure which is which.' She turned to go back up the stairs, saying 'Mrs Kennedy's had no supper. Ask Cook to make sandwiches and coffee and then ring for a taxi. It's much too cold and slippery underfoot for even walking around the corner.'

'If Mother owned a car,' Rosanna blurted out, spilling a frustration that had tugged at her all week, 'then I could drive her home.'

Phillipa checked, stared at her incredulously. 'Anna . . . can you drive?'

It was impossible to recall the words with which, by revealing a chip of her secret, she might have betrayed the whole.

'Yes,' she said shortly, praying that Philly would understand and ask no more.

The response was clear and gentle in the dark blue eyes so like her own. Phillipa nodded and went back up the staircase.

That night she slept badly. The loving knowledge in

Philly's eyes could not blot out a nagging, stupid fear. Carl's gleaming Bentley, somehow black spotted as a dalmation dog, driven by a faceless man, sped furiously along broad, moonbright roads, swerving and skidding away from huge snowdrifts that suddenly impinged upon their path only to disintegrate and retreat as quickly. All the while she heard a voice whispering, whispering (as Carl whispered when their lovemaking had reached its end and he was still inside her) 'Motoring . . . we'll go driving north . . . our honeymoon, Rüslein, will never end . . . .'

The next snowdrift was huge and went bubbling, like a whirlpool of cloudy water, to a peak. Sister Findlay leapt through the top.

'Late, Bland. You are late for duty. Call yourself a NURSE?' Her veil turned into Mrs Kennedy's best Sunday hat.

A cry came whimpering. 'It's the first time . . . .'

'The first time is one time too many!' Skinny arms in hospital blue grabbed at her.

She awoke . . . Philly's hand was on her shoulder, gently shaking.

'Hush, Anna . . . no reason to cry out. You were dreaming.'

The girl's hair was caught back in a rubber band. Rosanna recognised her dressing gown . . . a serviceable, royal blue wool bought in their seventeenth year. Her own, replaced by quilted satin, had been leaf green.

'I'm sorry . . . how silly to wake you. And Mother?'

'Not a murmur. It's four o'clock and *thawing*. Spattering with rain . . . see for yourself.' She pulled the window curtain to one side, gave her a tiny, ghost of a smile. 'Your nightmare's quite gone.'

Rosanna hauled herself up a little, pulling the eiderdown about her shoulders. 'Do you have bad dreams, Philly?'

'Never. Not yet. But when I do, Anna, I know you'll save me from them.'

Early in the New Year, Rosanna was transferred from

Mackintosh Ward to the ENT Out Patient Department and just before Easter to the Children's Ward. She enjoyed each new change and challenge. The rapture of her love for Sewerin and his ever more urgent passion in no way impinged on her powers of concentration and her practical ability. Her reports remained good and her marks for her written work, high. Neatly she divided her life in two, although sometimes using Carl's desk for writing up notes or planning essays. The small, maroon Standard tucked into the corner of a large public garage a road away from Flora's Tea Rooms gave her freedom but she never drove anywhere other than to Glenspeysie taking in turn all different routes.

Lack of close friendships with her fellow probationers helped keep the secret half a secret. Bland had been recognised as a loner right from her first week. The medical students had long since ceased trying to impress and nobody bothered to wonder where or how she spent her free time. It was inevitable the knowledge that she had a car should filter down the grapevine but she had always been so much better off than most that the fact was accepted as just another example of the luck of the well-to-do. On those days of deprivation when her time-off coincided with Carl's London appointments, she did as she had always done – ate cakes at Flora's and went to the pictures.

Philly's letters were full of the new curate at St Peter's. Wonderfully, his great aunt was Mother Superior of the enclosed order Phillipa felt most drawn to. Her comments on their mother showed her usual concern but no added anxiety. Magda Tallent had been on a visit; Ronnie had broken his collarbone riding point to point – his mount destroyed. Gladys had got engaged and Cook gone off in a huff. For Rosanna, the world beyond Edinburgh and outside the circle of Carl's arms seemed remote and she no part of it. Then the telegram arrived.

It was short. *Mother dangerously ill. Have cabled Father.* There was no need to add, please come. Rosanna went.

It was over by the time she reached the house – Mother already laid out in the pretty, frilly bedroom where so often she had pretended to be ill. Phillipa was blankfaced, contrite, dressed in black.

'Her heart was bad . . . even Dr Brodie didn't realise how bad.'

'Then stop feeling guilty. Doctors are supposed to notice these things but Mother cried "Wolf" so oten who can be to blame?' Seeing no change in her sister's woebegone face, Rosanna added astringently, 'Be honest . . . Mother was a lucky woman. She loved the life she wanted and managed to get . . . an invalid who wasn't ill. And when she *was* I doubt if she could tell the difference . . . had a quiet end.'

Some of Philly's tension eased. 'I've heard from Father. He's put his furlough forward . . . will be here in about three weeks. Something on his cable about *flying* part of the way. There will be all sorts of business to attend to. You'll stay, Rosanna?'

'As if I'd leave you. But I may have to go back for a day or two . . . to take an exam.' And be with Carl. She could not, even for Phillipa's sake, endure a separation of as much as a month.

David Bland looked even more handsome than his daughters remembered. And to the younger, who could make comparisons, unbelievably youthful. Not a single strand of silver streaked his thick, dark hair, the high forehead was unlined, waist unblurred by middle-aged spread and his eyes, the girls' inheritance, shone clear and blue in contrast to the suntan of his taut skin.

His attitude was straightforward and unsentimental. He went, with them both, to Angela's graveside and when Philly wept placed a comforting arm around her shoulders but he took no flowers. That evening he got down to business.

The masculine scent of cigar smoke and the sweet savour of malt whiskey vaguely reassured even Phillipa. She had grown accustomed to the incongruity of a man about the house and David's relaxed dependability helped to dispel her initial shyness. He guessed his other daughter would not be averse to a nip of her own but an offering glance towards Rosanna resulted in a just perceptible shake of the head.

'Cards on the table, children. I'd be glad, Philly, if you'd stay on in the old home if that's what you'd like – and for as long as you like. I've no wish to lose a foothold in the old country even if I rarely come back and property's a good investment. It may be larger than you need but I don't want the bother of looking for a smaller place nor lumber you with responsibility of moving. You've taken unselfish care of your mother but I've a notion you're not geared for change until you're ready for it. Right?'

Phillipa coloured, flustered and grateful. 'Th . . . Thank you, Father. I . . . I'd be happier staying here if you approve.'

'Good girl. I'll continue to pay all the outgoings as in your mother's time and increase your allowance to include housekeeping and pin money. We'll settle the amount when I've seen the household accounts but I don't imagine you'll be needing *two* servants.'

'Oh, no. Gladys will stay on until she's married but that's not for a year. Then I can manage with just a daily help.'

Surprise tinged his voice. 'You'd not be lonely living alone?'

She looked at him with limpid assurance. 'Why should I when I never feel alone? One day I wish . . . .'

He cut her short. 'That's another day and when it arrives just let me know. I have no intention of imposing my will on either of you but I do possess responsibilities. Now . . . Rosanna . . .' She felt his gaze narrow appraisingly. 'Making a career for yourself until you marry – which undoubtedly you will.'

She said, softly, 'Not part of my plan, Father.'

'I don't doubt but you've got one. Nor are you likely to fall in with anybody else's unless it suits you or break your heart for another's sake . . . bar Phillipa's. Too like me.' Unconscious pride warmed his words. 'So which will it be? An increased allowance or a lump sum? The first'll be less than Philly's . . . no home to run.'

She compressed a grin that sprang to her lips. 'I'll take

the allowance, please. As I don't intend to marry for years and years it might come to more than a single down payment.'

He looked amused and gratified. 'Good business thinking but . . . a bit of a gamble . . . .' Topping up his glass he continued, 'As for myself you're to know at once that I'm to be married . . . at St George's, Hanover Square, on the thirteenth of next month.' Philly's head came up. She was staring with eyes brimming with distressed disbelief.

'Little girl,' David leant forward and touched her hand which she pulled back as though a wasp had stung her. Without raising his voice but in a harder tone he went on, 'Don't let's pretend. Your mother and I lived apart for eighteen years by *her* choice. Angela had all she wanted for every one of those years and gave nothing back. Now I have a woman who wants *me*. So we're to marry as soon as we are able. I'm fifty-four years old; Pamela is twenty-three.' Philly's gasp was audible and horrified, Rosanna's steady gaze never left his face . . . no shock, no censure. He took comfort from the calm regard. 'You must, both of you, accept that I'm not prepared to waste one more day than is necessary in the conventional propriety of insincere mourning.' He turned to his younger daughter. '*You* don't disapprove, I gather?'

Rosanna's brows came up. 'Why should I? It's none of my business.'

Philly jumped to her feet, sobbed out like a little girl, 'Please may I go?' and rushed from the room.

Vexed and embarrassed David tipped out more whiskey. Rosanna leant across, took the tumbler from his hand. 'Here's to your future and your happiness,' and toasted him in one smooth, fiery gulp. Passing back the glass, she said, 'Give Philly twenty-four hours. In which to say her prayers and grow accustomed to the idea. You're a stranger called Father and she's a blessed innocent.'

'Which you are not?' He was pouring a second drink for her.

'Why ask so unnecessary a question? You knew from the first moment you set eyes on me that I wasn't.' She forestalled the query rising on his lips. 'What time at Hanover Square? If I'm in London, may I be there?'

Sewerin asked, 'What's your father's new wife like?'

'Surprising, physically . . . blonde hair, fair skin, turned up nose . . . not unlike Mother.'

'No surprise, Rüslein. A man's sexual inclinations rarely change.'

She sat up sharply, hair tumbling about bare shoulders. 'Is that true? Then you . . .' went stumbling into silence. Always she tried not to visualise Carl's wife – now an unwanted image intruded.

He tweaked the tip of her right breast. '*My* preference is for blue-eyed brunettes with long legs and bosoms as luscious and soft as whipped cream. Of whom you are perfection! My only wish is that your father is happy on *his* second honeymoon.'

Diverted and mollified as he'd intended, she said thoughtfully, 'The face may be similar but, my goodness, is the style different. She walked down the aisle on the arm of a man I do not know, dressed not in white – but, then, I doubt if she's a virgin – and carrying nothing in her hands. She wore peach silk and a tiny hat all feathers and a corsage of flaming orchids. I *bet* his second honeymoon is just as good as ours and lasts as long – all luck to him!'

Summer danced in – the Scottish days were long and light and all too often chilly. Rosanna moved to Women's Medical, Sewerin went on a conference to Blackpool and second year exams loomed large. A letter from Philly bothered her a little but she was too absorbed in filling Carl's absence with hours of needed study and revision to take sustained heed.

At lunchtime on Midsummer's Day she went into the dining room and took her place in the queue at the meal hatch. The two girls in front of her were speaking in subdued tones but easy to overhear.

'Have you heard about the accident last night?'

'In Casualty?'

'No, somewhere south . . . in Lancashire, I think. That aristocratic German surgeon everyone's mad about – what's his name – killed. Head on crash. They say an army lorry crushed his Bentley like a tank. Mackintosh is buzzing with it . . . Sister Findlay's got a face like doom . . . Mr Buchan's taking on his list.'

The nurse behind her buffeted Rosanna in the back. 'Get a move on, Bland.'

She walked out of line and from the room. Every part of her was icy cold. It wasn't true . . . it wasn't true. Carl was due back tomorrow . . . at Glenspeysie he would hold her in his arms . . . fill her with warmth and trusting love.

Blind to the corridors through which she passed she found the entrance to Mackintosh Ward swimming before her eyes. She pushed open the swing doors. Sister Findlay was seated at her desk.

'Sister . . . .'

The other looked up. 'Bland . . . what are you doing here?'

'I have to know . . . I heard . . . they're saying in the dining room . . . Carl . . . Mr Sewerin is . . . .'

Uncompromisingly, 'Yes, Bland, quite right. Killed outright in a road accident.' Her lips compressed. 'A waste . . . a dreadful waste.' Suddenly alert she caught at the swaying girl's arm. 'Come into my office. I know you're not one to make a scene. Brandy will help for a little while . . . at first . . . .'

Chapter 6

A fluttering outside the window distracted the girl's blank eyed attention. Two white doves alighted on the sill, the male sweet talking his lady and prancing up and down; she retreating, then sidling back to rub her bill against the feathers of his puffed out chest. Rosanna Bland stood up and walked towards the casement – the doves took fright and flew away.

She remembered the days following Carl's death as a blur – a slowed-down, out of focus, film moving in front of her eyes. She knew she carried out her duties well enough – no one complained – but the broken reality of her life kept cutting in . . . a knife that incised more deeply than any surgeon's scalpel. On the sixth afternoon, at the end of a lecture, Sister Tutor asked her to stay behind.

'I want you to report sick. Dr Benson holds his surgery in half an hour. Your Ward Sister has already spoken to me so I know she's in agreement.'

No spark lit the expressionless blue eyes but the girl's chin came up. 'I'm not ill.'

'That's for Doctor to decide. One thing's certain, you're not fit for ward duty. Why, child, you look as if you haven't slept for nights. I won't ask what the trouble is – believe your mother died not long ago. If you wish to report for a fortnight's sick leave I'll willingly endorse your application. Home is probably the best place until this little storm blows over.'

Rosanna felt her lips move in the rictus of a smile. 'Yes, Sister . . . thank you, Sister.'

She went directly not to Nurses' Sickbay but the store to fetch her trunk. Methodically she filled it full of her possessions. The pile of lecture notes and essays she divided neatly, fitting them in here and there but the text books she left stacked along her bedroom shelf. She hesitated over the half a dozen paperbacks alongside but finally tossed them in on top. Philly liked to read.

She fastened the locks and, lifting the clothes she had selected for the journey, placed them in a row along the trunk top. She unclipped her student cap and laid it on the pillow of her bed. With steel stiff fingers she untied her apron, pulled the butterscotch dress over her head, removed her sensible shoes and thick black stockings. Each garment she placed in correct order above the counterpane . . . the empty husks of half her life.

Fawn rayon stockings, high-heeled navy shoes, pale turquoise blouse, darker blue linen costume, navy swagger coat, soft beret hat automatically tilted over one eye, clutch bag matching shoes and coat and she was ready . . . ready for the next train south.

She gave Philly no warning of her arrival. When she opened the front door and walked into the drawing room the girl's already pale face grew even paler.

'Anna! How did you know I wanted you?'

'I didn't. I only know I need you to want me. Until . . . if ever . . . the storm blows over.' Wretchedly she made a parody of Sister Tutor's words.

Whatever the need for one another neither offered nor expected confidences. For mutual comfort's sake they reverted to girlhood, playing endless games of tennis on the garden court and, in the evenings, getting out the Sorry and Halma boards. For the most part of each day they were alone. Gladys had married sooner than expected – her new husband, employed by the Water Board, having been offered a Worker's cottage – but she still came every morning. No friends visited – Mrs Kennedy on a prolonged, possibly permanent, stay with a niece in Clacton. Rosanna was thankful to be saved the need for fending off inevitable questions but made anxious by Philly's agonised remoteness. She had resigned from the tennis club and divided her days between keeping the house spotless and attending church. It was her loss of natural serenity that troubled her sister the most . . . Rosanna not so absorbed in her own raw misery to fail to notice the strain and conflict blurring the calm of Philly's mouth and eyes. She recognised the difference that existed between their distinctive, private anguish . . . for herself, there was nothing so alive as conflict . . . every part of her was hollow. She might, every morning, dress with care, selecting with pernickety regard for detail, the right shade of belt, shoes and stockings to go with this and that but she felt the clothes she wore to be as empty as the uniform left lying on her bed in Edinburgh. I might as well, she thought dully, be wrapped in a winding sheet.

The local paper was delivered every Friday morning at breakfast time . . . Philly had not bothered to cancel the order of half a lifetime. Rosanna sipped her second, untasted, cup of coffee and turned the pages, listlessly. A small advertisement caught her roving eye.

'Philly, next Wednesday St Oswold's is holding its annual garden party. Shall we go?' It would be a way to fill an afternoon.

Phillipa's knife clattered to the floor. She stooped to pick it up. 'I . . . I'd rather not . . .' Rosanna couldn't see her face. 'S . . . Sister Poly might ask questions.'

'About what?'

'My noviciate . . . why I h . . . haven't . . . .'

Rosanna jumped in, but gently, 'And why haven't you? I thought it would have been all fixed up by now. You've done your duty to Mother.'

Her twin went very white. 'I . . . Anna, I'm not sure . . . .'

'Not sure you want to be a nun?' Incredulity swamped her voice.

Philly's cheeks flared hectic pink. 'I want, I want it more than anything.'

'Then why? – For Pete's sake you must *have* a reason.'

In a whisper, 'There was this letter you see . . . .'

'I don't. Tell me about it.'

'I found it, pushed down at the bottom of my jewel box, after Mother died.'

'She wrote it?' A flick of anger stirred the first positive

emotion for more than a month long.

'Yes.'

'*Show* me, Philly,' as near to a command as she would ever be.

She waited till the girl came back, tapping the table with her fingers, savouring the chance to feel *something*.

Angela had written on lavender paper in violet ink. Her hand was spidery.

My darling girl,

You know I've always held your best interests close to my heart. A mother's loving concern can never be severed – it is the silver cord linking a child to the mother who bore her.

Nauseating and not original. Angela had taken up the title of a play – not that Philly would know. Probably Magda had whisked her off to a matinée in Chester . . . Mother seized the chance to use evocative imagery for emotional blackmail. It was not hard to anticipate the next sentence.

My dearest wish and Magda Tallent's is that you and her Ronnie should become man and wife. She understands that whilst I live I cannot spare you but when I pass beyond this veil of tears . . . soon, my child, so soon! there can be no reason to hold back. It's a GOOD MATCH, Phillipa. The match of my dreams . . . don't fail me.

Your loving, trusting, Mother.

'It's,' Rosanna could think of only one word, 'monstrous!'

Philly flinched. 'No, Anna. No! You cannot blame her. Such old, good friends. What could be more natural?'

'Not natural – perverted! Why you haven't seen Ronald since he was about nine and we were six or seven or thereabouts.'

Uncompromisingly honest the reply. 'That's mainly *my* fault. Mrs Tallent keeps on asking me to stay but I don't want . . . .' She shivered. 'Even the name of the house scares me – TAURUS. So brutal . . . Yet how can I be so selfish as to ignore Mother's dearest, dying wish? Enter a convent knowing she relied on me?'

Rosanna refrained from saying – *Easily. By recognising who is the selfish one.* Dispassion was not one of Phillipa's strong points.

The girl looked at her with wounded eyes. 'I pray, Anna, I pray and pray and get no answer.'

The thought came like a flick of fire. 'Suppose *I* married him? What then? Mother and Mrs Tallent wouldn't care which daughter. Why Magda Tallent need not know.'

Phillipa went very still. She asked, on a tiny trail of sound, 'What are you saying?'

'Change places. You go to your convent. I take on Ronnie.' She knew it wouldn't matter. Carl was dead . . . *she* was dead. Walking around, making conversation didn't constitute *life*. Her mind, her heart, all the secret places of her being were empty of sensation. 'Think, Philly, think how often we have been mistaken for each other. Magda Tallent hasn't set eyes on me for two years or more. And if my intuition's right, her son is so indifferent to anybody or anything other than his horses he'll do as she says. Follow the line of least resistance. You'd be the nun you are meant to be, *I* fulfil Mother's last request.'

Bemused and a little frightened but not drawing back, Phillipa said, feebly, 'I c . . . couldn't take orders under false pretences. There's the legal side. Birth certificates . . . .'

'But once you're inside you're lost . . . to everyone beyond?'

'Y . . . yes. I suppose you could put it that way.'

Gentle pressure. 'And it's what you *want*?'

'Oh, Anna, more than anything, if . . . .'

'Right!' She was back in childhood, firmly steering the way ahead. 'Here's what we'll do. Give me your birth certificate or tell me where to find it so you can truthfully report its loss. Apply to Somerset House for a duplicate. There aren't any real obstacles, are there, Philly, to your being accepted?'

'No. Almost everything was arranged before I found Mother's note.' A little crack came to her voice. 'If I hadn't tidied the case I might have found it *afterwards*. I don't know which would have been worse. Only I can't,' imploringly she whispered, 'enter a convent unless my conscience is clear.'

'Give your conscience to me. Believe me, darling sister, you're handing me a reason to go on living. I've nothing left except to make sure *you* are happy . . . at peace.' She caught at Philly's chilly, pleading hands. 'Trust me, Phillipa, TRUST me.'

The capitulating answer was contained in the next words, 'I'll pray for you, Anna, every day.'

Beyond the window the dusky shadows of the house now darkened half the lawn – the doves strutted up and down in a patch of sunlight. Rosanna looked at her watch – twenty minutes to seven. She did not know at which hour of the evening convent nuns filed into the chapel for the sixth – or was it seventh? – service of the day. At Taurus, in the kitchen, the maids would be filling hot water cans ready to bring upstairs.

She crossed to the door and twisted back the key; then walked to the fitted wardrobe on the far side of the room, riffled through the dresses, pondering which one to choose.

Two were unworn – the rest Phillipa's. Every stitch she owned was Philly's excepting the shoes which were newly bought. The distinctive tread of even a twin made walking uncomfortable. She had disposed of all her own garments right down to stockings and underwear, bundling them up (including the squirrel jacket and hat) to be sent anonymously to an East End appeal for clothing. It was important that everything touching her skin should bear the print of her sister's personality. She had just lifted free a lemon, crêpe silk gown with an untrimmed V-neck, fluted cap sleeves and skirt flaring from hip to ankle when a tap came to the door. She called out, but so softly as to be unheard. The tap came again, more loudly. Quickly, embarrassment edging her voice she cried, 'C . . . come in.' So would Phillipa have answered.

The maid carried a copper, closed topped jug steaming

gently at the spout. 'I hope, miss, everything's to your liking?'

Not looking in her direction the girl stumbled out, 'Y . . . yes . . . Everything.'

When, half an hour later, Magda entered after the most peremptory of knocks, Phillipa was ready . . . waiting. The lemon crêpe was back in the cupboard – her second choice of puff sleeved turquoise taffeta drained all colour from the smooth curve of her cheeks.

They went down by a different, twisty stairway leading directly, but so unobtrusively as to be almost hidden, into the parlour. At first glance it seemed as large as the drawing room but with even longer, mullion windows and a lower, plaster ceiling. Quickly she recognised such spaciousness to be an illusion of the diffused light filtering through panes of coloured glass set in the west wall. The floor was covered with woven rush matting strewn with little, Turkish carpets. Their footfalls made no sound.

Both men sat in wide chairs flanking a stone fireplace filled with an arrangement of peonies and larkspur spikes. They rose as the women came towards them – Reginald a fraction faster than his nephew. He wore a plum coloured velvet jacket and pearl grey trousers . . . a tray with a silver cocktail shaker and thin stemmed glasses stood on a table close by his chair.

Magda said, bright and high, 'What have you got for us this evening, Naldo?'

'A welcome special.' He smiled at Phillipa.

Ronnie edged towards a corner cabinet. 'Not for me. Whiskey is the only drink.'

'You young Philistine. I keep telling you, not before dinner.'

Phillipa guessed the words formed an evening ritual.

'I'll take a glass of sherry when we're out for Mater's sake, but not,' with mulish emphasis, 'NOT in my own house.'

The drink she was handed was cloudy, tangy with gin. A variation of a White lady, she wondered, but said nothing.

Magda was smiling at her, offering a toast. 'To our very welcome visitor for whom we have waited so long.'

She looked down in confusion, holding her glass not quite steady in both hands. 'It wouldn't h . . . have been right. N . . . not until a year after Mother's death.'

Reginald commented, not completely hiding the amusement in his voice. 'I thought court mourning was for only six months.'

'I . . . I don't know . . . ' She sipped too fast and coughed. Ronnie came forward to slap her on the back but Magda forestalled him.

'I rather think, Naldo, that you've overdone your secret ingredient. Almost took my breath away.'

The girl covertly watched an exchange of glances between them. The man said, 'It seems a shame but I'll add some more orange juice.'

Phillipa's words came out in a rush. 'N . . . n . . . no. It's very nice. I was s . . . silly. Swallowing too fast.'

Ronald lounged back into a wing chair on the edge of the group, the tumbler in his hand already less than half-full – Ronnie Tallent gulped rather than savoured spirits. 'Not one of your more successful mixtures, Nunkie.' He swivelled round to face her. 'You had a jolly fast tennis service, too, I remember.'

'N . . . not really. Anna's a better player than me.'

'She *wasn't*. I could nearly always get back the ball *she* sent down . . . and that maid you used to have – what was her name?'

'C . . . Caroline.'

'But I don't think,' he looked aggrieved even in reminiscence, 'I ever won a game when you were serving. Used to get hopping mad.'

'Which,' his mother put in, 'was one of the reasons why you lost.' She slid the conversation forward. 'If this weather keeps up you'll be able to find out if you've improved. Naldo and I could make up a foursome – or the Triscombes from Poldinshaw.'

'Not a chance, Mater! The horses are going to need exercising and it's enough to know I'll have to dance at least once with boring Sheila Triscombe at this boring Silver Jubilee do you are so keen on.'

Magda said distinctly, 'You are to be *Phillipa's* escort at the Ball.' Her grey eyes flicked towards the girl. 'There really cannot be a more exciting time for you to come to stay. There's been no celebration in the County like it since before the War. It's to be held in the ballroom of the Lord Lieutenant's house.'

'Which,' Ronnie grinned, 'is not near as old as Taurus. *That* pleases the Mater no end.'

'But considerably grander . . . twice as large,' Reginald put in. Phillipa was beginning to recognise the lazy, laughing lilt in Naldo's voice.

His sister continued unperturbed, 'If the evening is mild the guests will be able to spill over into the grounds. I understand there's to be a refreshment marquee on the lower lawn.' She studied Phillipa's bare, upper arms. 'Jolly's in Bath have some delightful, little capes of silver and gold tissue. It would be as well to have something pretty to slip on when darkness comes. I thought we might take a trip in a day or two . . . for shopping. All my evening shoes are hopelessly out of date. I might even venture into fashionable sandals.' She leant down to appraise her guest's flimsy footwear, criss-crossed with narrow satin throngs and fastened about the ankle by a tiny, diamanté buckle. 'Charming.'

Awkwardly the girl shuffled her feet.

'Lord!' The exclamation came from Reginald's direction. 'That reminds me. Got something else for you, Mag. Finding the tile drove it clean from my head.'

Ronnie drawled out, 'What a song and dance you're both making about an old piece of pottery. Mother says she's going to have it fixed into the front porch wall.'

Magda said sharply, 'If you've no objection.'

He watched the remains of his whiskey as he swirled the glass around. 'What difference would that make?'

'Don't talk nonsense, Ronnie.' She might have been speaking to a schoolboy. 'This is your house and you are consulted about everything concerning it. If you would prefer, I'll make other arrangements . . . find another place.'

'Oh, stick it where you like!' He kicked out at nothing with his left foot, repeated, 'Only a bit of old tiling.' Looked at his uncle, 'What's the rest of your largesse?'

'Complimentary tickets . . . dropped into the shop today. For next Monday's performance at The Royal

Theatre. Luckes doesn't want them. Says his wife is averse to murder mysteries. They're in my room . . . I'll give them to you, Magda.'

Magnolia asked guardedly, 'What's the play? Not J B Priestley . . . I can never fathom all those hidden meanings.'

'Edgar Wallace. *The Case of the Frightened Lady*. Barbara Fitton's playing the chief female role.'

Ronnie showed unexpected interest. 'What – the woman who's supposed to look like Mater ? Bit of a comedown, isn't it – touring company in Bath instead of the West End?'

'Not everyone sees a resemblance,' Magda said mildly, 'I certainly don't myself. Perhaps, Ronald, you would like to accompany Phillipa to the show?'

'No fear!' The blurted words were past recalling but he pulled himself up sufficiently to offer an oblique apology, 'Not that it wouldn't be good fun but I've so much on my hands with the new horses.' Added for inconsequential emphasis, 'Would be different in the hunting season.'

Serenely his mother remarked, 'We'll combine it with our shopping expedition.' She held up her empty glass. 'Empty the shaker, Naldo. Lucy should be here any moment to say that dinner's ready.'

The dining room was on the far side of the house and reached by walking through the drawing room and across the dark hallway. It had the advantage of being close to the kitchens and a vaulted ceiling of wooden beams. The walnut dining table was capable of accommodating a dozen but only half was laid and with no place at either end. The couples sat at each side; Magda with her brother, Ronnie and the girl. At the bare end the polished surface reflected a pair of silver candelabra and their flickering flames. Even in the softly fading light of a summer evening it was a forbidding room. Phillipa wondered how it looked in daytime. When she came down in the morning she saw that most of the shadows had dispersed but only Reginald sat at the table. He rose unhurriedly to draw out a chair.

'Apologies for the absence of the rest of the establishment. Ronnie's in the stables . . . where else? And Magda's seeing to the fixing of the Taurus tile. 'Fraid you'll have to put up with just my company.'

'Th . . . that will be very pleasant.' The girl was looking at her plate as she sat down.

'What can I get you?' He flapped a hand in the direction of the sideboard. 'There's porridge, bacon and eggs, kedgeree or cold ham. The coffee's freshly made but if you prefer tea, I'll ring for some.'

'Thank you. C . . . coffee and toast will be nice.'

'Surely you're not slimming, Phillipa? There's absolutely no need.' He regarded with appreciation the slim waist and little, full breasts beneath thin cotton. Her dress was as softly coloured as yesterday's, its pattern of tiny green leaves replaced by equally small clusters of russet apples, the scooped neck and cap sleeves piped in the same colour.

He expected her to blush but the pale skin stayed cool and creamy. Instead words tumbled out. 'I th . . . think I will have some k . . . kedgeree, after all.'

As he reached the sideboard the unseen voice behind him came startlingly firm. 'Only a little, please.'

He scooped up two spoonfuls and returned to the table. Phillipa had already filled her coffee cup.

'Th . . . thank you.' Hesitancy back again.

Momentarily he was puzzled. The young girl, eyes averted, fumble fingered as she picked up her fish fork, did not equate with the voice he'd just heard . . . or *thought* he heard.

For a whole minute he waited then, aware that Phillipa was unlikely to instigate a start to conversation, asked, 'Did you get lost finding your way down?'

'N . . . no. I have, I think,' he was beginning to anticipate the two words which almost invariably formed part of her answers and felt a twinge of unfounded suspicion that their indecisive use was deliberate, 'a fairly good . . . wh . . . what's it called? . . . bump of locality. And the house is not so very large.'

'But strange. Don't you find it so?'

She looked straight at him – eyes dark blue and candid. 'This room, a little . . . but the rest . . .' she hesitated not from bashfulness but the need to find adequate expression, 'the rest is beautiful . . . bewitching.'

'Magda will be delighted to hear you say that. She *adores* Taurus – quite as much as she loves Ronnie.'

She asked quickly, 'Isn't that the same thing, for her?' then went stumbling on in quick confusion, 'I . . . I'm sure I'm talking n . . . nonsense but the house is so old, so . . . *everlasting* I can understand h . . . how much it means to her. It has a magic because it is so old. I've never lived anywhere built even one hundred years ago.'

'Women like to romanticise about everything – that's why I brought the terracotta tile. For when all's said and done, Pippa, houses are only bricks and mortar; fireplaces and furniture and the endless task of keeping both clean. Houses *trap* people.'

To stop the Rosanna part of her asking, *What then are you doing here*? she bit into a piece of toast. After a moment ventured, 'I . . . I suppose a house can be a sort of cage and cages can be safe.'

'Profound Pippa! Do you mind if I call you that?'

'P . . . Pippa? No one ever has.'

He probed gently. 'Don't you have a pet name at home?'

'Not any more . . . my sister's not there.' Forlornly she turned her head away from him.

He said the first words that came into his head for comfort's sake. 'If Magda has no plans for you this morning how about a game of tennis? I'm a lazy player but better than Ronnie.'

Her breath came in a little gasp. 'Thank you. I th . . . think that would be very nice. I'll . . . I'll go and change.' She got up so fast the movement jarred the table clattering the cups. She said, 'I . . . I'm sorry,' and went quickly from the room, head bent, shoulders stiff, feet in tan and white court shoes almost running.

Reginald frowned and rubbed his forehead with three fingers. Something . . . something didn't ring true. There was a hint of misery at the back of the girl's dark blue eyes but not the crushing misery of acute shyness. Her unexciting clothes were worn with a dash of elegance – the very fashionable tan and white shoes provided the evidence. He admitted to a fantastic impression that Phillipa Bland was living inside someone else's skin and immediately ridiculed so absurd a notion. Women, he had declared, were romantics. Could it be that at forty-five, he, Reginald King – that most level headed, self caring of men – was about to get romantic over a girl of twenty with a deprecating manner and the body of a wood-nymph? Mentally he kicked himself but, he was forced to admit, not hard enough.

Ronnie had spent a couple of amiable hours in the stables. The traveller for a firm of forage merchants dropped in not in the hope of making a sale but to share his new stock of dirty jokes and exotic picture postcards. At opening time they adjourned to The Bull for a couple of jars.

Ronald walked back to Taurus highly amused and pleasantly titillated. He went in not by the stable entrance but a small gate opening onto the road leading to the village. Sauntering through the gardens, immersed in reminiscent chuckles, he did not see the couple on the tennis court until his uncle's call, 'Good shot!' tugged his eyes in their direction.

Phillipa was facing him and preparing to serve. He sucked a surprised, silent whistle between his teeth. Beneath a short, white, pleated skirt her legs were long, shapely and bare, the hint of thighs roundly smooth. As she threw up the ball he could see the soft bounce of little breasts, firm and cherry tipped. The most explicit of the postcards slid before his eyes, superimposing itself upon his vision of the girl. He felt his heart begin the thump and a spurt of sweat trickle high between his legs. Ronnie's normally sluggish imagination took off in exciting detail.

He was aware of Magda's designs and, until that moment, had no intention of co-operating. Not merely from cussedness but for a reason his mother did not guess. Ronald Tallent could not make it in bed. Cheerful, uninhibited farm girl, enthusiastic, tricky slut, experienced, patient tart – the result – or lack of it – just the same. He pretended that it didn't matter but the humiliation of failure drove him to ride his horses all the harder.

He knew he'd have to marry someday – would look damned odd if he didn't – and now, for the first time he mentally acknowledged Phillipa Bland's physical existence. She wasn't likely, he was sure, to interfere with the way he ran his life . . . too easily dominated for that. But if she *belonged* to him – as much a possession as one of his hunters – with those sexy breasts and thighs no option but to share his bed might he not be able to . . . like other men?

Always quick – if not always wise – to make a decision when bidding for a horse Ronald made one now. He'd propose on the night of the Jubilee Ball but without giving Mater an inkling. Would do her good to be kept in a bit of suspense she'd have to conceal . . . on secret tenterhooks.

On the morning of the expedition to Bath, Magnolia, after the briefest of knocks, walked into Phillipa's room and asked, anticipating no denial, what dress she intended wearing to the Ball.

Abrupt speech flustered the girl, accentuating her stammer. 'I . . . I've brought two. I haven't d . . . decided yet.'

'Let me see.'

Phillipa fetched them from the cupboard. Most certainly neither was Rosanna's choice. Lilac lace, the pattern picked out in seed pearls around the high, scooped neck and the edges of the tight sleeves ending halfway down the upper arm, the full skirt falling straight from a natural, pearl trimmed waistline; the other, only slightly more dashing made of matt, pink silk with a shoulder frill in place of sleeves, a modesty plunging neckline and bare back and a skirt frouing from below the hips but clinging nowhere.

Magda dismissed the lilac (middle-aged girlie, her unspoken comment) and scrutinised the pink. 'What shoes?'

'S . . . silver sandals. And my purse.'

A nod of approval. 'Your taste's good, if a trifle unadventurous.'

It surprised her when Phillipa put the question. 'What will you wear, Mrs Tallent?'

'Black and silver tissue. It's not new but I've only worn it once when Naldo took me to some antique dealers "do" in London. You must wear the pink. We shall complement each other very well.'

She found the classical elegance of Bath enchanting and the efficient elegance of Jolly's department store comparable to Brown's in Chester or any of the quality shops in Edinburgh's Princes Street. The last she blocked from her mind – Phillipa Bland knew of nothing north of the English Midlands.

Magda was obviously a recognised and valued customer at Jolly's. In the shoe department the assistant lifted down box after box in an effort to please 'Modom'. The hidden personality of Rosanna was amused to watch Magda dithering between conventional buckled black brocade and up-to-the-minute, frivolous, criss-cross strips of satin. Eventually Phillipa diffidently suggested that a black slipper thronged above the instep might be a reasonable compromise. 'It s . . . suits your narrow foot, Mrs Tallent.'

'And in the latest but *subdued* fashion,' corroborated the close to exasperated assistant.

As she signed the account slip Magda observed, 'I've only just realised how much I've missed not having a daughter to come shopping with me. Now let's go and look at those pretty evening capes. To wear with your pink.' It was a statement not a question.

They ate a pre-theatre supper at the Royal York Hotel. Phillipa said, tentatively, 'P . . . please may I pay the bill? Father makes me a very generous allowance.'

'Of course, my dear, if it pleases you.' Magda stirred sugarless, black coffee and lit a cigarette. 'What does David think about Rosanna going all religious? I must say it came as a surprise to me.' It was her first comment on anything relating to Phillipa's family – perhaps because outside Taurus her thoughts shrivelled.

'I . . . I don't know. He thinks . . . I think . . . that we must make our own way. He's a stranger, really. A *generous*,' the girl repeated the word lest Magda think her unfilial, 'an *uninquisitive* stranger. In a way it's as if my sister were married which, in a way, she is. Father's responsibility, he believes, has ended.'

'And he has his own new wife to think of.' Magda's eyes narrowed behind a haze of smoke but she didn't ask about Pamela. 'Your father's a stranger to me, too. I married years before Angela met him. Then I couldn't go to the wedding . . . much too pregnant. And off she went to Singapore.'

The words slipped out. 'Not for long.'

'Your mother never was particularly adaptable. And the climate most unsuitable for European babies. A mother's first duty,' complacency in every syllable, 'must be to her children.' She stubbed out a half-finished cigarette. 'We should be going or we shall be late. I think it's so discourteous to be scrabbling for one's seat after the curtain rises.'

The play offered entertainment pure and simple – no social comment or hidden meaning to irritate Magnolia. Rosanna might have found the plot a trifle fatuous but uncritical Phillipa got caught up in the story. Parts of it made her spine prickle as though the shadow of a ghost passed over her grave.

The setting was Monk's Priory, an ancient house complete with secret panels, the ancestral seat of the Lebanons, and the action revolved around Lady Lebanon's obsession to ensure the continuation of the line notwithstanding that, Willie, her only son, happened to be raving mad *and* a multi-murderer. Coldly forceful, she coerced Aisla – the frightened lady of the title and a distant cousin – to agree to marrying Willie with the result that the poor girl took to sleepwalking all over the place.

Barbara Fitton (the declared resemblance to Magda fleeting and visible only in profile) played the central character with gaunt, aristocratic understatement. At the close of her impassively calculated speech to Aisla justifying the suggestion that she marry Willie and get herself with child by another man: 'You will be doing a wonderful thing, Ailsa . . . the line will go on . . . your children will be Lebanons; married to Willie they'll bear the Lebanon name,' a compulsive curiosity drew Phillipa's gaze from the stage towards Magnolia. In sideview her face was as calm and uncompromising as the actress's words.

There were guests for dinner at Taurus on the evening of the Ball. Major and Mrs Collinbury who rented the Dower House. The Major, a man with broken veins on his nose and a determinedly jocular manner, was retired from the Indian Army and an authority on decorative fowl which he bred in what had been the kitchen garden. Mrs Collinbury, who looked at least five years his senior, played the piano like a concert performer and bridge like a fiend. She substituted for the church organist and never turned down a chance to partner anybody in a rubber.

They had one son, in Australia, and lately had given up running a car. Magda suspected that without her invitation to join the Taurus party they would have been obliged to stay at home – the taxi fare for the sixteen miles to and from the Lord Lieutenant's home beyond genteelly hidden, straightened means. It was arranged that the Major and his wife should travel with her in the Rover; Naldo take the young ones in his Alvis.

Seated at her dressing table, with critical absorption Magnolia completed the symmetrical neatness of her hair and studied the touch of artificial pink on her cheeks and mouth. Archie wouldn't approve but a hint of makeup did marvels for tired skins. She reached for her drop pearl earrings and wondered about Ronnie's intentions. He had abandoned his horses for two afternoons in order to *just* beat Phillipa at a game of tennis and had vociferously applauded her stumblingly shamefaced admission that she couldn't play bridge.

'Good for you! No one under forty should bother with such a tedious way to pass the time. 'Specially not pretty girls. Cribbage – now that's different . . . ' and when she remarked softly that she knew the rules, was all enthusiasm. 'We'll be partners – take on these two intellectual card sharps!'

But other than those two occasions he never sought to stand close by her side or change his normal, horse ridden routine to entertain her.

The door to Magda's room stood in direct line to her dressing table – as if in extension to her thoughts it opened to admit Ronald, jacketless. He looked, in the subdued bedroom light, very like his father – minus the rock firm steadiness.

His request was Archie's. 'Give us a hand,' holding out his bow tie, 'thing's beyond me.'

Evening dress did not suit him. He was too short limbed and jerky in movement for the crisp, dark elegance of formal wear. All his limbs chafed to get back to breeches and a hacking jacket but he had washed and carefully parted his thick auburn hair and smoothed on a touch of brilliantine.

She made certain the pearl drops were perfectly and equally adjusted – held out her hand.

'This was the one task your father's valet never did. It needed a woman's fingers Archie maintained.' And when the ends were neatly tucked away she said, 'Tit for tat Ronnie. Fasten the clasp of my pearls.' Sat down again at the dressing table.

He came up behind her and bent down. She could feel the sticky warmth of his fingers on her neck. 'S'ppose these are the family heirlooms.'

She laughed at his reflection. 'Hardly. Your father gave them to me. *His* mother got missionary fever in middle age and sold all her jewels to help convert the natives. The only things left are a ghastly set of cameos I never wear. But Phillipa, with her mid-Victorian looks could . . . .

The windows were open and from the spinney the first nightingale of the summer began to sing.

'Philomel?' asked her son unexpectedly. 'The L. L. must be chanting hallelujahs that the weather's held.'

Magnolia stood up – a tall, slender, uncareworn woman in a black gown threaded with silver. 'It's a perfect night.'

'OK for you girls with bare arms and low backs.' His mother had neither. 'Pity we poor fellows – be sweating like pigs in a couple of hours.' He moved away, asking, again unexpectedly, 'How're we sitting at the dinner table?'

'What an odd question . . . you don't usually bother.' He volunteered no further remark. 'I'm in my usual place

Major Collinbury at my side, Phillipa on his other. That leaves Doris C between you and Naldo.'

'Thanks, Mater. Always the perfect hostess. I'll get my coat . . . see you in the parlour.'

The Collingburys walked up to the house through the gardens, their footsteps carefully paced by the Major so that they arrived at the exact minute of punctuality. He was resplendent in regimental mess kit and miniature medals; his wife's biscuit, figured velvet dowdiness redeemed by magnificent, square cut emeralds in her ears and on her left hand.

Everyone drank sherry in the parlour – Naldo's cocktail shaker strictly for family and Ronnie keeping firmly in line. Without prompting he escorted Mrs Collingbury into the dining room.

Magda had taken care over the meal and the flower arrangements. Cream of mushroom soup, roast leg of lamb, new potatoes, and the first picking of peas; strawberry flan topped in whipped cream, Cointreau spiked. To drink, a Veuve Cliquot. The glass and china on the polished wood were interspersed with tiny, fretted silver baskets frothing pink roses and feathery sprigs of maidenhair fern. A small cellophane box stood by Phillipa's place. Her evident confusion enchanted the Major who warmed to unsophisticated girls.

'What's that?' Magda leant forward to peer down the table.

'An . . . an orchid.' It was pure white and very large. Startled, she looked first at Naldo, then Ronnie.

The latter said, 'I didn't know what colour you were wearing. It's important flowers don't clash. White can't.'

'It's . . . it's beautiful. Th . . . thank you very much.' And, thank God, not a spray of carnations.

'I congratulate you on your taste, young man.' The Major's voice was breezily ambiguous.

The girl was fumbling with the pin.

Magda said, decisively, 'Don't bother now. I'll fix it after dinner,' but Collingbury cut in, 'Allow me, my dear.'

His stumpy fingers didn't linger and were surprisingly deft.

The Jubilee Flower Committee had done the occasion and the Lord Lieutenant's ballroom proud. One end wall was dominated by two three-quarter length portraits of King George V and Queen Mary, the gilt frames wreathed in silver leaves and white roses of York.

The whole theme was white and silver – the low window sills banked with a mixture of white blooms set in a waterfall of silvery fern and the windowless wall swagged in ropes of roses and tinsel cord. In the marquee, the pillars were twisted with silver ribbons, supper was served on silvered cardboard plates, the fairy lights in the garden were shaped like little, twinkling stars and the hostess herself shimmered in a sheath of lamé. Only the band provided a splash of colour with scarlet tuxedo jackets.

The Major gallantly asked Magda for the first dance and Ronnie did his duty by Mrs Collingbury. That left Naldo and Phillipa.

He smiled down encouragingly at her. 'The first is always the quickstep.'

It was Rosanna who answered but in Philly's gentle voice. 'I recognise the tempo,' stepped within the circle of his arms and was at once whirled into delight.

Naldo prided himself that he always made a poor dancer feel good and a good dancer like Ginger Rogers – Phillipa was very good. He had expected her to be inhibited, stiff, a chore to guide around the room but, perfectly relaxed and feather light, unhesitatingly she followed his lead, matching his steps even when he produced a series of what Ronnie referred to as, 'Nunkie's twiddly bits'. He was certain she enjoyed every lilting moment but never once did she smile . . . was not to know that only with Sewerin had she experienced such harmony of movement. On winter evenings, in the pine cabin, she had danced and danced in Carl's arms to the sound of his gramophone – not once in public, not once on a ballroom floor, certainly never in evening dress . . . her gown had been a drift of diaphanous chiffon, nothing underneath. When the music ended Reginald suddenly realised that in all her days at Taurus he had never seen her mouth in other than carefully held repose.

It puzzled him that he should feel such acute pleasure in her nearness, was reluctant to let her move out of reach. It was not, he admitted, solely the pleasure of one good dancer's encounter with another – he had wanted to stop and kiss her solemn lips.

It was a new experience to be puzzled by a woman. To resolve bewilderment required effort – effort Reginald King avoided whenever possible. It was, he knew, the girl's continued proximity that kept the riddle going . . . impossible to push her face from his mind. He argued – more often than he cared to admit – that Phillipa Bland's voluptuous body encased a pallid personality. But . . . but was it so? His experience was varied and noncommittal – virgins no attraction. Why then be intrigued and perplexed by an artlessly sexy and innocently charming child? Because – he watched Ronald lead her cloddingly onto the dance floor – because he didn't, couldn't (though in all fairness without reason) believe in her innocence. It peaked him that he should react so strongly to a veiled demeanour that in all probability concealed no more than inexperience and sexual modesty. All of which left him unconvinced. There were hints. Hints he couldn't pin down.

Major and Mrs Collingbury were dancing together and looking absurdly happy. He hoped they'd never need to flog those emeralds to make ends meet. But if they did he'd make an offer. Set in a diamond linked gold chain they would look superb above the cleft of Pippa's creamy breasts.

More rapidly than usual he ambled in the direction of the band. Would ask them to play a tango . . . that'ud sort out the dancers.

The Refreshment Committee hadn't stinted the champagne – a Bristol wine merchant one of their number. Ronnie, after four glasses, abandoned all pretence of circulating and monopolised Pippa. He had decided Naldo's abbreviation was a good one – Phillipa sounded too much like a saint and, God knew, it wasn't a saint he needed. As the evening progressed and he grew warmer and more hazy the conviction took root that *she was* what he needed. And Mater would approve. He was not over bothered about anyone's approval but Magda's would make life more amenable and if the marriage didn't work out he could shift the blame to her.

He was not so self absorbed and unobservant to fail to notice that his male acquaintances wouldn't have cut in if they could and he'd a sneaky feeling Nunkie Naldo was amongst them. Equally he was aware – not that it troubled him – that most of the local girls shied away from his advances. By marrying outside the County he'd be following Tallent tradition (for whatever that was worth!) and Tallent tradition was what Mater craved. At the start of the last waltz he and Phillipa – more by accident than design – were on the terrace outside the ballroom windows. He said, without preamble or so much as a finger's touch, 'Pippa, it would be a good idea if we got married. Will you say yes?'

The reply was cool, immediate and somehow disconcerting, 'Of course, Ronnie. That's why I'm here.'

The desire to kiss her faded . . . he felt trapped and outmanoeuvred. Phillipa – pale pink silk, orchid scented, mildly importunate, leant forward offering her mouth and the promise of breasts and soft, round thighs. Girlishly, she whispered, 'Don't you think we should go and dance the last waltz . . . afterwards tell your mother? She *will* be pleased.'

Chapter 7

Phillipa insisted, mulishly, with downcast eyes and Ronnie's off-hand support, on a quiet wedding. An exasperated Magda couldn't budge her – the delightful picture of a reception in Taurus gardens faded.

She complained to Naldo. 'A *quiet* wedding I'd go happily along with . . . *not* hole in corner. Why the girl wants a special licence – no banns. People will say she's two months pregnant.'

Reginald, who didn't want to get drawn into the discussion, answered sharply, 'Which won't matter – unless she is! Have a heart, Mag, she's self-effacing, her only sister shut up in a nunnery; father halfway across the world with a new wife four years older than his daughters! The poor kid can't be blamed for wanting no fuss. Just imagine how *her* side of the church would look.'

Acid dripped between the words, 'It seems to me, *you* are always prepared to take Phillipa's part. Perhaps she arouses suppressed paternal longings in your breast.'

He gave a weary, little laugh. 'Why is it weddings always bring out the cattiness in normally sensible women?'

She pressed on. 'And do you know whom she intends asking to give her away?'

Real alarm spiked his reply, 'You weren't expecting *me* to do it?'

'Don't be foolish!' Almost snapping at him. 'She must have an uncle or old friend somewhere in the Midlands. But, no – Major Collingbury.'

'Very suitable. He was with us the night Ronnie popped the question.'

'Exactly! All she wants in the church is four people – you, me, Major and Mrs C. It's unnatural.'

He applauded Pippa's commonsense. 'Stop griping, Mag. You picked the girl for her excessive shyness.'

'But is that what I've got? She surprises me sometimes.' He looked hard at his sister. 'After all that carfuffle about a *quiet* wedding and yet when I said, "I take it you won't be wearing white," she gave me one of those blank stares and answered, "But of course, Mrs Tallent. Mother wouldn't approve if I didn't."

He brought an uncomfortable conversation to an end by getting to his feet. 'You've accomplished what you and your school friend set out to do, so why complain? And there's no chance the whole village will stay away from the church. I suggest you combine the reception with your annual tenants' do . . . only mean bringing it forward a month. Pippa can't object to that. After all, she is the next mistress of Taurus. I'm surprised you didn't think of it, old thing. Not like you to lose your grip over a bashful chit of a girl!' As he walked away he wondered if the airy insincerity of his description had convinced or deceived her.

He was far from deceived himself – the more he tried to understand the personality of the young woman about to marry Ronnie the more baffled he became. It was a delightful bafflement pricked with excitement. Phillipa showed no trace of emotion – it came as a shock to realise that had she obviously fallen for his nephew, he would have moved out. The habits of an easy-come, easy-go lifetime were threatened and he didn't care. The riddle she presented was too fascinating. What made Pippa Bland tick? Ronnie Tallent wasn't the man to find out.

She bought all her trousseau at Brown's, choosing every garment with Phillipa's eyes. A plain, dead white, satin wedding gown with cowl neck and bell sleeves; chaplet of orange blossom to hold Mother's lace veil close to her dark hair. For travelling on honeymoon – to Torquay – a baby blue dress, small off-the-face hat the underside of the brim lined with pleated, petersham ribbon, black accessories and a silver fox cape – the gift of the groom.

Her nightwear was soft satin, turquoise blue and mushroom pink, cut on the cross like an evening gown and inset at neckline and hem with Richlieu-work motifs of ecru lace. In a brief mood of Rosanna defiance she purchased an autumn suit in light fawn wool with shoes, handbag and hat in the latest fashion colour of the year – London tan. The hat brim dipped provocatively and the pointed crown was pierced by a single, pheasant quill.

A cable to David announcing her forthcoming marriage but omitting the date and bridegroom's name elicited immediate congratulations, a transfer of money into her account and the request to put the house into the hands of a solicitor for letting.

She slept there only one night preferring to stay in a Chester hotel avoiding all possible encounters – with Gladys especially whom she glimpsed in the distance pushing out her new baby.

On the anniversary of Carl's death she went to a Fuller's café and ate cream cakes and lemon meringue pie until she felt sick. In the evening she telephoned Taurus.

Reginald answered. Magda was out playing bridge and Ronnie away on some unspecified horse spree.

Her voice was even more breathless than usual. 'Ev . . . everything's organised here. I . . . I've done as Father instructed . Would . . . would Mrs Tallent mind if I came down t . . . tomorrow? It's lonely here.'

He tried to gauge the depth of diffidence in her disembodied voice . . . was smitten by a silly longing to have her near.

'My dear child, with only ten days to go to the wedding? Of course she wouldn't mind.'

'It's . . . it's a little unorthodox, isn't it, to have the bride living in the bridegroom's home?'

'You're an unorthodox creature.'

'I d . . . don't think so.'

'I wish I knew, Pippa, what you think.'

She repeated childishly, intent on fooling him. 'Please may I come? Or . . . or would it be better if I asked Major and Mrs Collinbury if I might stay with them?'

She could hear the laugh in her voice. 'Because that might be more orthodox?'

'Yes.'

'Oh, heavens, you just turn up tomorrow. I'll talk it over with Magnolia and square things with the old boy.' On a sudden, unwarned impulse. 'Take the train to Bath – ring my business from the station. I'll be there – drive you here or to the Dower House. Which, Pippa, would you prefer?'

Primly, she answered, 'Whatever Mrs Tallent wishes.'

The wedding, everyone of the female villagers agreed, was 'proper luvly'. They were much in evidence (as Naldo had predicted) either at the back of the church or on the route from Taurus. Major Collinbury escorted the lilywhite bride and placed her hand in the vicar's with fatherly tenderness (poor little luvver – no dad of 'er own!). Master Ronald's voice was good and loud, the bride's inaudible ('which t'were modest and fittin'). With uncharacteristic imagination – or maybe because he couldn't get through the day without the smell of a horse – Ronnie had hired a landau and a pair of greys to drive them back to Taurus. The tenant party was waiting by the entrance door to clap and throw handfuls of confetti. In the drawing room Lucy, the head parlour maid, held out two glasses of champagne. Phillipa looked down first at her thin gold marriage band and then around the room. The thrill of ownership rushed in on her. Taurus might be Ronnie's, in *temporary* actuality Magda Tallent's, but in the future it would belong to *her*. She would cherish every stick and stone of it as she had cherished Carl's love. But this was different – no one's death could take the new, possessive, sweet reality from her as long as she gave birth to a son to hold that future safe . . . forever.

Ronald's arm slid around her waist – there were prickles of perspiration deep in the pores of his streakily florid skin. 'Drink up, lady wife. Remember you've just promised to obey me.'

She tilted her glass without speaking, her huge, blue eyes limpid and compliant. Her simple sheath of a gown just touched breasts and hips – if he could tear it off her now, fling her onto the polished floor amongst ruined shreds of satin surely then . . . *then* he would be able to . . . .

Phillipa moved her head and smiled past his shoulder towards Magda and Major Collinbury coming through the entrance by the screen. Frustrated and furious he made to fling away but she detained him with a swift clasp to his arm. Her fingers with the wedding band held him firmly . . . a soft, unyielding vice.

Gently, she murmured, 'Time for duty, Ronnie . . . before pleasure. You have to introduce me to all *our*,' the emphasis was subtle, 'tenants.' Then, as the others approached, he saw her, in the space of a shadow's flicker, revert to bridal bashfulness.

There was no one to whom Phillipa could throw her sheaf of lilies. She gave them to Doris Collinbury saying, 'Mater won't mind. The house is full of flowers.'

Naldo drove them away – the Alvis dragging a clattering row of tin cans and a worn out riding boot. They drove as far as the Red Lion in Somerton where Ronnie had left his little MG overnight.

Mindful of his nephew's lack of prowess behind a steering wheel Reginald had kept a hopeful check on the number of actual glasses of champagne Ronnie had consumed substituting almost empty for half full whenever the young man left a drink unguarded. But he doubted if the ruse had been successful. Ronald's unnatural ebullience increased his misgivings. He glanced at the couple in his driving mirror – caught a glimpse of Ronnie's flushed face. The cinnamon tweed jacket he'd chosen to wear with a Newmarket check shirt did nothing to cool the effect of fervid heat. By his side, Pippa sat pale and composed, his bare fingers clamped over her knee held from roaming any higher by a steady, black gloved hand. Naldo swore silently trying to block out the picture of her naked – available – on a hotel bed . . . providing the drunk young pup got them there safely.

At the Red Lion Phillipa floored him. Softly and restrainingly she said to her new husband. 'I'd love a cup of tea. And you could do with some black coffee. Go to the lounge and order a pot. *Plenty* of time to make Torquay.'

When he had, obediently, left them she turned to Reginald, 'Stop fussing, Naldo. *I'll* drive.'

He was stupefied. '*You* can?'

'Certainly. Been dying to ever since I saw that little beauty of an MG in the garage.'

Reginald took a circuitous route back to Taurus, went in by the side entrance and straight to the parlour where he poured himself a stiff brandy. Phillipa, he realised, had not stammered once since walking out of church.

The little devil! She'd fixed them all – mostly Magda.

The Imperial Hotel was on the sea front and patronised by Royalty. Princess Mary especially enjoyed the mild, South Devon climate, the unhindered view of the bay and the locals' lack of curiosity.

Five miles north of Newton Abbot, Phillipa, in the interests of self esteem, relinquished the driving wheel. Ronnie was able to sweep up to the hotel entrance with a suitably virile flourish.

The bridal suite was on the first floor with a balcony and private bathroom. A bottle of champagne in an ice bucket and a bowl of pink carnations stood on a little, marble topped table. The new Mrs Tallent told the porter who carried up their cases to take the flowers away.

The instruction unnerved Ronnie. The colourless, virginal creature he had assumed to be vulnerable to the crudest of male whims and advances had changed into a self composed young woman capable of giving orders without a hint of hesitation.

He'd not minded her driving – Ronald never minded abrogating responsibility in the cause of laziness and, consequently, felt no loss of face. But her immediate, quiet display of authority threatened his self confidence and aroused a frantic, secret fear.

'Why get rid of the carnations?'

She was pulling off her hat but with care so that not one dark hair strand should be disturbed. He wanted to yank out the hidden pins – send the whole mass tumbling down. With black locks falling over bare shoulders above round, pink tipped breasts surely . . . surely then ...? He clenched, unclenched his fingers . . . nothing more.

'I don't care for the perfume. Did you order them specially? *Orchids* are our flower.'

He said belligerently, 'No, I didn't. Nor did you carry orchids today.'

'Lilies are more suitable with virginal white.'

Thickly he growled out, 'Are you a virgin, Pippa?'

Even that did not shake her calm composure. Merely she answered, 'What an extraordinary question!'

There was something wrong . . . something she couldn't fathom. He hadn't budged since entering the room – stood with his back to the French windows, hands tight by his sides, neck stiff. Fishing in her handbag for her case keys, she said, 'Pop the cork, there's a dear. I may not approve the management's choice of flowers but I'd like a drink whilst I unpack. Soon be time to change for dinner.'

His words exploded. 'I don't want *dinner*. I want *you*. NOW. You are my wife.'

She felt cold . . . not shrivelled or unwilling – icily detached. Heard her voice acquiescent in reply, 'Of course, Ronnie. We're married.' And began to take off her clothes.

Still he didn't move . . . stared at her with devouring, desperate eyes.

Calculatingly matter of fact and unprovocative, she removed her dress, slip, panties – stood in high-heeled shoes, suspender belt, pale fawn stockings and brassière. As she reached behind to unclip the clasps he lunged forward, dragged her onto the bed, in the same movement scrabbling for her shoulder straps, pulling them down and her full breasts free. He tore at his jacket and trousers as if demons were after him – grabbed, slobbered, sucked at flesh and each breast tip.

With eyes wide and expressionless she drew him close, pressing her stomach and undulating, open thighs against him . . . felt nothing.

A shutter clicked up . . . vague, half formulated questions shifted, reformed themselves into answers. Ronnie Tallent was twenty-five. Ronnie Tallent had never had a woman. Ronnie Tallent was impotent. Here was a challenge for an ice cold heart and the knowing warmth of a soft, curved body. If Taurus were to have an heir the fruition lay within her hands.

She used them cunningly, as Carl had taught her for his delight . . . without effect. Ronnie sweated, moaned,-

submitted to every erotic trick until exhausted, humiliated, he pushed her away.

'No bloody good . . . if I'd dragged that white dress off you on the floor at home, might have been different.'

Drained and irrationally thankful (if any man, after Carl, should enter her not, please God, this maimed boy!), she said, unconvincingly, 'There's always tomorrow . . . another night.'

'No. Get this, my girl,' in weary shame he achieved a pathetic dignity, 'if not on my wedding night – never. I can mount horses – they rouse a heat between my legs – not women. You've done your best. Let's leave it at that.'

She sighed, said, 'Open the bottle . . . we must get dressed, go down to dinner . . . put on a show. This is,' wryly, 'our honeymoon. We're in the bridal suite.'

'Mater doesn't know.' It was a sudden, little schoolboy burst.

Comfortingly, she answered, 'No need . . . leave everything to me.'

Without looking at her he ground out, 'You're a good sort, Pippa.'

Dryly she replied, 'Then don't forget it.'

He ate a hearty dinner and slept beside her in the king-sized bed like a log. Phillipa lay awake listening to the rhythmic murmur of the sea. In . . . out . . . sand, shells, water moving until eternity. She believed Ronnie's 'Never again'. But what of Taurus? Tallents at Taurus for five hundred years. She caught a wisp of an echo she couldn't identify. Taurus needed an heir . . . she needed a man. Ronald's frantic, inconclusive fumblings had aroused an ache she thought had died with Carl.

Slowly she ran her fingers along the base of her throat, over breasts, waist, hips . . . deeply into the most secret part of her. She was not yet twenty-two – fifty years lay ahead if the Bible predicted true. Fifty years without a man? It made no sense and now . . . now there was Taurus. A man . . . but who?

Suddenly she smiled. Why Naldo! Naldo whose indolent good humour would never make demands. Whose kinship to Magda would add spice to the affair. *Naldo, of course*. Relaxed and contented as a cat who's glimpsed the cream jug she curled herself away from Ronnie and tipped into dreamless sleep.

It was a strangely pleasant five-day interlude. They ate breakfast on the bedroom balcony and on the first morning went looking for a riding stable that took Ronnie's fancy. Found one a few miles short of Ashburton. She left her husband complacently choosing his hack and drove off to explore. This formed the pattern to be followed each fine day. She visited the, as yet uncompleted, Abbey at Buckfastleigh and bought a bar of sungold, monastic beeswax; spent two hours wandering in Exeter Cathedral and the Close; another two walking beside the River Dart. In mid afternoon she collected Ronald and they searched out farmhouses serving Devon teas and sat in the sunshine demolishing a pile of tuff cakes with homemade jam and clotted cream. In the evening they danced to the hotel's three-piece orchestra.

The one rainy morning they spent in the games room playing unskilled, vigorous table tennis with another honeymooning couple. On the last day, Ronnie, having got wind of a horse sale at Kingsbridge, drove off alone. She filled the time strolling along the promenade and looking at the shops.

To outward eyes they appeared as normal newly-weds. Away from Taurus – or was it Magda? – Ronald seemed more relaxed, less moodily abrupt, aware of the need to hold in place a conventional façade. What had passed between them – or rather its lack – was never mentioned. Phillipa guessed that with the disclosure of sexual inability behind him, Ronnie would blot out its memory and settle for the undemanding status quo without regret or thought for another's feelings. That suited her. She was happy to play at husbands and wives – when the time came Ronnie, needs must, play mothers and fathers.

They arrived back at Taurus in the early afternoon. Ronnie greeted his mother with a perfunctory kiss and immediately went off to the stables.

Magda said, 'He hasn't changed,' and led the way indoors. In the hallway she realised that she was still alone. Irritably she turned back. Her daughter-in-law was standing by the entrance porch, right hand resting lightly on the Taurus tile. The sight annoyed the older woman. 'Come along, Phillipa. He's a piece of pottery not a pet.'

The girl did not move beyond lifting brilliant eyes towards Magnolia. 'Where's Naldo?' she asked.

Now anger brought a sharp edge to her voice. 'In Sandwich . . . playing golf. Why ask?'

Phillipa gave a vague, inconsequential smile and said, 'How nice . . . I wondered, that's all,' let her hand fall limply to her side. 'Sh . . . shall we go in?' The near whisper was familiar . . . should have made Magda feel more comfortable. Somehow it didn't.

She would have been even less so had she cause to go into the garden before breakfast on the following day.

Phillipa awoke early. Ronnie, impatient to be with his horses, climbed into breeches and riding boots without regard to disturbing his wife. When he had gone she rose and dressed quickly, tying the laces of tennis shoes and slinging a fawn cardigan around her shoulders.

She went down by the parlour stairway. One of the maids had drawn back the curtains. The room was drenched in splinters of coloured light, an arrangement of feathery white spiraea and spikes of buddleia stood in the fireplace and there were bowls of sweetpeas on two of the occasional tables. Faint perfume and gentle brilliance spun a web of benediction.

The drawing room door to the terrace was bolted. With the pride of ownership she pulled them aside. Very slowly, without a sound or footfall, she stepped onto flagstones, over the gravelled drive and across the soft lawn. Without looking back she sauntered to the end of the grass – turned around.

She could see the whole of the south front and a gleaming hint of stained glass in the eastern wall. Early morning sunlight sprinkled grey stone with specks of gold dust and painted the slanting edges of the porch roof in a gilded line. Beneath the eaves the tiny, deep set oratory window seemed no more than a secret shadow and beside the dusky entrance the Taurus tile glowed as though warmed by an inner fire. The only other colour touching the pale walls was a frame of yellow roses trailing and spilling up and around the parlour's unstained, foliate glass.

This was, apart from its smaller companion above, the only delicate, elaborate window in the whole façade. The rest were older, simpler, higher off the ground, the stone mullions straight and solid, unconcerned with decoration – private windows built to bring a flow of light and the touch of seclusion to family rooms behind the narrow panes. Strangely the change of style, the fanciful additions, in no way detracted from the sweet perfection of the house.

Phillipa began identifying every downstairs room – the upper floors were still in part a mystery to be discovered. Soon, she promised, every one would be as familiar to her as her heartbeats. Her eyes moved as would the sun, from east to west; the parlour, the door and two windows to the drawing room – she could just glimpse the honey edge of brocade curtaining. Next the spikey porchway, then the dining room – one window here set not dead centre in the wall (there were two above). The maids, she guessed, would be setting the table for breakfast but the glass too opaque and she too far away to see them . . . did they, however, notice the dull, still figure staring so intently in their direction?

Still skirting the boundary of the lawn she walked around to face the west wing. The first two windows she recognised as those of Magda's study – a room to which no one was invited although she suspected Naldo wandered in. Further along, a third was kept almost permanently shuttered – the gun room. Most of this part of the wall was smothered in wisteria . . . pale green leaves and a very few, late, violet coloured tumbling flowers. A single frond had reached the tip of the tiles and was creeping towards one of the little dormer windows. Seventeenth-century Tallents wanted more rooms in their brand new wing but out of the family's way. An unintended intimacy and charm added to the western aspect of their home. In high summer morning light, they were tipped with a flick of gold but how, she wondered, would they look under a sheet of snow? The seasons stretched before her . . . the forgotten pleasure of anticipation.

Enchantment . . . magic. 'I am a weaver of spells; I am a dreamer of dreams'. Where had she read or heard those words? Maybe they had yet to be written or had slipped, unbidden as a dream, into her head. She gave a little, twisted smile. Philly did not believe in magic. There was nothing, she said, other than the love of God. Rosanna Bland asked nothing but the love of just one man. She did not recognise that Sewerin had bewitched her senses . . . she understood this lovely house could fill an empty heart. Men died and love was lost . . . Taurus was indestructible. She would never be lonely again.

Intentionally tactless, Magda had not moved out of the fresco room with its medieval wall paintings and big, four-poster bed – nothing could better underline her unchanged position as mistress of the house. Ronnie had got himself a wife . . . no more than that.

With equal intention Phillipa waited a week – which coincided with Reginald's return.

They were gathered in the parlour watching his elegant act with the cocktail shaker, Ronnie fidgeting as usual although his amber eyes looked calmer, some of their moody heat evaporated. The girl was wearing a dress Naldo hadn't seen – a spur-of-the-moment Torquay purchase of white crêpe narrowly edged in black, all cool sophistication. It was the sight of her that prompted him to mix straightforward White Ladies.

Ronald said, 'I'll try a drop of your fiendish concoction, Nunkie. Pip persuaded me to experiment a bit in the hotel.'

Naldo curbed his surprise and an instinctive revolt against the possible ambiguity of the words. 'How was the Imperial?'

'Very expensive.'

'Just as well that honeymoon's come only once.' He was handing a drink to Phillipa and saw her eyes flicker, then grow very still. The old conjecture grew that it would not have been his inept nephew who had robbed her of innocence. A corner of her mouth twitched in a semi-smile of amused understanding.

Still looking at him, she said, 'About the fresco room, Mater . . . when will you be moving out?'

There was a silence filled with chips of ice. Then Magda gave a little, splintered laugh. 'Whatever prompts you to think that I shall, child?'

'Because it's customary. Even more customary for the Dowager to move into the Dower House. But the Collinburys are there . . . we mustn't disturb them.'

Abruptly Magnolia got to her feet . . . part of her cocktail splashed down the front of her dress. Never had Naldo seen his sister's elegant composure so shaken. Caught between anger and mortification she flapped an ineffectual handkerchief at the stain and glared at Ronnie. He sat contemplating his shoes as though calculating their worth on a second-hand stall.

'Ronald.' The name a whip crack. 'Is it *your* wish that I should leave my home?'

Phillipa's voice came dripping honey. 'How absurd! Major and Mrs Collinbury can't be expected to move. It's merely the fresco room I'm speaking of.'

She rounded on the girl. 'The question is academic. Ronnie, I'm sure, would not wish to dispossess his mother after nearly thirty years. *He* doesn't care *which* room he sleeps in.'

'And I am equally sure Ronnie is aware of what is fitting now he has a wife. What room did you occupy, Mater, when thirty years ago you came to Taurus as a bride?'

Magda cut in guardedly, 'I had no mother-in-law.'

Phillipa shrugged and smiled in her direction. 'That fact is academic. Your husband was master of the house.'

Ronnie pushed aside his barely tasted drink and crossed the room to the cupboard. With his back to the women he poured whiskey and muttered, 'She's right, Mater. *I* don't mind what room I sleep in but I have to think of Pip – she's my wife.'

Dangerously quiet, Magda asked, 'Am I to take it you

intend to support Phillipa in this . . . whim?'

He gulped at his brimming tumbler. 'Not a whim – tradition. You're all for tradition, Mater. Can't have it both ways y'know.'

Naldo sensed rather than saw the girl's smile of triumph because, carefully, he kept his eyes away from her sleek face but in so doing encountered Magda's look of smouldering, grey capitulation. He expected no appeal and received none. With tightly held dignity Magda said, 'I must go and change my dress before it's ruined. Start dinner without me – I'll be happy to miss the soup course.'

'Oh no, Mater!' Phillipa's exclamation, deceitfully breathless, robbed her of even so small a relief, 'We can't do that. Just ask Lucy to hold dinner till you're ready. It would be such a shame to spoil your pretty gown. Don't hurry,' the smile was icing sugar smooth, 'Naldo can always mix another cocktail.'

'Perhaps,' her mother-in-law commented bitterly, 'you'd care to take over the ordering of the meals as well as rearrangements of bedchambers?'

'Good gracious! Whatever gave you that idea? I'm sure the servants would resent it.' As Magnolia's stiff, stalking back disappeared up the little, hidden stairway his wife turned to Ronnie. 'Tomorrow we must discuss with your mother *which* bedroom she'd prefer – have it refurnished. The way *she* wants. We must be very careful not to let her feel ousted in her own home.'

Like hell! Reginald's outburst held no sound. He couldn't judge which emotion was the stronger – pity for the first rout of his sister's life; admiration for Phillipa's dexterity. Well, well, little lady, he speculated, what shall I find you doing next?'

The next thing she did was overtake him at high speed on the main road to Bath. Just short of Midsummer Norton he saw the MG drawn into the side of the highway, Phillipa standing by the bonnet. He pulled up.

'Trouble?'

'Not with this little beauty. Whoever persuaded a lousey driver like Ronnie to buy such a dream of a car?'

He ignored the unwifely comment. 'Why stop?'

Her face was all smiles. 'To attract your attention. I want to see over your shop. This way avoids diplomatic manoeuvering.'

His mouth twisted in response. 'But not the necessity of travelling in convoy.'

'Don't you believe it. There's a garage half a mile back. I'll ask the owner if I can leave the MG on the forecourt and collect it later. Give him a quid for concession. We'll go together.'

He said, 'You're adept at taking every trick.'

Gravely she looked at him. 'Not yet, Naldo . . . I'm learning.'

He parked just out of hearing distance and watched her charm the man in overalls. Her face, framed by a bright cotton handkerchief she had tied under her chin peasant style, was very earnest. First she filled up with petrol, then, before handing over the money began talking confidentially pointing first at his car, secondly an empty space at one side of the forecourt. The man was slow to understand . . . he scratched his head. She went through the pointing routine again and, suddenly, his face split into a grin, he nodded vigorously and walked across the tarmac preparatory to seeing her back neatly alongside a battered Austin Sixteen. A ten shilling note changed hands and Phillipa rejoined Reginald. He leant across to open the passenger seat, she shrugged off her creamy, short jacket, tossed it into the rear and slipped in beside him. Her dress was the leaf sprigged cotton, her shoes white, flimsy sandals. Beneath the pale silk of her stockings he could see toenails painted a flamboyant red.

'What a helpful man!' She untied the ends of her head scarf. '*Covered* in grease. Do I smell of engine oil?'

'No . . . lilies of the valley.' He concentrated on turning the car around and then, as they gained speed, said reprovingly, 'You shouldn't drive that nippy little car in high-heels.'

'I don't . . . except for those five hundred yards just now. Stockinged feet.' She stuck them out in front of her, wriggling her toes. 'Which will be far too chilly when autumn comes. I must buy some decent driving shoes.'

'It would appear,' the remark was more than conversational, 'that Ronnie has no objection to handing the use of his car over to you.'

Her reply came serious and flat. 'I think he's relieved. Got a feeling he's afraid of anything he can't kick in the flanks and shout at, "Git up there!"'

A devil in him prompted the question, 'Does that include my sister?'

She answered flat, 'Don't try to trick me, Naldo. Remember I'm a twin, too.'

His eyes were on the road ahead. 'Identical. Not me. There's the difference. Magda's not the other half.'

'You don't feel any need to protect her?' The words more an affirmative than a query.

'Christ no! Why should I?'

It was Rosanna who laughed. 'That's a relief!'

He said, 'You're a strange young woman.'

'A Gemini . . . a Gemini in Taurus. Don't you find that to be something of a challenge?'

Reginald was as quick to pick her up. 'You're offering me a contest?'

'Good gracious, no. Surrender.'

He stopped the car. 'Let's get this straight. You've been married to Ronnie not much more than a fortnight and, unless I've read the signals wrong, you're giving me a big, green light.'

She laughed again. 'Oh dear! Such a lack of subtlety. I do apologise. Would you prefer I flutter "come-hither but don't-touch-me-quite-yet" eyelashes? Christ – to use your personal choice of blasphemous idiom – I'm telling you my new husband isn't any good . . . impotent . . . can't raise a hope.'

He froze, staring at her. A hundred niggling, half admitted, mostly ignored suspicions whirled around and clarified.

'Naldo, Naldo.' Her huge blue eyes were disturbingly remote yet near to pleading. 'What have we got to lose? You're . . . hot for me. In the most gentlemanly fashion but, decidedly, *hot*. I know, so don't pretend. If I couldn't break through poor old Ronnie's maternally induced inhibitions in five days of naked, *marital* seclusion who, in God's name, could? I'm good in bed . . . I'm *very* good. You know that without so much as touching me. I've seen the confirmation in those cloudy, grey, *intrusive* eyes.'

He moved to kiss her but she retreated a little. 'Don't mistake me, I'm not speaking of love but *pleasure*. What was it Sarah Churchill wrote? "My lord was in such haste he pleasured me in his boots". How *lovely*, Naldo.'

His knowledge of history was sparse but he was pushed to put the record straight. 'Sarah Churchill *adored* her John.'

She brushed the words aside. '*Adoration* is the last thing you want. Admit it – you'd run a mile.'

He felt his lips twitch. 'But only in the most gentlemanly fashion.'

'Of course, providing that proved fast enough.'

He took her nearest hand and held it close to his mouth. 'And where, Pippa, do you propose we take our pleasure? At Taurus?'

'No!' She sounded genuinely shocked. 'You've two antique shops. If I leave Magda in full control of the house there will be plenty of time lying idle on my hands. What more natural than that you should suggest I help out in the business – now and again?'

'What a resourceful girl you are! It could be arranged. Not in Bath – Luckes is always there. But the Taunton shop . . . now that has a flatlet above.' The conspirational smile in his eyes made the grey deepen. 'I was thinking of turning the rooms into an extra store. Yours is a much better idea.'

'And I've the car, so getting there and back is no problem.'

He kissed her fingers teasingly; asked in the lightest of tones. 'You've done this before?'

For as long as it took to blink her face went dead – a mortality so fleeting that in recollection he considered it a whim of his imagination. But Reginald King was not given to whims. Then, as fast, the warmth came back into her mouth and eyes.

'Oh, no, Naldo . . . nothing, ever, quite like this.

Magnolia moved out of the fresco room on the day Ronald took delivery of two new hunters. Her first reaction to Phillipa's proposal to refurbish a bedchamber (patronising . . . it was patronising!) had been to ignore the scheme and move lock, stock and barrel into the nearest large room. It was Naldo who jolted her towards her customary commonsense.

His remarks came jauntily. 'Shouldn't be a martyr, Mag. You're not the type and a hair shirt's most unbecoming. Ronnie won't notice and I shall look the other way.'

Sharply. 'And what will Phillipa do?'

'Not, I think, change her mind.'

'Everything else has,' his sister said and left him.

Neither hurrying nor deliberately slowing her steps she made her way to the study. It was long and narrow, reached through the dining room and opening out of a passageway containing also doors to the kitchens and gun room. Two-thirds along the inner wall a carved, stone fireplace was piled with fir cones and little logs ready for kindling on top of a bed of soft, pale ash. All the year round the place smelt faintly of wood smoke. A sofa just large enough for two was set at right angles to the hearth and, on the left, a deep armchair and padded footstool. There were book shelves in an alcove and a low coffee table scattered with Magda's favourite reading – *The Tatler*, *Sphere*, *Illustrated London News*, *Britannia and Eve* and *Vogue*. At the far end of the room, a small door opened into yet another stairway leading to the first floor. She had made it as much her personal domain as it had been Archie's in his lifetime.

Testily she sat at her desk tucked between two waist-high, mullioned windows. Knowing it to be her day for household accounts Lucy had already placed a small coffee tray to one side of the blotting pad. Magda reached for an exceptionally early cigarette and filled her cup. She refrained from adding sugar – a bitter taste suited her mood. She inhaled, frowned and thought back over all those tedious visits to the house in Cheshire; Angie's voice always plaintively demanding, her daughter doing exactly what she was told.

'I don't know, Magda, what I'd do . . . how to survive, without Philly. But I would never, never stand in her way of a happy marriage. It's just that, sometimes, I have these dreadful, bad dreams, when my head's especially painful. I really think those sleeping draughts the doctor prescribes make them worse. A nightmare in which I have just *one* daughter – Rosanna. *She* has no consideration for anyone's wishes or feelings other than her own.' The words had become a continual lament during the last two year's of Angie's life.

With a jerk Magda tapped the ash from the tip of her unenjoyed cigarette. Last evening's cool young woman in her white, black trimmed dress *could* have been Rosanna. Such a stupid fancy increased her bitter, hard held anger.

Another picture intruded – her daughter-in-law, on return from honeymoon, standing by the entrance porch stroking the prancing, terracotta bull. Almost she regretted having the thing fixed.

Again she inhaled deeply but without soothing pleasure and, with a stiffer jerk, crushed the half stub onto the ashtray. Naldo was right and she shouldn't have needed him to tell her that there was nothing to be gained by sterile ungraciousness. But . . . but a new, raw vulnerability left her almost defenceless. However . . . her eyes narrowed on the thought . . . she could make things displeasing. Take Phillipa up on the remark, 'Which bedroom would you prefer?' She'd prefer the one the newly weds were occupying and would be delighted with the prospect of having it done out right through – down to a change of carpet . . . probably fitted wall to wall. It would be a silly, little victory obliging them to move twice before possessing the fresco room and about as satisfying as her last cigarette but necessary if she were to retain some self-assertion.

Her mind slid back to Angela. She had described Taurus, its history in detail and room by room to a flatteringly attentive friend. It would be quite in Angela's character to impress upon her malleable daughter the significance of the bedchamber with the wall paintings and four-poster bed as being the one where, as Mrs Ronald Tallent, she should sleep. Phillipa's mother had dominated the girl all her life . . . it would be unnervingly natural that her influence should reach beyond the grave. Magda's appreciation of Angela's pallid forcefulness helped make so fanciful an explanation plausible. No other was possible . . . Magnolia Tallent could not admit that her own judgement had been at fault.

So she took her time over the new arrangements, spent a great deal of money and deliberately, provocatively, changed her mind more than once as to colours and furnishing materials. Phillipa showed no impatience, offered no opinions and agreed to every one of her suggestions. The apples were red on the orchard trees when all, at last, was ready. Magda walked out of the fresco room with an angry pang and the vow never to enter it again except to see her first grandchild.

Ronnie had asked Paul Gifford, the veterinary surgeon, to look over his new mounts and come in afterwards for a drink. Neither the Tallents nor the house impressed Gifford – Ronnie's vet's bills were high but often for the kind of care Gifford would have preferred not to need to provide and his preference was for modern homes with clean, straight walls and large paned windows. There were two people in the parlour – Mrs Tallent seated on a stiff backed chair, a cigarette between thin fingers and her brother, drawing the heavy curtains against the darkening sky.

The men were acquainted – they belonged to the same golf club but rarely played. Naldo from lack of energy, the vet too much hard work.

He was struck by Mrs Tallent's lack of colour and wondered if she had been ill. He couldn't recall so many streaks of iron grey in her carefully waved hair. Her dove silk gown, the skirt agingly crossed by two deep bands of frills, didn't help – nor the marcasite pendants in her ears.

She asked in her usual, clear, crisp voice, 'What's your verdict, Mr Gifford, on my son's latest extravagance?'

'No extravagance, Mrs Tallent. *If* he doesn't ride them

too hard.' The last was spoken for the record – not from conviction. Already he'd put down two of Ronald's mounts. Privately he hoped the young bruiser would break his own neck before ruining another horse's back or legs. At once he pulled back the thought. A dark girl in a pale golden yellow dress had come into the room from some entrance he couldn't define. Would wish widowhood on no one.

Ronald called, 'Pip, come and meet Gifford our worthy vet.'

He never felt more than scornful amusement at the young man's arrogant dropping of a prefix to his name but he saw the girl's eyes flash.

She held out her hand saying, 'How do you do, *Mr* Gifford,' the emphasis slight but sufficient and he found himself skilfully drawn down into a comfortable chair as King placed his favourite early evening tipple – very dry sherry – onto a table by his side.

For conversation's sake he asked, 'Do you hunt, Mrs Tallent?'

Ronnie answered for her. 'Great Scott, no! Pippa doesn't know one end of a horse from another.'

'But certainly how to handle a fast car.'

She looked at him in calm enquiry.

'I've seen you – and you've passed me – on the roads hereabouts.'

She laughed. 'It's just as well I don't have a secret life.'

'Vets,' he answered mock seriously, 'know how to keep their council . . . like GPs.'

Her smile moved sideways like the tilt of her head. 'That's a relief! What car do you run, for the record?'

'Huge great Austin,' Ronnie cut in, 'like a hearse.'

'It has been . . . on occasions.'

Magda said, 'What a morbid turn this conversation's taking, I don't care for it.'

'No more do I, Mater.' Young Mrs Tallent was quick to agree and as quick to turn to him again. 'You'll be seeing a lot more of me, Mr Gifford, on the road – especially to Taunton. Reginald's asked me to help out in his shop.'

'What?' Ronnie's mother sat up even more stiffly. 'You know nothing about antiques.'

'No more do I, Mag.' Naldo put a cocktail into his sister's hand. 'That's never stopped me selling 'em. I think she'll be an asset.'

'I hope so.' Phillipa was still smiling at their guest, 'if Ronnie doesn't mind. You don't mind do you, Ron?'

'Good Lord, why should I?' Her husband sounded disinterested. 'Stop you being bored. 'Spect the hunting season must be boring if you don't ride. Think it's a good idea. Gonna pay her a wage, Nunkie Naldo?'

'Just commission. So don't imagine, young pup, that you can cut down on Pippa's dress allowance.'

Magda said frostily, 'It's hardly usual for a Tallent of Taurus to serve in a shop.'

'Oh, but Mater,' the words came breathlessly, 'you run the house so efficiently . . . even arrange flowers better than I can. There's practically nothing for me to do around the place. And an antique business isn't a *shop* now, is it?' Her dark blue eyes opened appealingly.

The veterinary surgeon was uncomfortably conscious that a snare had been set – a net cast to catch someone. He was being used as a decoy in a family affair which was none of his business. He cut the unwelcome involvement short by finishing his drink and standing up. Tonight there would be no spoken thanks for hospitality. 'The animals are calling.' He turned to Ronald. 'One of your tenant farmers – Elias Sumption – nasty case of mastitis.'

The young man's grin twisted into a leer. 'His cattle, Gifford, or his wife?'

The Taunton shop was situated centrally and unobtrusively close by the Castle and its adjacent hotel. The flat above had a private, back entrance but no parking space. Reginald arranged that Phillipa should leave the MG in the Castle Hotel parking lot. His own car, he left a quarter of a mile away at Wilton walking to the business through the town park and along the High Street. This was his custom in both cities. He enjoyed a leisurely stroll and the distance gave him an excuse to stay at home when the weather was cold or rainy. Now it proved fortuitous.

Phillipa drove to Taunton twice a week – on Tuesdays and Fridays. She never entered the shop except, occasionally, with Naldo. After parking the MG, she unlocked the flat door opening out onto an almost completely secluded yard and let herself in. She was never sure if she would find Naldo waiting.

The two knowledgeable, dear, old queers who ran the business were totally incurious. Schoolmasters who, for perceptible reasons, had been required to take early retirement, they were too grateful for the chance to augment their meagre pensions to bother what went on upstairs.

The larger of the two rooms which Reginald used as an office was a cluttered conglomerate of bits and pieces . . . large, roll top desk, badly misused Regency sofa, a round Benares brass table, an accountant's stool and a prettily upholstered nursing chair. The smaller had a wide modern bed and a view over the Castle tree tops. She was content to spend hours lying against a pile of pillows watching the leaves turn from yellow, to bronze, to brown . . . finally drift away leaving the brittle, black skeleton of twigs and branches. It were as if some of Philly's passivity had seeped into her limbs.

For her lover passivity did not exist. With greedy arms and smiling, parted lips she reached towards him. Lacking a hint of inhibition she possessed the tender ability to prolong, without dulling, the tide of passion and a promise never to disappoint but always lead him above the peak of expectation. He did not ask, nor wish to know, who had taught her such erotic charm . . . found more troubling her adroit refusal to be serious. Always she laughed, cried out in pure enjoyment . . . never love. Yet he knew her not to be emotionally cold. When in the New Year the old King died, she wept. Watching her tears, Reginald could not crush an intuition that she would never weep for him.

It was foolish, he recognised, to feel deprivation. Always he had wanted women voluptuously responsive but unattached to heart strings. She gave him just that – superbly. But as the months went by sexual delight alone – no matter how accomplished – ceased to be enough.

Increasingly, however, it became difficult to guard his eyes when he was with her. Ronnie, following his usual winter routine of riding his horses into the ground four days a week in pursuit of fox or stag and snoring in a chair by the fire in the evenings, noticed nothing. To Magda, after weeks of niggling disquiet she couldn't pin down, the truth burst like a starshell.

It was a mild, February night with a gusty wind that, now and again, threw handfuls of rain against the windows. Ronnie, for once, was quietly asleep; Phillipa playing Patience with a set of nineteenth-century French cards she'd brought back from the shop. Her dress was the black edged white, her finger nails varnished pillar box red. In the soft light of the parchment shaded standard lamp her neat hair gleamed like polished silk. Magnolia glanced up from the latest *Vogue* reaching for a cigarette and saw Naldo, who had gone to refill his brandy glass, standing by her side. He was looking down not at the cards but the girl's cameo clear profile. His expression checked his sisters movement – froze her right hand foolishly in mid-air – tender, longing, hungry and, unbelievably, *committed*. He lifted his own hand and briefly caressed the girl's bare shoulder. Phillipa raised her head, blue eyes reproving, her mouth mischievous but gently shook her head, once. Reginald moved away and Magda groped blindly for her cigarette.

Dear God that she should have been hoodwinked so easily! And yet . . . and yet, *Naldo*, her level headed, indolent Naldo and the girl she'd wished her son to marry.

By the end of twelve hours, Magda's sick incredulity had turned to frozen wrath. It was a Tuesday. She stood by the window of her study and watched Naldo's car disappear down the drive. Then, by the little stairway, she went up to the fresco room and opened the door without knocking or a word.

Phillipa was seated before the dressing table adjusting a cherry red, angora beret.

'Good gracious, Mater.' Calmly. 'Is something wrong?'

Magda shut the door. 'Wrong? It depends on how many

interpretations are put on the word. In my book, there is only one. I think it would be as well if I drive with you today into Taunton.'

The blue eyes widened . . . not a hint of alarm. 'Of course, if that's what you wish. I'll gladly show you over the shop. Or maybe you want to buy some things? Hatchers is the best department store.'

Her mother-in-law said wearily, 'Don't play games, Phillipa.'

The girl turned round facing the older woman. 'If you want to talk in riddles, do be so good as to give me a clue.'

Harshly the words came rapping out. 'Clues! This house has been littered with clues since God knows when and I never picked up on one until last evening.'

Still calm – even a little amused. 'What and where last evening?'

'In the parlour. I saw Naldo look at you.'

'Great heavens, Mater. He does that all the time.'

'Not intimately . . . naked . . . with *lover's* eyes.'

The amusement drained away. 'That was foolish of him.'

'You don't deny it?'

'Deny what?'

Magda's fingers twisted with the longing to grab the girl by the shoulders, shake her till the smooth head flopped like a rag doll's. She pressed them against her sides. 'That you and he are . . . lovers?'

Phillipa stood up preparatory to fetching her jacket of tight, black astrakhan. 'Yes, it's true. We go to bed together.'

'You . . . you . . . little . . . .' a splintering gasp, 'I can't find the words to describe what you are!'

The younger woman let her coat fall, swung round and came to the other's side. She grasped her elbow with tight fingers. 'I think you had better sit down . . . there are things you must know.' Propelled Magda down onto the dressing table stool.

Dispassionately, keeping her gaze fixed on the aging, raging features, she said, 'Firstly, Magda Tallent, your adored Ronald who spends all his time with his legs across a saddle, rushing all over the countryside isn't capable – not for his life's worth – of competently straddling a woman. I could get an annulment for non-consummation of marriage. Think of the scandal.'

The woman went deadly white – even the lips were colourless. Phillipa walked swiftly to her husband's wardrobe, opened one door, filled a glass from a whiskey bottle on a shelf and took it back with her. Magda gulped, choked on the fiery liquid . . . some of the warmth flowed back into suddenly withered cheeks.

'That's . . . that's no excuse.' The words were shaky but game. 'My own brother . . . abusing my hospitality.'

'Come off it, Magda! It suited you to have him living here.'

Magnolia regained some of her authoritative energy. 'It will have to stop. Reginald will have to leave.'

Phillipa said gently, 'Mater, you don't understand. If not Naldo, someone else.'

'Promiscuous!'

'Not at all. I can live quite happily without sex, much as I enjoy it when it's going on. *Taurus* can't survive without an heir. Remember the play we saw in Bath? *The Case of the Frightened Lady*. Think back on Lady Lebanon's speech . . . the actress who looks like you. "Aisla, you will be doing a wonderful thing . . . the line will go on . . . your children will be Lebanon's; married to Willie they'll bear the Lebanon name." *I'm* not a frightened lady. It will be a pleasure to keep Taurus safe.'

Her mother-in-law said feebly and without hope. 'Perhaps Ronnie should see a doctor . . . .'

'Can *you* see him agreeing. It suits him the way things are. And you can be quite certain he'd never admit a child of mine wasn't his. Be practical, Magda, this is the best way. Only four people would know the secret and Tallents at Taurus be assured unto the third and fourth generation.'

Magda put her hand onto the corner of the dressing table and levered herself up to stand on legs that felt like water. 'I don't wish to discuss the matter any further. It's . . . disgraceful.'

'Of course, we won't,' Phillipa soothed, 'after all, everything has been said.' She reached for her coat, swinging it around her shoulders. 'I really must be off to Taunton or I'll be late.' She winked. 'Maybe make a child this afternoon.'

Chapter 8

On the second Thursday in June, Phillipa knew for certain she was pregnant. The next afternoon she told Naldo. He stared down at her with a mixture of astonishment and unexpected delight.

'You're sure?'

'Dr Bates confirmed it yesterday. Will be all over the village by tonight.' She gave a half chuckle. 'Lucy's aunt saw me coming out of the surgery. I shall tell Ronnie and Magda this evening at cocktail time. I suggest, for Magda's sake, that you are not there. Have one of your rare dinner engagements – a business associate in Bath will do.'

Way outside her drift he answered, 'This changes things.'

'It certainly does – no more keeping shop. The mother of the heir to Taurus must stay at home, rest and think beautiful thoughts.'

Bemused and excitedly adoring he looked at her unaltered nakedness – smooth, flat stomach, small, proud tipped breasts. It was incredible . . . wonderful that she should be carrying his child. 'I never dreamed,' his words the whole, simple truth, 'that this could happen. You said, right from the beginning, that you'd take care of things.'

'So I have . . . just as I pleased.'

Still he didn't hear her. 'We must go away together – to the South of France or maybe America. I knew I loved you but not until this moment did I realise how much.'

Her reply came patiently. 'You haven't been listening.'

'To every word . . . I'm going to be a father.'

'No,' she said, 'Ronnie is.'

He felt as if a cold fist had thumped the left side of his chest. 'What . . . Pippa . . . are you saying?'

'That the child I'm carrying is my husband's. I'm prepared to swear to that in any court of law.'

Now the bunched fingers were pummelling hard, catching at his breath. 'You are implying,' the astounding, agonising conviction grew, 'that you've used me to make a child for Ronald.'

'Only incidentally – in truth for Taurus. And, Naldo, we've had lovely times together.'

He reared away from her soft limbs and stormed out savagely, 'What do I care if the whole shebang has to be sold up because there isn't a single Tallent left?'

She began to twist her tumbled hair into its customary neat knot at the nape of her neck. 'You may not. *I care*. Taurus is the only thing I care about.'

'Not me?' He barely recognised the sound of his own voice. 'Not me, one little bit?'

'Come on now, Naldo, that wasn't in the deal. *Pleasure*. That was the contract we made. Which you've had in good measure . . . running over the edges, so don't complain.'

'And what,' he asked ice cold and breathing hard, 'if your baby should be a girl?'

She shrugged. 'There will always be another time . . . another man.'

'Not me,' the shout tore through his lungs. 'Not me!'

He flung himself out of reach but, placatingly, she caught at his naked arms. 'Don't be too hurt, Naldo. Or judge me too harshly.' Her blue eyes swam midnight dark with unshed tears. 'When I came to Taurus to marry Ronnie . . . never mind why . . . I had nothing left. Not a thing except to breathe in and out and pretend to be alive. You say you love me, but is it love that pervades every moment of your day? When you awake is your first thought, "Phillipa"? At night is it my face that swims before your eyes as you slide into sleep? I doubt it. *Women* love fiercely, *invasively* . . . not men. Magda understands this. *Her* love is not for a man . . . *people* leave her cool underneath. Cool as you have always been and still are although you daren't admit it at this moment. All Magda's love is for Taurus which is why she's willing to ignore our liaison.

'I understand, too – how well I understand! Taurus is beautiful, indestructable . . . a magic house. I cannot bear that we should be parted . . . that I should lose *another* perfect love.'

He read a host of secrets in her pleading, ravaged face and, raw from the hurt she'd dealt him, capitulated. He lifted her hand from his arm and dropped it onto the pillows. 'You're wrong, Pippa. I'm not the cool man I once was. Making love to you has changed all that . . . bewitched my senses; trapped my heart. But you win. I'll go to France alone.'

There was much to gossip about in the village that autumn. Mrs Ronnie's coming baby; the uncle going off abroad so sudden. Sold up his shops and living in France now, they said. Most agreed he probably couldn't stand the prospect of a baby squalling about the place – 'im bein' a bachelor. The Abdication when it came took a poor second place of interest though. 'In'nt Mrs Ronnie's hairdo like that Mrs Simpson's?'

Reginald gave his car to Ronnie. 'You'll need it for a family, pup.' He wondered if Pippa would feel any regrets or qualms whilst driving it. She didn't.

Magda joined two more committees – one The Diocesan Care of Unmarried Mothers – and refused to knit for her first grandchild. As the Abdication crisis slowly broke and culminated, she looked at Phillipa with new eyes . . . Wallis Simpson. The hairstyle, the immobile features, were on every newsheet but even Magnolia, in half resigned defeat, could not concede a likeness to the blunt Transatlantic jaw and hard, carefully painted mouth.

In mid-December, Ronnie was brought home slightly concussed and Paul Gifford had to put down another maimed hunter. Phillipa, unshakably serene, wore maternity dresses in navy blue and mossy green with tiny, detachable white collars and cuffs. She carried the baby easily but in the last two months grew very large. Ronnie taunted, 'That kid'll be cart-horse size, Pippa, not thoroughbred.'

After Christmas, she went out rarely except down to the Dower House for tea. It had been tacitly accepted that Major Collinbury would be the infant's godfather.

One bitterly cold afternoon she mentioned that one of

the estate's small houses on the edge of Somerton had become vacant. Fully repaired and redecorated it would be much easier to keep warm and, with a long, adjacent paddock, ideal for the Major's decorative chickens. Collinbury, pressed for every pound, jumped at the idea but his wife slowed him down.

'We should need, Phillipa, to see the building first.'

'That's easy. Dr Bates says it does me good to take the car out for a gentle run. I'll pick you up tomorrow at half past ten. We'll have lunch at the Red Lion afterwards.' Her insistence was mild but very firm.

As they watched her walk away down the drive the Major said, jerkily, 'Don't look a gift horse in the mouth, Doris. With my diminishing income any place smaller would be a blessing. Forget about keeping up appearances, don't let pride ruin our chances.'

His wife patted his hand. 'My dear old Dick, that simply won't happen. We must leave the Dower House soon. Now there's a family on the way, Magda will need to move in. What a blind, old fellow you are!'

Magda learnt of the move from the Vicar's wife. As treasurer of the Mothers' Union she stayed behind after the January meeting to check the annual accounts and discuss plans for the Easter outing. The two women had little in common except a desire never to leave things to the last minute.

Ruth Pobberell said, '*How* we shall miss Doris Collinbury when they go to live at Somerton. Just about the time of the outing, too. Ah, well,' as wife of a pathological pessimist Ruth forced herself always to look on the bright side, 'our loss will be St Michael's gain. And I hope, about then, to be enrolling your daughter-in-law. How is Phillipa? Not long to go now. You must be getting quite excited.'

Magnolia, her reactions swift enough to check vocal surprise and veil the anger in her eyes, answered blankly, 'Yes . . . quite excited.'

On her way back to the house she called in at the estate office. Kelly Watts reluctantly pushed aside a ledger and stood up. Magda sat down without ceremony.

'What's all this about,' her tone stabbed like a bodkin, 'the Dower House . . . the Collinburys moving out?'

He had been expecting her enquiry and had thought himself prepared to answer but found it wasn't so. He and Magda Tallent had worked together too many years for him to relish her usurpation, inevitable though it must be. He stumbled over the first sentence. 'It's . . . it's a little large for them – they're aging and, I think, not too happy financially. Now that Miss Lemon has gone permanently into a nursing home Mr Ronnie thought the house in Lion Lane would suit them better.'

'*Mr* Ronnie?'

He looked uncomfortable. 'Young Mrs Tallent conveyed her husband's wishes . . . Ronnie was out with the Quantock Staghounds.'

'I see . . .'

Her looks, he thought, were growing gaunt and tight – the sallow tint of skin more apparant, the marcelled hair wispy with grey streaks fading out the brown.

'I would appreciate,' she said, 'being kept informed of estate changes.'

The frost in her voice peaked him. 'I'd assumed,' it was not entirely true, 'you would have known – it being a family affair. Major Collinbury, I understand, is going to be the baby's godfather.'

She gripped the thin fingers of her flashing left hand about her handbag and compressed her lips together. Unguardedly she muttered, 'That's news to me.'

Watts felt embarrassed. The outward signs were that tranquil, blue eyed Mrs Ronnie and her mother-in-law got on well. No one knew better than he that Magnolia was an unemotional women and Ronald unreliable and disinterested in everything other than those poor, bloody horses of his. He had been surprised when his pretty, young wife came enquiring, innocently, about available Taurus property but the surreptitious implication had been that she was acting on Magnolia's behalf. She hadn't entirely convinced him . . . now he knew for sure it wasn't so.

'I seem,' he said, 'to have stepped out of line.'

Magda stood up. 'Forget it. It's done now.'

He opened the door for her and she walked away like an old women. As dignified and graceful as ever, but *old.*

Phillipa's son was born on 20th February – the cusp of Pisces. He weighed eight and a half pounds, was completely bald and resembled no one. Exhausted – the labour had been protracted – and triumphant that her baby was a boy, she cradled him in her arms. 'Carl . . . my beautiful, beautiful Carl.'

'Carl!' Magda demanded. 'What sort of name is that?'

'Nothing wrong with it.' Ronnie was bored and fidgeting to get back to the stables. 'If that's what Pippa wants.'

She watched his stocky, belligerent shoulders push their way through the drawing room doorway and went herself to the study by the longest, roundabout route.

Slowly she walked through each room looking about her as though for the first time but with the fierce, possessive pride of familiarity. In the parlour, the fire had already been kindled – the hearth asparkle with applewood flames and the scent of orchards.

She left by a small door close to the foot of the concealed stairway which opened onto a narrow corridor leading back to the hallway and screen. Then across the dining room, into the kitchen/gun room passage and, eventually, her narrow, private domain. Despite iron grey skies and the winter bleak garden beyond the window – the snowdrops were finished, the crocuses yet to bloom – inside the room was cosy. The curtains, looped back with golden cords, were Tudor pink and the fire, on its bed of ash, burnt constantly from October to Easter time.

Magda sat at her desk, rubbed chilly fingertips together. She drew a plain piece of paper towards her, unscrewed her fountain pen and began to write in swift, long looped letters:

TALLENT. On 20th February, at TAURUS, to PHILLIPA, wife of RONALD EDGAR TALLENT, a son.

That would put paid to premature, wide disclosure of his unsuitable, appalling name.

She flipped through the pages of her desk address book for the *Daily Telegraph's* phone number, noted it at the bottom of the sheet and went back to the hall and the telephone in its confidential alcove. She dialled the number and dictated the announcement.

Replacing the earpiece on its hook she went into the kitchen to ask for a pot of coffee to be brought to the study.

An open bottle of wine stood on the scrubbed deal table – all the staff were in the room including Greedy, the gardener/chauffeur. Cook looked shamefaced but said, defiantly, 'Wettin' the baby's head, ma'am.'

Magda gave them a wan, comprehensive smile. 'I see you've used the best sherry. Coffee will do for me. In the study.'

The fire needed tending. She stirred the ashes under two logs and added half a handful of fir-cones. Taking her writing case she sat in the armchair . . . lit a cigarette. When Lucy brought the tray and set it on the table she said, nervously, 'We should have asked your permission first, madam, but Cook got a bit carried away.'

Her head bent over the writing paper she replied, 'Nonsense. Mrs Ronald doesn't have a baby every day of the week.' *Or any other day* – I'll see to that. Made no attempt to crush the vicious thought.

The ink from her pen seemed to flow too fast . . . she wrote carefully, this time to an address near St Tropez. The words were self defensive, formal and very few.

Dear Naldo,
This morning at 9.45 Phillipa was delivered of a son. He weighs over eight pounds and has been given the name of CARL. Mother and child are doing well.
Your affectionate sister,
Magnolia.

Only in the P.S. did her guard slip.

The winter here, drags on. You, I imagine, are wreathed in the scent of mimosa.

When, ten days later, a box of golden flowers arrived she took them, jealously, to her own room. Standing the vase on the window sill she looked through and past the feathery puffs of blossom to the barren parkland beyond the mullioned window panes.

Spurious sunshine. A spurious Tallent to inherit her life's dedication. A Tallent of Taurus who was not a Tallent at all. No comfort in the thought that the boy's father was no secret stranger but her twin. She had so carefully ordered, planned and deployed the participants in her life and for the future . . . and all for nothing. Taurus was slipping beyond her grasp.

She stared more closely at the shower of golden glory . . . now each flowerlet seemed like a shiny star suspended in a crowded, burnished milky way. Suppose . . . suppose she wrote to Naldo – 'Coming to join you.' He didn't – couldn't *love* the girl. Prudence, when Pippa told him she was pregnant, had sent him overseas. The cool, undemanding relationship between brother and sister had always been so harmonious – like their dancing across a ballroom floor. A foreign country could not change the wordless bond they shared.

But even as the thought spun in her head she knew that she would do no such thing. She was, invisibly, but as irrevocably, attached to the stones of Taurus as the terracotta tile set into the entrance porch.

The persistent brightness and insidious perfume of Naldo's gift dazzled her. Momentarily she closed her eyes and shook her head trying to dispel not only the shimmer of little flower lights but the silly notion that it had been the tawny, raised impression of a virile bull that had set in motion the bitter tumbling of her ordered world.

As spring advanced the country became gripped in Coronation fever. Even those most ardent supporters of the abdicated Edward VIII were obliged to admit that a spectacular ceremonial which included an enchanting Queen Consort and the presence of two fairytale Princesses was preferable to that of a glum faced, bachelor monarch. Prince Charming of Wales had ceased to be charming months before his accession.

The papers and magazines printed little else, the shops were full of souvenirs, school children over the age of eleven were expected to produce albums commemorating the event, street parties were planned, decorations put up. On wasteland in towns, and hilltops close to villages bonfires were built so that the day could end in the celebratory blaze of beacons. Carl was entitled to a Coronation mug and Ronnie named the nervous, black gelding bought to replace the hunter that had been destroyed, Rex Imperitor – quickly shortened to R.I.

Phillipa was in no hurry to have her baby christened. Magda kept her own council. Carl gained weight so rapidly he quickly outgrew the family christening robe. Better that he should be carried to the font in a gown fashioned from his mother's bridal train than Victorian Tallent fine lawn and Honiton lace.

He was a vigorous, contented child, rarely crying, smiling early and treating whoever happened to be holding him with impartial placidity. It was not possible completely to crush angry resentment – equally impossible to dislike the tiny boy. Magda would never love him but she could, with even a degree of pleasure, tolerate his unobtrusive presence in the house.

Ronald virtually ignored his son's existence being absorbed in the black gelding – the best point-to-pointer he'd ever owned, he reckoned. The animal's increasing nervousness he disregarded. Prone, since Carl's arrival, to drink more whiskey of an evening, he teased Phillipa about her nursing mother's big breasts. 'I liked 'em smaller, Pip.'

She withered him with a gentle but distinct, 'You didn't like them any way, my husband dear,' and immediately insisted that he help her and Magda decide on the baby's second name.

'For Pete's sake!' Petulantly he crossed and uncrossed his legs. 'I don't ask you to think up names for my horses! Let Mater choose.'

'Well, Mater?'

Magnolia, not looking at the girl, said flatly, 'I suggest David. After your father. You've broken with Tallent tradition so why not go the whole hog?'

Phillipa contemplated her mother-in-law and calculated that the cigarette between her fingers was the twentieth of the day. She was tempted to test her reaction to the proposition 'Reginald' but that would be cruel. Phillipa didn't feel cruel. She felt not happiness – very much doubted if she would, after so long, recognise the sensation – but a rosy satisfaction. So rosy it touched exultation.

She looked slowly around the parlour. Heavy tapestry curtains covered the coloured window glass, only the standard and one table lamp were lit so that all the corners of the room were deep in shadow. This is the womb of the house, she thought, and the chapel. Rosy . . . rosy for Rosanna; exultation was for Philly. It mattered . . . mattered as much to her as the stewardship of this lovely, magic house, the honey sweet existence of a baby called Carl, that Philly should be safe. She had known, without a spoken or written word passing between them, from the moment of crossing Taurus threshold, that Phillipa was secure within the closed walls of her chosen heaven. She . . . Rosanna . . . had made it so.

She gave a small, unguarded sigh and Magda glanced up at this unusual hint of weakness.

'I think, Mater,' the words came fast and firm as if in contradiction of the sigh, 'as the Major's going to be the baby's godfather it might be a happy thought to call him Richard Carl.'

The older woman was surprised. 'In *that* order?'

'The order's not important.'

Ronnie laughed nastily. 'You're awfully keen on buttering up the old fella, Pip. First he gives you away, then you fix up his moving out of the Dower House.' His words snapped the fragile beginnings of accord between his wife and mother. Magda turned away to crush out her unfinished cigarette. Ronald blundered on, 'when's the gallant if decrepit Major going to do his latest stuff, Pippa?'

Without thinking she answered, 'Coronation Day.'

On the morning of the 12th May, 1937, Magnolia awoke early. A blackbird singing his heart out disturbed her. She lay, eyes wearily wide, on a tolerated bed in an expensively furnished room above the parlour. Even after the passing of more than a year she was still, in the moment of gliding up from sleep, puzzled by unfamiliar surroundings . . . the outline of the window in the wrong place and what had happened to the heavy bed hangings? It had been easier to accustom herself to the unshared expanse of the four-poster when Archie went to war (even a secret relief as always she had clung to the edge of her side disliking to encounter naked, hairy, masculine legs in sleep) than the loss of the fresco room.

After interminable moments of liquid song she reached for her fobwatch suspended from its little stand on the bedside table . . . twelve minutes past six. In half an hour she would ring the bell for Lucy to bring an early pot of tea. Without enthusiasm she contemplated the day ahead. As chairman of the Church Flower Committee she had been able to temper the lady arrangers' patriotic fervour by insisting that red, white and blue blooms be placed in separate, well spaced vases instead of mixed all together. The flowers around the font were pure white . . . roses, lilies of the valley and a few, late freesias.

Phillipa had told Greedy to fetch the Major and his wife at noon and had ordered a buffet luncheon in the dining room with tables set out on the terrace and top lawn. Her daughter-in-law showed none of her bridal reticence – over twenty people would drink the baby's health excluding all the household staff who were to join them when the cake was cut. Nor inhibitions in her choice of dress. Ankle length, coral crêpe silk with a loose fitting jacket. The below elbow sleeves, lavishly trimmed in ostrich feathers of a darker pink and to complement and not quite hide her neat, dark hair, a huge, slant brimmed hat, the small, flat crown hidden by a swathe of plumes.

Magda, resigned to providing a contrast, asked the dressmaker for a navy blue coat with a shawl collar to be left untied displaying a crisp, white, organdie jabot beneath. Her hat was tiny, tight fitting and edged with chenille spotted veiling.

A photographer was coming when they returned from church and before Carl demanded his two o'clock feed and in next week's local paper, alongside the county Coronation celebrations, a blurred picture would appear. *CHRISTENING PARTY AT TAURUS HOUSE* – the instruction that only the name was necessary persistently ignored – *RICHARD CARL, infant son of MR AND MRS RONALD TALLENT* . . it was inevitable.

And afterwards when the child had been handed over to the nursemaid, Phillipa feeding him now only night and morning, luncheon would be eaten and the champagne drunk: a toast to the baby; toast to the King and Queen; then they would all troop down to the village green and watch the children run races, eat their party tea and be presented with their Coronation mugs.

The long, demanding day would end at nightfall with all the adults and older children cavorting round the bonfire built on Horn Tip Hill. It was part of the estate but a place she'd visited less than half a dozen times in all her years at Taurus – a place with a pagan name and the whole proceedings would look ridiculously pagan. Ronnie, as landowner, had been asked to light the pyre but if he stuck to his original refusal she would be obliged to trek up the hill and graciously join in. Phillipa wasn't the sole mistress of Taurus yet.

She looked again at her watch – ten to seven. Rang for Lucy.

Phillipa heard the blackbird when she went into the small night nursery (which had been Archie's dressing room) to give Carl his six o'clock feed. The baby was already awake and cooing. She changed his napkin with difficulty because he kept kicking up his little, fat legs and tangling plump fingers in her hair which fell about her shoulders. Cradling him, still laughing and leaping, in her arms she crossed to the window, pulled back the Bo Peep patterned curtains and settling into the low nursing chair, popped a rosy breast tip into his not over interested but willing rosy mouth. The blackbird sang as if his heart would burst . . . Philly's face swam into unreal focus.

At this lovely, secret moment of the morning Philly would be on her knees in a cold chapel . . . . Phillipa Tallent held a nuzzling, warm child close to her heart. When a nun was accepted into the community did she not take a new name . . . what would be her sister's name in Christ? Would she wear a wedding ring? The Rosanna-that-was looked down towards her own, hidden beneath her baby's head. A band of gold as sterile as her sister's. Philly's circlet provided protection from a world that frightened her; Mrs Ronald Tallent's the chance to bear a child called Carl, named after the man who had been all the world Rosanna wanted. Suddenly, uniquely, she felt grateful to Naldo.

When she returned to the fresco room Ronnie was gone – his pyjamas in a heap on the floor by his side of the bed. She felt a quiver of disquiet. Usually if he went out early in the morning it was to ride one of his horses to dropping point and himself sweating with the after-effects of furiously dissipated energy. Then he would flop into the nearest chair and snore for an hour or two. Her husband *must* be clean and respectable in time for his son's christening. The carefully constructed façade must not be seen to crack.

Magda was in the dining room spreading honey on her toast when she got back from the stables.

'Where is he?' the question was guarded.

'Practising jumps in the paddock. Told Warren the gelding needed schooling . . . *today*.'

'Today, it would.' Her mother-in-law's voice was wearily resigned, her smile twisted. 'I'll go down when I've finished my coffee. You concentrate on the flowers for this room and keeping yourself pretty.' Bitterly. 'No one will look for me this afternoon.'

The row of chafing dishes were all full. Phillipa helped herself to kedgeree, thought again of Naldo. 'Your brother,' she said against her better judgement, 'he's all right?'

The reply came coldly. 'I'd inform you if he wasn't.'

The rest of the day passed anxiously. A morose but acquiescent Ronnie got dressed in a pearl grey suit and did his duty to the family name. Greedy had a puncture on the way to Somerton – the child's godfather and his wife, emeralds flashing beneath a neat, black hat, arriving last and five minutes late for the service. His godmother – the Vicar's wife who should have known better – got the order of names confused. A registered Richard Carl Tallent left the church baptised Carl Richard which brought a snigger from his mother's husband. The photographer was new to his job and pernickety. He insisted that a shot be taken of *grandmother* holding the little mite between the happy parents. Three generations of Tallents in front of a house a dozen generations old would make good copy in the local press. The pretty mesh trimming Magda's hat might help to shade the anguish in her eyes but made her head ache. Florrie, the second housemaid, dropped a dish of Russian salad, the estate manager's shy, teenage son, Bernard, broke a champagne glass and Sir Ashley Merrivale, who had been at school with Archie, took ten minutes to propose the baby's and the Loyal toasts.

They were, thankfully, lowering their gasses when Ronnie lunged forwards. The skin on his cheeks was tight and shiny, the hazel in his eyes glistening like polished glass. He faced them all . . . straddled his thick legs.

'Ladies and Gentlemen,' he announced.

His mother knew he wasn't drunk. Ronnie when drunk became monosyllabic and fell asleep but there was sufficient alcohol inside him to produce possible, unpredictable, verbal abuse. The muscles in her neck tensed – the small hat felt like an iron weight about her brow. She glanced at Phillipa. The girl's face was composed, lips even smiling a little but the big, slanting brim hid the expression in her eyes.

'Ladies and Gentlemen. There is one more toast that must be drunk before the party breaks up and we go our separate ways.' Magda's mouth twitched, all those who lived in the village would be walking down to the children's Coronation tea. 'I want you to drink the health of the one person responsible for these celebrations today. *She* who asked Phillipa to Taurus. *She* who,' an insulting hint of hesitation presaged the next word, '*encouraged* me to propose marriage. I won't ask Pip what prompted her to answer "yes".' Ronald rocked a little on splayed feet and grinned. 'Carl Tallent's existence, Ladies and Gentlemen, owes nothing to me. He is his grandmother's creation.' Lifting the glass of champagne in his not altogether steady right hand he disregarded the fact that most of the other glasses were empty. "I give you – now – Mater! The cleverest woman in Somerset.'

Phillipa came quickly to his side, linked herself to his free arm, only Ronald knew with what a cold, restraining touch. 'Magda, dear,' her clear voice soothed the ripples of embarrassment, 'Ronnie's put it very badly. Not much good at making speeches, are you?' Gave the young man a wifely, little shake. 'There was really no need to make one at all but it's a lovely idea to drink your mother's health, so . . .' her smooth smile slid over everyone. 'Let's do just that, shall we? The toast is Magnolia Tallent.'

Major Collinbury, tipping an empty glass, called out misguidedly 'Speech . . . spee . . .' His wife, more perceptive and troubled by the frozen look on Magda's face, trod on his foot, stemming the flow.

Phillipa, still linked to her husband, said with a sweet expression and in words no one else could hear, 'I should drink some strong coffee if I were you before climbing onto one of your gees . . . you might fall off.'

It would have required overt physical force to pull his arm away. He confined himself to a spiteful retort. 'Don't try to teach me a business, Pip, I *do* know about.'

For the second time that day there were chafing dishes on the sideboard. In order that the domestic staff could join in the evening's celebrations Magda had instructed that a supper of mixed grill with croquette potatoes be set out in the dining room so that the family could help themselves.

The room was empty. Since the village members of the christening party had drifted towards the green with its trestle tables and noisy, excited youngsters Magda had not set eyes on her son. When she had returned from the children's tea (to which, without her preknowledge, the nursemaid had carried Carl, all smiles and white satin, to receive his Coronation mug and be photographed once again) she swallowed two aspirin and lay down on her bed in a darkened room. Her headache had shrivelled to tiny spots of pain on each side of her eyes but the stale taste of champagne lingered on her tongue. Now, in the dining room she remembered there was a bottle of Vichy water in the sideboard cellaret – she poured a glassful; went to sit at her accustomed place at the table. *Where* was Ronnie?

'Taken out Rex Imperitor.' Phillipa's quiet voice answered the unspoken question. 'That's the last you, Mater, are likely to see of him today – or me either except snoring in our bed.'

The girl had changed into a mid-calf length dress of flowered ninon. She carried a fawn, lightweight wool cloak and her shoes were black with unusually low heels.

Magda's words came wrung out from her like hand-washed linen. 'Thank you for your timely . . . intervention this afternoon.'

'Nonsense.' Brisk, impartial. 'It was as much in my interest as your's – and Ronnie's – that no one should guess a truth stupidly blundered out.'

'Did they . . . anybody . . . guess?' It was an old woman's sigh that finished her sentence.

'Not as long as I am Ronnie's *loyal* wife. And I shall be, Magda, for the rest of all his days. Do you believe me?'

A bewilderment newly admitted tinged the answer. 'I don't understand sexual passion. Perhaps if I had . . . and Archie . . . Ronald would have been . . . different.'

'*I* understand. For me there is no passion without love. Only physical gymnastics.'

'Didn't you love Naldo?' It was hard to ask.

'Naldo was a means to an end . . . to give me Carl. *And* Taurus an inheritance. That is within your comprehension.'

'It should be but – I cannot. He's my twin . . . too close. *Poor* Naldo.'

Phillipa said shortly, 'I'm a twin too, remember?'

She crossed to the sideboard, filled two plates . . . one kidney, a chop each, mushrooms, tomatoes, potatoes . . . brought them back to the table.

'Eat that – you picked at things this afternoon. Then go to bed. I'll do the necessary at the bonfire.'

'No. Not yet, Phillipa. *I'm* still mistress of Taurus.'

'Of course.' The tone was conciliatory. 'We'll go together. In Naldo's car.'

Horn Tip Hill marked the western boundary of the village and Taurus estate. It was a flat topped hump detached from a wooded escarpment to the north. From the summit, it was possible to look across the flatlands away to Barrow Mump and Athelney. Nearer at hand, possible to pick out most of the village houses although Taurus was tucked out of sight together with the Vicarage and church.

Horn Tip was bare except for the lowest slopes clumped in hawthorn bushes afroth with flowers. Those who took the steeper, southern pathway which eventually twisted like a snake, were obliged to push through a thicket of fragrant, milk-white blossom.

The easier route to the top lay on the escarpment side. Not only was the incline gentler but ridges of grass here and there formed a natural series of steps. There were, amongst the oldest inhabitants, those who would not climb the easy way. No one could tell the origin of the name HILL TOP but local custom insisted it had been the site for human sacrifice – carried out by a spiketopped bull's horn. It was said that the high priests approached by the northern way – the people scrambling up the steep side of the hill. At the top one would be selected (always a youth or maid) and offered to placate – what god? There was a chance of returning down the southern slope . . . northwards brought the means of death.

Others, more bawdy, declared the name derived from the fact that it was the place where most of the village girls lost their maidenhead.

A jumble of cars filled a corner of the field containing the gate onto the pathway. Phillipa drew up alongside the Vicar's dilapidated Morris. Magda, a pale wraith in the dying day, a soft, grey shawl wrapped around her head and shoulders, carried a torch. They walked up the hill side by side – ahead, a group of near adults chattered amongst each other. Almost at the crest Magda paused for breath.

'I've been up here so few times . . . not once since Archie's last leave. The going was better, then.'

Phillipa, panting herself, exclaimed, 'This is the *easy* way?'

'But it *is*, Mrs Tallent!' Young Victor Pobberell materialised from a cluster of shadows. 'The other's a scramble. You're just in time. They are going to light the bonfire now!'

A figure with a blazing brand – impossible to identify in the dusk – stood by a high peaked pile of branches, bits of old packing cases, broken chair legs and sundry tags and jags of wood. 'Now everybody,' it shouted, 'Three cheers for the King! Hip, hip, hooray! Hip, hip, hooray! Hip, hip, HOORAY!' and on the third he thrust the flaring, flaming pole into the base amongst the dry pine cones and twigs. There was a moment's anxious hush . . . then a tongue of fire shot up the centre. The hard effort of a whole month was burning merrily.

At almost the same moment, across the vale, another twinkled into flame.

'Hip, hip, hooray! Hip, hip, hooray!' The young ones were linking hands and dancing in a ring. Phillipa found her own suddenly clutched by the Vicar's uninhibited son and whisked along. 'God Save the King! Long live the King!' he shouted – and kissed her with lingering audacity. Behind them a more scholarly voice kept chanting, 'Vivat, vivat, Rex Imperitor Georgus.'

Somewhere far below a terrified horse whinnied . . . and again. Phillipa pulled herself free, ran to the edge of the circle peering down the southern slope. The grey mist of a summer's night swirled before her vision; behind her, the crackle of flames and laughter and cries and excited chanting voices.

Magda was by her side. '*Where* is he?'

'I can't see, Mater. Surely he'd never try . . . to ride up the hill?'

'Don't you reckon you know him better than I, his mother?' The words came bitterly. 'And yet you say surely not?'

Rex Imperitor shrieked again – some of the dancers heard the frantic sound . . . half the noise and singing stopped. The more timid clung to their partners.

Forcing the sweating, thorn gashed gelding up the slope, Ronnie looked upward – saw the dark forms of two women outlined against a red and sparkling sky. He yelled and dug his heels in, yanking up the horse's foaming mouth and drove him – plunging, swerving, rearing – to the top.

Two pairs of masculine hands pulled Magda and Phillipa out of his way. Rex Imperitor, past controlling, rushed on, legs flailing, eyes staring, Ronnie, screaming, swearing, firm upon his back.

At the edge of the flames the horse stopped dead, leapt sideways, came crashing to the ground. It screamed once, kicked out twice, twitched twice more and then lay silent and unmoving. Ronnie, still in the saddle and as silent, pinned irrevocably beneath a scorched and steaming flank.

The hands that had caught Magda turned her head away. 'Not now, Mrs Tallent. Come with me'.

Strangely she recognised the voice. Hector Mackay, the schoolmaster, whom she'd never liked.

Phillipa had thrown her rescuer aside . . . ran to the heap of horse and man. People were trying to heave up the shattered creature, lift Ronald clear. She shouted, 'No, no, get the animal away but let him lie. Until we know what's happened.' And then, as someone yelled, 'Douse that bloody bonfire!' again, 'No. No. We need the light . . . torches, torches so that I can see.' She went on her knees amidst smuts, broken grass and the smell of horse, felt a ladder run up her right stocking from shin to thigh, put her fingers round her husband's wrist . . . counted the heartbeats. 'Dr Bates . . . is Dr Bates here?'

An unknown voice answered. 'Not *Dr* Bates but I am one . . . you're a sensible girl.'

Someone in the darkness said, 'That's his wife.'

'Brave, too . . . now leave things to me.'

Mrs Ronald Tallent got to her feet – let herself be drawn away . . . gently but not too far.

'I must wait . . . I won't leave until I know.'

Mrs Pobberell was by her side. 'Of course, dear, if that's what you want.' And one of the village women murmured,

'Have a sip 'o this, luv . . . always bring a tea flask with me.'

Close by someone was sobbing . . . not Magda? Where was Magda?

'My mother-in-law. Is that Magnolia crying?'

'No, some hysterical schoolgirl. Victor's found Lucy . . . taken them both back to Taurus.'

At the back of the crowd there was muttering. 'Reckon us 'ad better look for a hurdle . . . fer Master Ronnie.'

She heard her own voice, without effort, loud and clear. 'Yes, that would be most fitting. Not the first Tallent to be carted home that way,' and the horrified hush that followed the words broken by a jumble of pitying remarks. 'There, there . . . poor soul.' 'Terrible shock for 'er. Enough to make 'er lose 'er mind.' All of which, as suddenly, petered out.

'Mrs Tallent?' He was standing by her – the man who'd said he was a doctor. She looked into his face . . . couldn't see the colour of his eyes but the hair above a high forehead was silvery grey. In the smoky haze and for a swimming moment she thought the figure to be Sewerin . . . almost reached out her arms to him. He saw, in return, a pale young woman, dark hair still pinned neatly into the nape of her neck; eyes huge, blue and filled with an incredulous hope that flicked out as if an inner light had been extinguished . . . realised at once that there would be no point in pouring out syrupy, sympathetic assurances to this girl. 'I'm sorry, Mrs Tallent.'

'He's dead?'

'No . . . badly injured. Back broken . . . chest crushed. You saw that, I think. I've sent your estate manager to the nearest farm to telephone for an ambulance but I doubt if your husband will survive the journey down. I'm truly sorry . . . there's nothing else we can do.'

'Where will you take him?'

'Hospital . . . or home if you prefer.'

'You are saying it's merely a matter of time?' And when he nodded, 'I understand. If that's the case why not a hurdle? There's been more than one Tallent carried home on a farm gate before today.' She pulled the cloak off her shoulders. 'Put this under his head.'

He said, 'If you wish it.' It would, he conjectured, make little difference.

There was a stirring amongst the men. Phillipa did not see but guessed that half a dozen moved off towards the nearest boundary fence.

The doctor touched her briefly. 'I must get back to him. I see you're well looked after here.'

The women made acquiescent, reassuring noises.

She asked, feeling no pity other than the detached compassion of the Casualty Ward, 'Is he in much pain?'

'Not yet. Barely conscious. My wife's fetching my bag from the car. I'll give him a shot of morphine – hopefully before he's fully round.'

'Your wife,' the question burst from the back of her mind, 'is she an opera singer?'

He jerked up his head in astonishment then bent to look, with professional concern into her face.

'Don't worry, Doctor, I'm all right. It's . . . just you remind me of someone I once knew. Is she?'

'Nowhere near as glamorous. A nurse, Mrs Tallent, as I rather think you were.'

Phillipa gave a little crack of laughter. 'Good gracious, what a strange idea. I was nothing before I married.'

'A nothing? Oh, no, not that,' and as he walked away, he said softly to the nearest figure, 'Find out if anybody's got some brandy. That girl needs something stronger than sweet thermos tea.'

Magda was standing by the entrance porch when the ambulance came up the drive. Lucy had tried to persuade her to rest on the sofa in the study but Magnolia was too restless to stay indoors. She told the maid to turn on all the downstars lights and, in their feeble blaze, walked up and down the terrace, along to and back from the dining room windows, all the while tying and untying the ends of her shawl. When she heard the approaching motor she reached out for support. Her fingers encounterd the raised outline of the bull. She tore her hand away as if burnt by the terracotta tile.

Mesmerised, she watched the white vehicle grind to a stop. The strange doctor was the first to step down. He turned, offered his hand to Phillipa.

Her daughter-in-law's hair had become slightly awry, the skirt of her dress, stained and drooping . . . no cloak covered the flimsy ninon on shoulders and arms. She walked towards Magda, the man still hovering behind her.

'Mater . . . come inside.'

'He's dead . . . Ronnie's dead?' It was a little, whispering, truncated wail.

'Yes . . . before we left the hilltop. It was easy for him, Magda, *easy*.' She tried, dumbly, with the secret of her hospital experience to make the other understand the *blessing* of such ease. Out of the blue, she comprehended that Magda never had seen the finish to a life, was an innocent in the presence of death.

Magnolia Tallent turned away. 'Gone . . . all gone . . .' The Taurus tile, glowing beneath the warmth of the porch lights, rushed up towards her eyes. She ducked her head, spat full on the massive, lowered shoulders and fainted into a heap across the threshold of her home.

The local paper had a field day. *FATAL ACCIDENT AT CORONATION BONFIRE. Local landowner and sportsman dies on the day his baby son is christened.* Then the photograph of Magda holding Carl flanked by his parents. Even the nationals included a paragraph. *TRAGEDY IN SOMERSET ON CORONATION DAY.*

Phillipa felt nothing other than an incredulous acceptance of unexpected freedom. Magda moved and looked like the ghost she had resembled on the pathway up Horn Tip Hill.

The Vicar talked comfortingly of the life beyond, read the burial service and committed Ronnie's mortal remains to the Tallent family vault. His father's grave was marked by a white cross in a French cemetery. Carl crowed and bounced about on his cot mattress.

The two women rarely spoke – Phillipa absorbed in making plans; Magnolia controlling the turmoil of her grief.

At the end of July, Phillipa said, 'I'm taking Carl and the nursemaid to the seaside for three weeks. That should give you plenty of time, Mater, to make the move into the Dower House . . . get at least two rooms comfortable before sorting out the rest. The place has stood empty long enough and it will do you good to be occupied. I've spoken to Watts about the Dower Fund . . . all tied up and ready for your independent use. Lucy, I'm sure, will be happy to go with you.'

Anguish had smudged Magda's eyes and trapped the corners of her mouth. Phillipa quashed the stirrings of compassion. Taurus was *her* house now, in trust for her son. Magda must have felt now as she did when Archie failed to return from the War. Rosanna-that-was didn't intend to allow the rescued shipwreck of her life to be capsized and flung about as flotsam through softheartedness. Magnolia Tallent had, with cool deliberation, engineered marriage for her son to a girl whom she could dominate – or so she'd thought. Philly she would easily have crushed, but Philly was a nun.

Her mother-in-law was staring into her face. 'I can't . . . I can't believe you can be Phillipa!'

The response in her blue eyes was blank. 'Oh come, Magnolia . . . who then?'

'God knows,' came the rough edged, hopeless reply, '*I* don't.'

When she returned – Carl weaned and having cut his first two teeth – Phillipa found only the servants in the house and the study stripped of all furniture save for a few books on the shelves and a small table standing ostentatiously in the centre of the barren room. Magda had placed a marble backed ledger on its surface, *The Inventory of the Contents of Taurus*. A note was pinned on the front page.

I have marked every item that I have taken. All are my personal property with the exception of the dining room portrait of Ronald's father. I assume that this is of no interest to you but if you wish, it shall be returned. In any case it will come back to the house on my death. No signature . . . not even the initial M.

On the following afternoon, Phillipa walked through the gardens to the Dower House. Her mother-in-law, a straw hat tied beneath her chin, was on her knees energetically weeding the herbaceous border. Her dress was unrelieved black but the smudges were fading from beneath her clear, grey eyes.

'Come in, Pippa, and have a cup of tea.' No enquiry after Carl. 'You won't mind, I'm sure, to have discovered I've taken Greedy with me as well as Lucy. I shall still need to use the Rover and he's too old to want to change his ways.'

She led the way through the drawing room French doors, tossed her hat and gardening gloves onto the floor just inside and briskly crossed the room to press a green enamel bell push beside the Adam marble fireplace. The chair and sofa from the study had been recovered – the latter in honeycoloured linen; the other, with its stool, a deeper gold, patterned by swirls of creamy, jade and bronze brown leaves. The carpet, green and caramel, Phillipa recognised as having come from the bedroom Naldo used to occupy. A coffee table was strewn with magazines . . . the uppermost *Homes and Gardens*. Archie's portrait hung in an alcove to one side of the mantleshelf. The wall of its companion was empty but Magda had stood a gold plinth topped by an arrangement of gladioli and gypsophila to fill the blank space.

She turned to face the younger woman, saying without malice, 'You've won, my dear. Taurus is yours. But this house is mine by right. With Kelly Watts' help I've gone into all the legal ramifications affecting a Dowager's tenure. Unequivocally my possession until I die. So in future, kindly check if I'm at home when you wish to call.'

Her cheek twitched in a wintry, little smile then she continued composedly, 'I'll be pleased to spend such time as you wish with your little boy but Carl is no concern of mine. I shall attend church – sit, as always, in the family pew and I'll dine, by invitation, at Taurus for appearances' sake. Appearances *are* my concern. We are neither of us fools, Pippa . . . We understand each other.'

Ironically, for Rosanna-that-was, some of her sense of triumph faded to be replaced by an unwilling twinge of admiration. Phillipa made her answer slowly, 'Yes, Magda, we do . . . at least in part.'

'Which is the only part that matters any more.' With all her old gracefulness Magnolia sat at one side of the sofa, gestured towards a small, armless, button-backed chair by the open window. 'Sit there. It's very comfortable and you can just glimpse the tip of Taurus rooftop through the trees. Dick and Doris Collinbury are most interested in the changes I propose to make here. I doubt if you'll make many to Taurus.'

'No . . . I won't. That was never my intention. It wouldn't be right. After five hundred years in the making.'

Magda Tallent laughed. 'You sound just like one of those characters in that awful Edgar Wallace play.'

Chapter 9

There *were* changes at Taurus – small but talked of in the village. Phillipa moved out of the fresco room. She had always disliked the faded mural frieze of flowers and leaves and the Tudor hunting scenes depicted on the tapestry hanging to the bed. Gone with Magda, was the need for scoring points.

She chose to occupy the room first shared with Ronnie. A sealed up communicating door she had reopened. The room beyond made into Carl's night nursery.

For daytime she reorganised the study ordering a high brass guard to fix exactly in the fireplace, converting the lower shelves of the bookcase into a toy cupboard, carpeting the whole with hard wearing oatmeal floor covering and buying only furniture with smooth, round edges.

She exchanged the Alvis for a biscuit coloured Lanchester and bought a little, Morris tourer as a runabout. She attended church regularly sharing the Tallent pew with Magda but emphatically declined to join the Mothers' Union.

From an artist living in Cheddar who occasionally hunted with the Mendip Farmers Foxhounds, she commissioned a portrait of Ronnie. She gave him a handful of photographs and drove up to his studio three times to watch progress and help assess the right colours of hair and skin. On her last visit the artist offered to paint her without a fee. When she declined he felt disproportionately disappointed.

His wife, who had watched the final exchange, remarked, 'Just as well. That girl would be a menace when in the mood for sex.'

The husband was quick to jump in her defence. 'There is absolutely nothing menacing about Phillipa Tallent. She has an interesting face. A challenge to paint . . . the expression . . . not quite a Madonna's.'

'I'll agree with that,' his wife said.

He sounded hurt. 'I wanted, merely, to produce a companion piece. Not a thought of sex.'

'That, my dear, is because Phillipa Tallent wasn't in the mood.'

The finished portrait was delivered to the Dower House.

In the first week of October, Carl began to crawl and Phillipa engaged a German nanny. A thin young woman at the end of her twenties, called Helga, with impeccable qualifications, a good command of English, empty brown eyes and a gold band on the third finger of her right hand. Phillipa asked if she were married.

'No, madam,' the words came carefully, the voice as drained as the look in her eyes. 'I was to be, but my fiancé was taken away one week before our wedding day. You see, he couldn't keep his mouth shut. I don't know where he is.'

'This ring is his mother's. She gave it to me just before I left for England. I did not want to take it but she insisted . . . became distressed. In the evening she walked into the river and drowned. Perhaps I should have stayed . . . to comfort her. Irwin was her only child. But it's too late now.'

Carl accepted Helga's care with his usual impartial sunniness. She looked after him with professional calm and uncloying devotion. Phillipa, for reasons she didn't explain, encouraged her to speak to the child in German. As the weeks went by, she was gratified to see the young woman's cheeks fill out, vitality return to her expression – the eyes no longer dull and blank and to hear her pretty, clear, soprano voice singing nursery rhymes to the baby. Learning that the girl could play the piano she purchased a small upright for the day nursery and gave her a book of English nursery tunes. The word got round that Mrs Ronnie's German girl was 'wunnaful good at the keyboard'. The Vicar, still missing Doris Collinbury's services, asked if she would be able to stand in when the church organist was sick or away. Helga said, 'Yes' and, diffidently, enquired if it would be possible to join the choir. It was more than possible – welcome. Then the congregation learnt that she could sing like a bird. The solitary bass in the sparse men's line, not a local boy, invalided from the Royal Navy with a duodenal ulcer and running a successful market garden on the road to Street, suddenly contemplated the pleasure of a musical wife.

Once Arthur Liston made up his mind he pursued it doggedly. He made certain that he never missed Evensong (Helga, because of her nursery duties attended Matins erratically) and afterwards ran her back to Taurus in his van. She never asked him in. This he accepted, guessing that, having no sitting room of her own, he would be under interested scrutiny in the kitchen. Every Sunday he suggested that on her day off they go together to the pictures. Every Sunday she refused. He was an imperturbable and gently persistent young man who never scored her feelings with reproach or impatience. Just before Christmas she asked, 'The Carol Service in Wells Cathedral . . . would you take me if madam lets me have the time off?'

'Of course! And we can have supper afterwards . . . there's a nice, small hotel not far from the Cathedral.'

She hesitated. 'I don't know . . . perhaps better . . .'

He cut in, not sharply but with a touch of anxiety, 'What is it, Helga? Ashamed of me?'

She looked up, horrified. 'No, Arthur! Why should I be?'

'I guess,' he said slowly, 'in Germany you were more Mrs Tallent's kind.'

Bitterly. 'In Germany I was an outcast.'

He didn't understand her . . . the sense of protectiveness grew.

Again she hesitated. 'It is that . . . I must tell you. During the singing I may weep. It is Christmas time and . . . this is not my country.'

It will be *your* country, he vowed, if *I* have anything to do with it. Aloud, refraining to touch her, he said, 'Don't fret yourself about that. There'll be many in tears . . . remembering the lads who never came back from the

Western Front. Now stop getting yourself in a tizzy. Ask Mrs Tallent the moment you get in . . . must book up for a table . . . always full up after Carol Service.

Phillipa was in the parlour, playing an intricate game of Patience with her tiny, hand painted, French cards. She smiled at her child's nurse. 'Not a murmur, Helga. Sleeping like a Botticelli cherub.'

The young woman blurted out, 'Arthur Liston's offered to take me to Wells Cathedral . . . at least *I* asked him. Now I'm not so sure.'

Phillipa put the remains of the pack cupped in her left hand face down onto the table top. 'What is it you're not sure about?'

'If I should go. Irwin . . . I shall feel close to Irwin if they sing *Stille naght, Heilige naght*.'

'Didn't Irwin know you were going to England? To work here?'

Brokenly. 'We were coming together . . . it was all fixed. Afterwards . . . afterwards they didn't try to stop me.'

Feeling out of her depth, Phillipa asked, 'Did Irwin want you to come to England?'

'He said so, he said so, over and over again. *There's no place here for you, or me*. That's why I went when the permit came through.' Her mouth began to tremble. She dropped her face between her hands. 'But *he* has no other place now, my Irwin.'

'And Arthur Liston – he's the dark man in the choir?'

The hidden face nodded.

'Arthur Liston wants you to go out with him and you want to say "yes"?'

'I do . . . he's kind . . . and faithful . . . and *straight*, as Irwin was.'

'Was, Helga?' The first time use of the past tense startled her.

'I think . . . I feel . . . he's dead, Mrs Tallent. He is the sort they *have* to kill.' She shuddered. 'God knows what they did to him before that.'

The question came unbidden. 'Helga, do you know of a man called Carl Sewerin?'

The girl pulled up her head. 'I . . . don't think so . . . yet,' her fine, very thin brows contracted, 'the name's familiar.'

Very flat. 'He was a very clever surgeon.'

The temples cleared. 'A specialist . . . in chests. He lectured Irwin in his second year.'

'Your fiancé was a doctor?' The girl had never offered information about her past life nor had Phillipa asked.

'Just qualified. We met when I was doing a special course in children's diseases.'

Phillipa picked up the cards and turned the first one upwards. Jack of Spades. 'Go out with Arthur. We cannot, for all our longing, call back the dead.'

She expected the girl to say, 'Thank you, madam. Goodnight, madam,' but she went on talking. 'You *know* your man is gone. You saw him die.' Phillipa's Jack of Spades went firmly onto the discard pile. 'I feel . . . here in my heart . . . and my head *tells* me Irwin's dead. But I have no . . . what word I should use? Fact . . . a printed paper.'

'Official confirmation.' Phillipa kept her gaze fixed on the seven of diamonds in her hand.

'I want . . . I want, very much, to go out with Arthur. He's in love with me and I could love him – not like Irwin but enough to make him happy. What is the purpose of my life, Mrs Tallent? Carl will not need me for many years and then I must move on . . . start again. It is hard without my family . . . a home. But what . . . suppose that Irwin *is* alive . . . may need me one day? He will not be the Irwin that I knew . . . no one can be the same after years of what they do. But, if I am *Arthur's* wife, that would be betrayal.'

Phillipa put the seven on a black eight. 'There must be some agency to write to for information.'

'It would not be wise. I have brothers and a sister back in Germany. Not good for them for me to be trying to find out.'

Phillipa asked disbelievingly, 'It is as bad as that?'

'Worse, madam, if you are a Jew.'

For the first time since Sewerin's death she wondered if

his brother-in-laws had got out . . . turned over another card. The Ace of Spades. As though concentrating on nothing else she put it to one side and dropped the two on top. 'Someone else could make enquiries? Someone who has no connection with your family?' Rosanna-that-was could. Irwin was a doctor – the Medical Faculty at Robert Carnegie should be able to help. Especially if he were a former student of Carl Sewerin. 'That would be safe?'

'Y . . . yes. But who?'

'Leave it to me.' She scooped up the cards – the silly game had reached stalemate. 'Write down Irwin's full name, his qualifications, where he studied . . . everything important. Bring it to me in the morning. When you came to England . . . was it fixed where you would be together?'

'He had an appointment. House Surgeon – the General Infirmary in Leeds.'

That was better – there would be no need to identify the reason for writing by mention of 'my sister Rosanna'. She repeated, 'Leave it to me.'

'You're very kind, madam.'

'Not so very kind. It will suit me well to have you living close to Taurus.'

The marriage, eighteen months later, caused critical comment in the village and satisfaction to Phillipa. No one disliked Helga but ' 'er's *German*. That Mr 'Itler up to no good.' The euphoria succeeding Neville Chamberlain's PEACE IN OUR TIME statement had fast evaporated. Few believed war to be inevitable, fewer that it wasn't likely.

' 'er's a *refugee*,' the best informed insisted but, 'Makes no difference. Still German!' The mother of a maiden rising thirty, sniffed. 'What did Arthur Liston find wrong with *English* girls I'd like to know!'

The newly-weds' home stirred even fiercer comment.

' 'Course it's Mrs Ronnie's business 'oo she lets Taurus 'ouses to but Arthur's got a 'ome of 'is own.'

'You see it? Scarce large enough to swing a cat.'

'Plenty 'as to start in nothin' larger – young folks shouldn't 'ave grand ideas.'

Arthur Liston's home was a squalid brick box of a bungalow. It had done him well enough as bachelor – just inside the market garden gates – but he'd no intention of taking Helga there. He was conscious of, but in no way disconcerted by, the small gulf separating their social backgrounds. His main trouble was, that all his capital was tied up in the business and he needed to be on the spot. He hadn't the nerve to ask Mrs Tallent for a lease but when she offered him Bramble Cottage he jumped quicker than a racehorse.

But her reason for the offer soon became apparent. 'I'm not being generous. You'll pay me a fair rent and I shall expect Helga to take charge of Carl either up at Taurus or in the cottage most days a week. It will be good for him to get used to a change of environment. As he's bound to be an only child I want him to go to kindergarten early. She's ideally qualified to run a nursery school and my friends with young children are keen to join. I shall look around for suitable premises and put in the necessary finance.'

Feeling as though buffeted by a strong and unexpected breeze, Arthur said, 'We plan to start a family of our own.'

'Of course you do. Easy to combine. Helga won't run the thing single-handed.'

Feebly he asked, 'Have you talked to her about this?'

'Not yet. Wanted first to find out if you were willing.'

Willing? She hadn't put a single proposition to him, simply laid conditions on the line. He began to reassess his opinion of Mrs Phillipa Tallent and half wished he hadn't given up his independence so easily. She was smiling at him blandly – it was too late now. Bramble Cottage was every young woman's ideal – oak beams, inglenook, modern kitchen and bathroom. Once married that would be the time for gentle, firm, masculine self assertion. He'd pay a year's rent in advance, take a close look at the terms of the lease and keep an eye open in the neighbourhood.

Leasing the cottage to Liston gave Phillipa the greatest

pleasure – greater even than the positive conclusion of eleven months of correspondence between Mrs Ronald Tallent and Basil Tatlock, Esq., FRCS in Leeds.

She hadn't been sure how Helga would react to the bold statement that set her free.

This is to confirm that Dr Irwin Helmut Holthaus, aged 28, died in the camp hospital at Lunerburg on 24th September, 1937. Cause of death: Pneumonia.

She had prepared herself for either quiet relief or a rush of anguish – neither happened. Helga went the colour of unbleached linen and sat down without permission.

'Madam . . . I need to go away and mourn.'

Rosanna-that-was felt a twinge of envy. Hidden grief brought no respite of pain. She asked, 'Where?'

'I don't know . . . maybe by the sea. The sound will help.'

Briskly Phillipa said, 'You can have three days. Go and pack your bag. I'll ring the guest house where I took Carl last year, reserve a room for you. And run you to the station. When you come back,' she put her fingers briefly around the girl's arm, '*Not another word.*'

Helga lifted her head. 'I do not need to promise, madam. There will be no more to say . . . or think about. Mrs Arthur Liston will have no *remembered* past.'

When she returned her right hand was empty of its thin, gold band. Intercepting Phillipa's questioning glance, she answered, 'I went for a walk along the cliffs . . . climbed over a stile. It must have fallen off.'

Grudgingly the mother of the thirty-year-old maiden admitted it was a very pretty wedding – 'though 'course *green's* an unlucky colour for a bride.'

Helga's dress was made of white organdie over a slip the colour of apple leaves. She wore a tiny, stiff, Dutch-style bonnet and carried a posy a blush pink roses grown by Arthur and tied with pale green satin streamers. At the church porch Carl came running up to present a big, silver horseshoe. Phillipa had borrowed Greedy to drive the newly-weds in the Lanchester to the reception in the village hall. Magda, on her way to an afternoon's bridge, watched them pass. Next day, as she left morning service with Phillipa she congratulated the young woman on the expertise with which she had manipulated matters to her own satisfaction.

Her daughter-in-law responded with an amused, lopsided look. 'As you did, Mater, when inviting Phillipa Bland to the Jubilee Ball.'

The other's smile was equally twisted. 'There I miscalculated but, unintentionally, *not* to the detriment of a future for Taurus.'

The half admission startled Phillipa – she shot a quick look into her companion's face. Magda looked calmly back but made no further comment. Feeling a thread of warmth between them the younger woman said, impulsively, 'Come up to Taurus and have lunch. Carl's very civilised at table now.'

'Thank you, no. Ronnie never came to adult meals until well after five.'

'Your nannies didn't get married.'

'One did – and was quickly replaced. Who's looking after the child now?'

'Fanny.'

'Then there's no reason why she couldn't give him his lunch.'

'None at all. But I prefer to supervise him myself.'

'You always did. I confess I was most surprised when you engaged a full-time, qualified children's nurse.'

'*And* a German!'

'You had your reasons, Pippa. You always have your reasons.'

Magda's remarks rankled as she guided mashed carrot into Carl's ever-ready, little mouth. Congratulations were in order . . . life was going exactly as she wanted.

Two months later, the Second World War broke out.

Twenty-four hours afterwards the village was drenched in evacuees from London's East End. Three, extremely, bulky, luggage-labelled, little mites were deposited at Taurus: one was in tears and another made a puddle on the hallway floor. But bedtime explained the bulkiness – each child had been sewn into layers and layers of clothing.

The Dower House was one of the few homes to escape the flood. Magda's clout in the County was greater than her daughter-in-law's and she had the foresight to offer the dining room as headquarters for the local WVS organisation. The garden outbuilding where Major Collinbury bred his ornamental chickens became an Air Raid Warden's Post.

It was difficult to sustain initial feelings of pity for the evacuees. The children in Phillipa's home were miserable; none had ever seen an indoor lavatory let alone a bath with hot water taps. They hated the food (missing a diet of chips, tinned salmon and condensed milk), were scared by the green quietness of the countryside and the animals in the fields whilst the one boy in her care was disruptively inquisitive and foul mouthed. Phillipa kept all the upstairs rooms locked (it was impossible to keep him out of the parlour) and put Fanny, with an increase in wages, in charge of the children. She took Carl to spend all day at Bramble Cottage.

Helga's evacuee was a bright, four-year-old called Shirley, who slotted, without effort, into a life away from streets and close packed houses and treated Carl with older, sisterly patience.

The expected bombing of London failed to materialise and at the end of a couple of weeks, beligerent parents turned up and took their offspring home. Phillipa, grateful for an empty house was aware of the vulnerability of so many unoccupied rooms. She suggested that the East End teacher, who had accompanied the older children doubled up in the village school where more than half remained, move from his tiny, cottage back bedroom into a larger, bedsit in Taurus. He stayed for three months, then left to join the RAF. By which time the number of evacuees still in the village numbered less than six. One was Shirley – her father was away in the Army and her mother enjoying her freedom too much to be bothered with a four-year-old.

Phillipa revived and revised her ideas for a kindergarten. The garden at Bramble Cottage was wide – sufficiently spacious for an extension to form the basis of a nursery classroom. There was stone, cement, timber and labour available on Taurus estate. These were the months of the phoney war following Hitler's successful invasion of Poland. The only action took place at sea, in Europe nothing happened. Pathetically convinced of the invincibility of the Maginot Line, public and politicians waited to see what he would do next and no one was over insistent on enforcing building permits.

Arthur hesitated to dig in his toes, inhibited by a secret pestering of the Admiralty to rejoin the Service – for shore if not seagoing appointments. It would be as well for Helga to have her days occupied should he be sent somewhere inaccessible to wives such as Scapa Flow and, in any case, probably wiser for her to stay where she was known and accepted than be an unwelcome German amongst patriotic sailors' families.

He tried to persuade himself that growing food was not only a reserved but a vital occupation (most of his flower production lost to vegetables). Without success. He couldn't forget the years spent as a member of His Majesty's Navy before he earned his living digging about in the earth. It was back to the Navy that he wanted to be even if the price was being separated from Helga. He prayed she would understand . . . not feel betrayed.

By the end of April the schoolroom was ready. The first children – Carl, Shirley, two Merivale granddaughters, whose mother had returned to her parents' home whilst their father was with the BEF in France, and a boy and girl living on the Somerton side of the village – were enrolled on the day the German Army entered Belgium.

Whilst the broadcast news became worse and worse – German tanks rolled westward, Neville Chamberlain resigned, England became a haven for fleeing European monarchs, France collapsed and the little boats made possible the miraculous rescue off Dunkirk; while the new Prime Minister, Winston Churchill, rode high on a flow of defiant, nationally responsive rhetoric – the innocent half-dozen daubed paint on big, thick sheets of paper, chanted action songs and played in the sandpit. Britain had not been invaded since 1066 – the newly formed Local Defence Volunteers paraded with broomsticks and manned road blocks with unloaded firearms. These children were the stake for the future. With the ignorant, arrogant insularity of an island, not one person doubted that the future was safe.

Phillipa fought a private battle with her patriotic conscience . . . whether or not to enrol as a VAD at the local hospital. Prudence won. Phillipa Bland had no experience of nursing – Rosanna-that-was would give herself away. She offered the use of her car for ambulance duty . . . ferrying Out-Patients to and from the hospital. For this she received an extra petrol ration and for taking elderly worshippers to church, a couple more coupons per month.

Magda worried about Naldo . . . had received no letter from him since early in May. France's accommodation with the conquering power – the division of the country – did not allay her fears. What would Naldo do cut off in what was no longer voluntary exile from England? She spoke no word of this to Phillipa – her brother's name was never mentioned in their superficial, conversational exchanges.

For those living in England during the summer of 1940 time possessed a dreamlike quality. Every day, from rise to setting, the sun shone in a cloudless, paintbox blue sky, the air shimmered with heat, the gardens overflowed with flowers and danced with butterflies and never had roses been so beautiful or abundant. Uniforms were to be seen everywhere but most of the girls still wore brightly coloured, cotton dresses and on innumerable green pitches throughout the land, men in white played the lazy looking but deadly serious game of cricket whilst their women folk cut sandwiches and checked that the tea urn was boiling.

Only on the forbidden beaches with their coils of barbed-wire, iron spiked tank traps and hidden mines was the threat of invasion evident and even there reality remained remote, the menace across the Channel incomprehensible and, what was more, downright cheeky. Was not one-third of the World Atlas coloured British red? Did not Britannia rule the waves? – none but the Government and Chiefs of Staff knew *how only just*. The ordinary, civilian public exhorted by a barrage of posters to 'Be Like Dad, Keep Mum', 'Dig for Victory', 'Join the WRNS and Free a Man for the Fleet' and questioned from a multitude of hoardings, 'Is Your Journey Really Necessary?' went about their ordinary, ordered lives now made extraordinary by a sense of waiting.

Once in a while a random German bomber flew over in daylight, dropped the odd bomb and sprayed a second eleven with machine-gun fire. Arthur Liston opened up and spring cleaned his tiny bungalow as home for a Guernsey refugee who had been directed to help him run the market garden. The Merrivale grandchildren went with their mother to join their father at Matlock Spa and were replaced at school by three little boys of naval families stationed at the RNAS eleven miles away.

Phillipa, with no man to worry over and Taurus all to herself, was utterly content. Especially on a golden, August morning. Often she awoke early and, making sure Carl was sound asleep, walked the length of her lovely, quiet home. Every room possessed an individual, inviolate, untouched quality. Although cradled in the heart of Puritan country Cromwell's men had not laid a finger on stick or stone and the faded, flowery friezes in the fresco room breathed survival from an earlier Civil War – that of the Roses. That particular morning, the air fragrant with the heady scent of jasmine, she lingered in the parlour.

The room was dim but speckled with muted, reflected, multicoloured eastern sunlight. A copper vase of flame and ivory gladioli had spilt their lowest flowerlets onto the top of a little polished table. At the moment of her stooping to scoop them up, on Portsmouth Station, a weary eyed traveller in a crumpled coat and battered trilby hat boarded a north-bound train. By an uncomfortable, circuitous route Reginald King had returned to his native shores. He did not telephone his nearest, his twin – the personal devil that had tweaked at his tail for the last four years drove him to find Phillipa, first. His thoughts were of nothing else as he shrugged down into the corner of a third class compartment and lit his last Gauloise cigarette . . . nothing except that he must look for a barber; get a decent shave and haircut.

It was Phillipa's duty ambulance morning. She drove Carl in the Lanchester to Bramble Cottage (the Morris runabout laid up for the duration in one of Ronnie's stables) and then, alone and on impulse, back up Taurus driveway. The eternal, silver grey walls of the house shimmered in the sunlight as she drove past, the parlour mullions looked feathery and insubstantial. She left the estate by the home farm exit.

Now only a tree lined road lay ahead of her. Carl would stay with Helga for his lunch and afternoon nap and once she had ferried her old dears to and from hospital the rest of the day was her own until teatime. Perhaps she would go to Wells, wander around the Cathedral, watch the Bishop's swans gliding on the palace moat.

Although she rarely visited the little, Cathedral town, even in its narrow streets, she felt close – almost hand in hand – with Philly. Strange that in the five years since she'd seen her sister – doubted if in anonymous black habit and white whimple she would recognise her face – never, never had the two of them quite lost a thread of touch. She wonderd, with a tenderness that reached back to their childhood, if Philly needed to do penance for such a firm intrusion into her ordered thoughts . . . at Taurus the link was gossamer thin.

She stopped the car alongside a field gate flanked by a single holly bush. Already the branches were clustered with little berries – not the bright red that would light up the tree at Christmas time but a translucent, greeny grey barely visible amongst the shiny leaves.

She relaxed her clasp on the steering wheel and sighed with pure pleasure. This year Carl would be old enough to appreciate and join in the magic and excitement. She would get the estate's carpenter to make the present of a Noah's Ark . . . paint the animals herself. Allow the tiny boy and, perhaps Shirley, too, to help hang the decorations on the tall fir tree that by years of old custom stood in the corner of the drawing room; start a new custom of her own – a wreath of holly and ivy and silvered cones fixed to the dark wood of the front entrance door. She would put honey scented candles in the porch and light the tree on Christmas Eve when the carol singers came to call. With luck it would be a frosty night . . . she closed her eyes and formed the picture of her lovely house, silvery walls and roof glinting in starshine, the porch washed mellow gold by candle glow and the bright tree twinkling behind narrow window panes that had watched how many hundred Christmas tides?

A passing lorry brought her eyelids up – briskly her mind slid to the problem of finding stocking fillers. The traditional orange and nuts presented no difficulty but the shops were fast emptying of toys. A trip to Bath might be a good idea.

The thought swung her back to Philly . . . the dark of early Christmas mornings. It had always been Rosanna who crept to the end of the bed they shared, pinched the bulging stockings and crawled back with the whispered news, '*He's* come!' In a convent was Christmas Day different from any other? Did the instinctive, intuitive, loving transference they shared bring a spark of temptation to the dedication of her sister . . . temper, harm, her sweet obedience . . . jeopardise her soul? It might be safer, for Philly's sake, to avoid the charm of Wells . . . put herself beyond the other's easy apprehension. She would go back to Taurus, pick the last of the summer's raspberries, take them to Bramble Cottage to share with Helga, Shirley and her incomparable, little Carl. But first she'd lunch alone at The George and Pilgrim in Glastonbury.

Her wristwatch showed almost three o'clock when she turned into Taurus drive – later than she'd planned. But a mediocre luncheon had been enlivened by the attentions of a lonely, army officer who'd tried to pick her up. The dining room at the hotel had been full – it was market day. Quite legitimately he had asked if he might take the vacant chair at her table for two but from then on his eyes had shown undisguised approbation and his talk amusing persuasiveness. About Ronnie's age, fair, with a carefully tended but Cavalier flamboyant moustache, he mentioned (without soliciting sympathy or admiration although both were inherent in the information) that he had returned from Dunkirk to find himself submerged in a bucolic boundary of the West country retraining his regiment and bored to death. Phillipa sidestepped his advances, accepted a Drambuie with her after luncheon coffee, failed to provide her name but dropped, in passing, that she often took lunch at The George and Pilgrim . . . on a Tuesday. From now on, she decided, she would. The stirring of lighthearted sexual attraction warmed her.

She drove along the familiar last lap of her journey with her vision on the way ahead but her mind elsewhere until she saw a straggly huddle of figures about the curve that hid the approach to Taurus front porch. They parted to let her through. She caught a glimpse of upturned, pale faces and, puzzled, glanced back at them in her driving mirror. They had regrouped and stood staring after her. Irritated she turned her eyes to the front.

Ahead there was nothing . . . nothing that made sense.

She saw two piles of splintered stones, a gaping hole, a lingering pall of dust, a stationary, unneeded fire engine, Kelly Watts, Palmer, the air raid warden, the village bobby, the boy who helped in the garden, two or three others . . . one, a figure in a scruffy, shabby raincoat and a tip brimmed, dirty trilby hat, bending over the rubble where the entrance porch should be.

The Lanchester stalled . . . she was out on the driveway stumbling almost to her knees. What, what . . . Christ! what had happened? This morning all had been silvery light; a five hundred year-old, lovely, *harbour* of a home. Now . . . now . . .

The policeman and the warden came up on on each side of her. The policeman took her arm.

'German bomber, Mrs Tallent. Direct hit. No one's hurt and kitchen's still standing, mercy knows how. I've sent Cook and Fanny down to the Dower . . . they're all shook up. Madam's not in . . . doesn't know about this yet. Lucy'll look after them . . . tell her when she gets back.'

She felt as though fighting a bad dream. 'It's crazy . . . why, in God's name, *here*?'

Palmer sounded excitedly important. 'Just the one aircraft . . . a Heinkel 102. Ditched his load . . . *jettisoned's* the word. Our boys must have been after him.'

'Gone!' The word came out in savage, twisting incredulity. 'TAURUS gone! Nothing . . . nothing left.' Her whole world went tumbling upside down.

Somebody urged her onto the grass lawn . . . advised her to put her head between her knees . . . she flung them away.

'One, bloody, silly bomb . . . *my* home . . . *my* Taurus.'

The policeman reiterated ploddingly, 'Kitchen block's still standing . . . no lives lost.'

Wildly she looked around. 'It can't, it can't . . . tell me, it cannot be a total wreck!' The panelled drawing room, the mysterious, colour flecked parlour, the secretive stairways, the fresco room . . . surely not all swept away in one shattering, explosive moment?

A fireman said authoritatively, 'No telling yet, madam. Not safe to go inside and ascertain.'

The policeman was still holding her arm with fatherly care. 'You must be thankful, Mrs Tallent, that you and the little boy weren't at home.'

'Thankful!' The hysteria of despair shredded the words. 'Taurus is my life.'

'I think,' the fireman said, 'someone should go for Dr Bates.'

'A doctor!' even more wildly, 'What use is a doctor to mend centuries of stone and love?'

A voice seeped out of the mist that seemed to swirl behind her eyes. 'Stick to the stone, Pippa, if you want to keep your head. And remember the love.'

Dazedly she looked in its direction.

The policeman said, 'It's Mr King, madam.' Attempted a feeble joke. 'Arrived just as the bomb went up.' Stepped back to let Naldo take his place.

'What are you doing here?' His presence all part and parcel of her nightmare dream. Naldo was a thousand miles away.

The old, faintly mocking smile was recognisable on a face grown thinner and hollow-eyed. His clothes were scruffy to a degree the offhandedly spruce Naldo she remembered, would never have tolerated. 'Returned by devious routes to serve King and Country and, in the nick of time, it seems, rescue a damsel in distress.' In the same bantering tone. 'Pull yourself together, Pippa. Taurus ain't the end of the world.' He turned to a pair of mightily relieved officials of the law and fire brigade. 'I'll take care of Mrs Tallent. You say the kitchen's still safe so someone cut along and make a good, strong pot of tea.' To the bobby, 'Pop down to the Dower House, make sure nobody blurts out the news to my sister – including my return. She's no idea that I was on the way back.'

The fireman said, 'We'll have to stay . . . carry out a proper survey.'

Which seemed to Naldo pointless but he answered, 'Fine. Mrs Tallent and I will take a little walk. The tennis court should be far enough . . . a bench to sit on there.'

Unresisting and as limp as a rag doll, Phillipa let him lead her across the sunny lawn. But always she looked over her shoulder towards the nightmare behind her. As they passed close to a sprawling buddleia tree, the brittle branches spiked with musky, pale mauve blossoms, a myriad butterflies floated upwards in a rainbow coloured cloud. Dazed and dazzled she clung to his firm, cool fingers.

When they reached the unmarked tennis court he gently pushed her towards and down onto the unvarnished, wooden seat parallel with the empty, left hand net post.

'Tell me,' she said, pleadingly, 'tell me it isn't true.'

'And if I did, would you believe me?'

'No . . . no . . . no.'

'Then stop asking stupid questions.'

She flung up her head. 'You're cruel!'

He kept his voice flat . . . empty of emotion. 'As you were to me, remember? I *loved* you, Pippa. Gave you a child and you cared for nothing save Taurus.'

Suddenly she began to shake – so violently he caught at her to save her from falling off the bench. He made a circle of his arms drawing her close, his lips against her hair, murmuring baby words of comfort. In France he had dreamed of holding her . . . not like this.

When she grew still she whispered on a wintry thread of sound. 'Yes . . . I cared for Taurus. It's beauty . . . *permanence* . . . gave me back a reason for breathing in and out; a purpose for opening my eyes each morning . . . for putting one foot in front of the other.'

He held her away at arm's length, searched her stricken face. 'Tell me *now*, Pippa, who was the man whom you loved so much, so exclusively, you'd no feeling left for any other . . . only sticks and stones? Who *was* Carl?'

Her reaction to the name was instant. She jerked out of reach and onto her feet. 'My baby! I must go to my baby! Someone will have told Helga about Taurus . . . she'll be wondering what's become of me.'

Approvingly he patted her arm. 'Good girl! Concentrate on the living.'

A new thought swung in – rocked her a little. 'Living! Where shall I go? I've nowhere to take Carl . . . no place left!'

'Don't be foolish. Go to Magda . . . The Dower House.'

She spoke in words chipped out of rock. '*If* I am invited.'

'No one talks of invitations at times like this. And The Dower is part of the estate.'

'You don't understand. I've no *right*, there. Magda's tenure until she dies . . . it will be up to her.'

Lightly he said, 'It'll look damned odd if she doesn't take you in. In any case, only for a little while. It's quite possible that a part of Taurus can be salvaged . . . the kitchen block's untouched.'

Bitterly she began walking with fast, short steps away from the tennis lawn. 'Continuity can't be rebuilt. And since when has a Tallent lived in the *kitchen* block?'

Hurrying to catch up he called out, 'The first Tallent shared his dwelling with his cattle.'

Against her will she slowed her pace. 'What sort of man was he? Can you guess . . . apart from a house builder?'

'Certainly not a whiner . . . and rumour has it, Pippa, as I conjecture you already know, the first Tallent was a bastard of the Earl of Devon.'

Phillipa stopped dead. 'And the *last* Tallent is *your* bastard.'

Softly he answered, 'He isn't a Tallent at all. So much for continuity.'

She gave a hopeless, little sigh. 'I tried . . . it was so beautiful I tried to make it true.' Pathetically she turned to him. 'I don't know, Naldo, what it is that I must do. Tell me, tell me . . . please.'

He didn't touch her. 'I can ASK you,' he said, 'to take a chance, bring the boy and come away with me. I don't know where I shall be going or what I shall be doing but who can, with any surety, these summer days? When you awoke this morning you never guessed that before the sun went down your magic world would be reduced to a heap of ragged rubble. Let Magda pick up the pieces – she'll make a better job of it than you. For Magda, Taurus was true reality – for you the lovely substance of a dream. She lost it to you – give it back. When the war's over, *if* we survive, and Carl's a man, he can be offered the choice of accepting his dubious inheritance. Providing,' his lips twisted, 'there's an inheritance left.'

She took a long time answering . . . with sick panic he wondered if, silently she would reject him once again and turn away. At last, not looking at him, 'It wouldn't be fair, Naldo. I don't love you.'

'Rot!' Relief brought out the word in a little shout. 'I'll be the judge of what is fair. And you've forgotton how it feels to care for something that breathes and responds to love. Maybe, or on our travels, you'll find a man who touches the frozen part of you. It's a chance I'll take. I offer *no strings*, Pippa.'

'The boy,' she said, 'we have the boy. He . . . he deserves a mother and a father. I know how it was . . . could be . . .' She lifted her chin and faced him squarely . . . blue eyes, dark and unfathomable as the midnight sky, lashes spiked with tiny, stars of tears. 'When we leave here he will be no longer CARL . . . our son, Richard.'

Naldo let out a long, slow, glorious breath.

Purposefully she began walking towards the ruined house. 'I shall take nothing of Taurus with me. Nothing at all. Only the clothes I stand up in – the rest are under a pile of ancient dust. It's all Magda's now.'

Surreptitiously he reached into his raincoat pocket, drew out the terracotta tile he'd found, unscathed, lying by the shattered porch wall. He ran his fingers over the outline of the virile, challenging bull – tossed it deep into a clump of azalea bushes before following her.

Caroline Gray

Alix Wantage was born into nobility, wealth, opulence . . . and the stale prospect of an arranged marriage to someone she could never love. But when she was thrown from her horse while out hunting, Clark Hale, a brash, young American photographer was there to lift her spirits and, with outrageous forwardness, steal her heart.

So begins Alix's remarkable story. Banished from the country by her aristocratic parents, she and her lover arrive in the exotic and dangerous wilderness of Malaya to seek their fortune in rubber. And throughout a life of hope and passion, despair and tragedy, Alix proves again and again that she is a woman with the courage to turn her dreams into sparkling reality . . .

Also by Caroline Gray in Sphere Books:
FIRST CLASS
HOTEL DE LUXE

0 7221 6342 8 GENERAL FICTION £2.95

From the bestselling author of SISTERS

Cousins

SUZANNE GOODWIN

Elizabeth Bidwell led an enchanted life on her uncle's beautiful and rambling estate, Merriscourt, deep in the heart of the languid Devonshire countryside. She longed to become mistress of Merriscourt one day, but her handsome, charming cousin Peter – who was destined to inherit the estate – would only flirt and drop half-promises.

And when distant cousin George Westlock arrives from India with his stunningly attractive godchild Sylvia, Elizabeth soon realises that her life and hopes will change dramatically. For Peter is captivated by the sylph-like newcomer, as all the Bidwells are, and Sylvia, a woman who knows exactly how to get what she wants, is determined that Peter and Merriscourt will be hers . . .

0 7221 4093 2 GENERAL FICTION £2.95

Also by Suzanne Goodwin in Sphere Books:
SISTERS